D1000766

INVITATION TO LIVE

Invitation to Live

LLOYD C. DOUGLAS

 This book, while produced under wartime conditions, in full compliance with government regulations for the conservation of paper and other essential materials, is COMPLETE AND UNABRIDGED

GROSSET & DUNLAP
Publishers   *New York*
By arrangement with Houghton Mifflin Co.

COPYRIGHT, 1940, BY LLOYD C. DOUGLAS

ALL RIGHTS RESERVED INCLUDING THE RIGHT TO REPRODUCE
THIS BOOK OR PARTS THEREOF IN ANY FORM

PRINTED IN THE U. S. A.

TO MY WIFE

Contents

INVITATION TO LIVE

1. Legacy

IT WAS a serious occasion and Barbara's eyes were misty, but she couldn't help smiling when she heard the concluding article of her great-grandmother's will.

Even Mr. Leighton himself, though he did not alter the prudential tone with which he had done appropriate honor to this lengthy instrument, grinned dryly while reading the final paragraph.

And it is my further request that at eleven a.m., on the first Lord's Day subsequent to her graduation from college, the said Barbara Breckenridge shall present herself, unaccompanied, at divine services in Trinity Cathedral, Chicago.

Resuming his gravity, Mr. Leighton folded the impressive document, pocketed his pince-nez, and said, 'I wish to extend my congratulations, Miss Barbara, upon your very valuable legacy.'

Barbara accepted the distinguished old attorney's felicitation with a little nod and an inarticulate murmur of thanks. She had made no pretense of being surprised to find herself the heiress to approximately half a million, for there never had been any secret about Grandma's intentions in this matter.

The vivacious and expensively gowned Alicia Grayson, Barbara's mother, beamed happily on her lucky child.

Though Alicia had been bequeathed a mere fifty thousand by her grandmother, she wasn't jealous; for Peter Grayson was immensely wealthy and Alicia had all the money that was good for her. And perhaps a little more.

'But how quaint!' she remarked. 'How very odd — Grandma sending you to church — in her will!'

'You may have noted,' observed Mr. Leighton, 'that this final provision is in the nature of a recommendation rather than a requirement. If Miss Breckenridge should find it inconvenient ——'

'No, no,' interposed Barbara. 'I'll do it. It's little enough, after all she has done for me.'

'Of course, dear, that changes our plans for your house-party,' Alicia reminded her — 'but I daresay that can be arranged. We'll have to notify everybody that it's postponed a week.'

'Thought you were sailing for France on the twenty-fifth,' said Barbara.

'So we are, but you can have your house-party without me. You can ask Aunt Marcia to come and chaperon you.' Alicia laughed. 'Fancy your going all the way from New York to Chicago — to attend church! Grandma certainly was a queer old darling. Did you ever know anyone just like her, Mr. Leighton? Brimful of the funniest little notions.'

Mr. Leighton made a small basket of his interlaced fingers, gazed into it reminiscently, and replied, 'Madame Breckenridge did occasionally express some unique ideas — but they usually made sense. Now — take this one, for example. It is not as strange as it seems. You may recall, Mrs. Grayson, that about two years ago your grandmother spent several months in the home of your Aunt Victoria in

Chicago. While there, she was a regular attendant at the Cathedral services, and was deeply impressed by the wisdom of Dean Harcourt. And it occurred to her that Miss Barbara, at the close of her college days, might be greatly benefited by one of these inspiring talks.'

'Oh, I agree that the request is not unreasonable,' said Alicia, 'and Barbara should by all means comply with it for Grandma's sake, though it is a bit of a nuisance that it had to come at this particular time. Perhaps some other Sunday would do as well. And what assurance did Grandma have, six months ago, that this Dean Harcourt would be in town — and in his pulpit — on the — what is it? — twentieth of June?'

'Dean Harcourt is a cripple, Mrs. Grayson,' explained Mr. Leighton, patiently. 'He does not travel. He is invariably in his church on Sundays. I think Madame Breckenridge felt quite safe in her forecast that the Dean would be on hand.'

'But ——' pursued Alicia, in a puzzled voice, 'having gone that far in planning some good advice for Barbara, why didn't the precious old dear notify Dean Harcourt of his opportunity to recondition this young flibbertigibbet?' She patted Barbara's hand and smiled fondly into her eyes.

'Motherrr!' scoffed Barbara. 'How silly! Grandma wouldn't have dared to suggest such a thing. Imagine — asking a clergyman to single out some person in church — and go for him! Grandma was brave, but she would never have had the nerve to do that!'

'Well,' drawled Mr. Leighton, 'she did; for I helped her compose the letter. It was done the same day she added this last paragraph to her will.'

Barbara's blue eyes widened.

'Do you mean to say that I'm expected to sit there in church and have this man preach at *me* — as if I were the only one present?'

Mr. Leighton said he supposed that was one way of putting it, and there was quite a little pause before Barbara found her voice again. She glanced up anxiously at her mother, and said, 'Of all things!'

'Perhaps there won't be many there,' consoled Alicia. 'I don't believe you'd be so dreadfully self-conscious, darling. Likely there will be just a handful of people — scattered about — in a big church.' She turned to Mr. Leighton, who had drawn a little smile. 'That's the way it would be, don't you think, Mr. Leighton? Barbara could sit quite apart from anyone else. How many people will be there?'

'Probably about two thousand,' he replied casually. 'The Dean is quite a popular preacher, it seems.'

'Two thousand! Holy Saints!' Alicia stared into her daughter's incredulous face. 'Your great-grandmamma certainly did arrange something nice for your moral improvement. Dreadful! Well — I'll go with you, darling, and hold your hand. And we'll ask Aunt Vic to come with us.'

Mr. Leighton slowly shook his head.

'Sorry, Mrs. Grayson, but she is instructed to go alone. . . . And now, Miss Barbara, may I venture to inquire whether you confidently intend to do this? For I am expected to notify Dean Harcourt of your decision.'

'You may write him,' muttered Barbara, mechanically, 'that I'll be there. And if he wants to identify me — in the audience — tell him I'm the one that looks scared.'

And she was scared, too. The Breckenridges were not a

church-going family. Barbara's father, who had died when she was twelve, was a lovable and generous man, considerate in his treatment of the people who worked with him and for him, and wisely known for his philanthropies, but he was an agnostic, as his father had been.

Peter Grayson, Barbara's stepfather, was an excellent fellow, but all the days of the week were alike, except that there was usually a little more social activity in his house on Sundays. And if Alicia thought about the church at all, it was in connection with weddings, christenings, funerals — and the Easter parade. They owned an expensive pew in a fashionable church, but the ushers felt quite safe in seating strangers in it.

Barbara had arrived in Chicago late Saturday afternoon. Aunt Vic had not been notified of her coming. It was much better to stop at a North Side hotel and say nothing to anyone about her presence in the city. She had her return reservation on the Limited for three o'clock Sunday afternoon. It was a shabby way to use Aunt Vic, but Alicia had agreed that this plan would obviate a lot of explaining. Vic would make a joke of it, and probably tell everybody.

As the hour drew near, Barbara's nervousness increased. She had risen early and dressed with care — in unrelieved black crêpe. It seemed a suitable costume. And she wore a small black veil which, fortunately, was modish at the moment. There wasn't a scrap of color on her, or in her cheeks either, as she set forth on foot for the Cathedral.

Mr. Leighton's disquieting prediction about the size of the crowd was correct. While still a full block away, Barbara could see them pouring out of private cars, taxis, and busses, and streaming across the park, hurrying up the broad stone steps, and funneling through the great Gothic doors — hundreds upon hundreds of people massing to hear poor, defenseless little Barbara Breckenridge learn what was good for her frightened soul.

Wouldn't it be dreadful if this Dean Harcourt had announced, a week ago, 'Next Sunday we will have with us a young lady who hasn't been inside a church — except once, as a bridesmaid — since she was christened. I have promised one of her relatives that I will preach a sermon directly to her. All the rest of you will be welcome, of course.' ... Oh — he couldn't have done a thing like that! It wouldn't be fair! But maybe he had! Barbara's knees were trembling, and her steps grew slower and shorter as she joined the throng. Nobody had paid any attention to her yet, but they probably would — the people seated with her — when they saw her agitation.

The organ — hidden away some place high up — was playing softly. Almost everybody seemed to know where he was going and needed no direction. Barbara hesitated and an usher beckoned to her. She followed him, hoping he would seat her in one of the rear pews, but he kept going on and on — and on. It did not occur to her that the black ensemble, mistaken for mourning, was entitling her to special consideration. Her steps lagged, but the usher stood waiting for her at the third pew, almost directly beneath the massive pulpit. She took the only unoccupied space beside an elderly couple. The old lady leaned forward and gave Barbara a sympathetic little smile that startled her. The smile seemed to say, 'Well — you're here — poor child. But don't worry too much about it. We're all your friends.'

Then everybody stood up and the choir came down the

broad central aisle, singing. And when the choir had filed
into its place in the chancel, two young clergymen assisted
an older one to a tall-backed chair. Barbara remembered
that Dean Harcourt was a cripple. She was fascinated by
his face. It was seamed and crisscrossed with lines that
told of much pain endured, but there was an expression of
serene strength such as she had never seen before. The
people beside her tried for a while to help her find the places
in the book, but presently gave it up. Barbara sat and
knelt and stood when the others did so, but didn't take her
eyes off Dean Harcourt's face. Her heart had calmed down
to normal. She wasn't frightened now. Indeed she was
glad when the people put the little black books back in
the racks and it seemed to be time for the sermon.

As soon as the Dean began to speak, Barbara knew that
all her fears had been groundless. Apparently he had decided not to preach to her, after all. The very first sentence
made that clear enough.

'I shall be talking to you today,' he said, 'about the
special privileges of the poor.' Barbara felt that she was
going to be interested in this unusual topic; for she had
never suspected that poor people had any privileges at all.
That was why they were pitied: they had no privileges.
They couldn't go to college, couldn't have nice things in
their houses, couldn't have pretty and seasonable clothes,
couldn't travel, couldn't entertain — and, consequently,
couldn't hope to have many friends. It was too bad.

'The most valuable possession,' Dean Harcourt was saying, 'is sincere friendship, and only the poor can be certain
that they are loved for what they are — and not for what
they own.' This idea had never occurred to Barbara before,
and she didn't take much stock in it now. There was

Patricia, for example. Patricia didn't love her because she was well-to-do. Patricia would be her loyal friend if she lost every cent she had.

'I am not saying,' continued the Dean, 'that the rich have no friends, or that because a man is wealthy his value to others is estimated by what he can do for them materially. Plenty of rich men and women have friends whose sincerity is beyond all question, especially if they have come by their wealth through personal effort, after having been poor enough to be sure of the loyal comradeship of those whom they had known and cherished before they became so prosperous. I suppose it is only the people who have always been rich, who have inherited large wealth, who will never be sure, who will never know whether they are loved — for themselves alone.'

Probably some kind of socialist, reflected Barbara. What are people with money supposed to do in order to find out whether they are liked? Give it all away, maybe?

'Of course,' the Dean went on, 'if the rich man has a friend, who is known to be on comradely terms with a few poor men, this might help him determine the value of that friendship. He could say to himself, "Smith's friends aren't selected on a basis of their possessions. Perhaps he likes me, and would like me if I owned nothing."'

That sounded fairly sensible, and Barbara found herself calling the roll. Patricia Foster, her room-mate in college, certainly liked poor people. That is, she certainly had nothing against them, though it wasn't likely she knew very many; not as chums, anyway. This was a disturbing thought. Would Patricia have anything to do with her if Barbara were poor? For a while she didn't hear what the Dean was saying, being occupied with her own dismaying meditations. She went through the list of her closest associates — both boys and girls. There wasn't one of the lot who — so far as she knew — had friends without money. And that went for Barbara, too.

Oh, of course, she had tried to be kind and generous with the girls in the beauty shops and the saleswomen in the stores; and, naturally, the servants at home. But there wasn't one of them who could be called a friend.

'The poor inevitably miss a great deal of the pleasure enjoyed by the rich,' the Dean was saying, 'but the greatest of all satisfactions is theirs for the asking. It is to be feared that sometimes, in their wishing they had more money, they do not appreciate this one supreme joy that the rich cannot know; cannot command; cannot buy — for it is not on sale.'

Barbara began wishing she hadn't come. From now on, she said to herself, she would probably doubt the sincerity of every friend she had. What right did she have to believe that Dick Morton — or Pinkie Powell — had any genuine interest in her? The suspicion began to be annoying! Perhaps Tim Wainwright was interested only in her financial support of his players when he invited her to come this summer and join his colony at Provincetown. Maybe she had been fooling herself when she accepted compliments. Maybe she hadn't a bit of charm — apart from her pretty clothes! And now she had this to worry about. It wasn't very nice of Dean Harcourt — to hand her this fret.

She didn't hear much of the rest of it, and presently it was done. There was some more praying and singing, while Barbara told herself that once she was out again in the sunshine she would forget about it. For it was nothing but a precious lot of nonsense.

But the sunshine didn't help very much. Barbara thought she would stroll leisurely up the boulevard to the Drake, but she found herself walking very fast, her steps keeping pace with her thoughts.

The luncheon menu looked inviting, but she had no appetite. She was terribly lonesome. She bought a few current magazines and carried them to her room, absently turned the pages, gave up trying to read, and held her diamond-studded wrist-watch — graduation gift — to her ear, thinking it might have stopped. It was only one-forty-five, much too early to go to the station. That long railroad trip would be a bore. She looked for quite a while at her own reflection in the mirror, wondering whether she was pretty. Many people had said she was — but how was one to know? She had never been so thoroughly upset in her life. Dick was always telling her she had lovely hair. Well — if it was — that could be accounted for by the expensive care it had. Suppose she was too poor to patronize these experts? Suppose she had to curl her own hair, or put up with a cheap permanent at rare intervals? Then — how pretty would it be?

Suddenly a new idea gripped her. Dean Harcourt had got her into this dreadful dither; and, being responsible for it, perhaps he was the right person to consult about a solution. She certainly couldn't go on this way! It was quarter after two now. If she was going back to New York on the Limited, it was time to pack.

Barbara wasn't sure whether churches had telephones, but she looked in the book and Trinity Cathedral was there; there three times. One was for the verger, one for the Parish House, one for the Dean's Residence. She tried that one. A man with a high-pitched voice and a pronounced British accent said this was Mr. Talbot.

'Are you Dean Harcourt's butler, perhaps?' inquired Barbara.

'No, Miss. I am just one of the curates.' There was a perceptible trace of amusement in the tone. 'Would you like to convey a message to Dean Harcourt?'

'I don't suppose I could speak to him.'

'Not now, Miss. He is resting.'

'Does he ever talk to people — privately?'

'Oh, yes, indeed, Miss ——'

'Miss Breckenridge.'

'Ah! You are Miss Barbara Breckenridge. The Dean said that if you called up, I was to request you to come here at four-thirty for tea. Will this be convenient?' After a lengthy silence, he said, 'May I tell Dean Harcourt to expect you?'

'But' — stammered Barbara — 'he doesn't know me.'

'Oh — that's quite all right,' shrilled Mr. Talbot. 'He will, you know. You come right along.'

'Very well,' said Barbara, uncertainly. So — he had been expecting her to call him up, had he? So — he mighty well knew he had played the deuce with her peace. Well — it wasn't a very polite thing to do. She wished she had gone to her train. There was still time. But she had promised. She would have to keep her engagement — for Grandma's sake. It was a pity that Grandma couldn't have stopped doing absurd things when she died.

The Talbot person let her in, and without asking for her name preceded her down a long hall and opened the door to a large library. The Dean was seated on the other side of a huge mahogany desk. Talbot disappeared and Barbara walked slowly across the room.

Dean Harcourt pointed to a massive churchly-looking chair and she sat down tentatively on the edge of it. Neither had spoken, so far. Barbara wasn't sure whose turn it was. Perhaps he would know — and do something about it.

'Dear me!' sighed the Dean. 'College graduates keep getting younger and younger. When I graduated, they were quite elderly — and they were wise and serious.'

'I know I'm not very wise, sir,' admitted Barbara, 'but I'm awfully serious.'

'Just now, you mean,' said the Dean. 'Wouldn't you like to take off your hat? Put it there in the closet, so you won't look quite so temporary.' He pushed a buzzer. 'Do you like tea?'

'Oh, so-so,' replied Barbara, from the little dressing-room where she had paused before the glass to pat her hair. 'I'm not passionate about it.' It was very easy to talk to this man.

'Cinnamon toast, maybe? Or would you rather have scones? We have both.'

'Both, then,' said Barbara, lounging in the chair that was three sizes too big for her. 'I'm hungry. I ate no lunch. That,' she added, reproachfully, 'was your fault.'

'I know,' confessed the Dean, 'and I didn't enjoy doing it. In fact, I too lost my appetite. It's just coming back now. Let's have a couple of poached eggs: what do you say?'

'It's a good thought,' agreed Barbara.

There was a tap on the door and a tall woman, well past middle age, evidently the housekeeper, came into the room.

'Mrs. Crandall,' said the Dean, 'my guest is Miss Breck-enridge.' They took this for an introduction, and smiled at each other. 'We find ourselves in need of a little more nourishment than you usually provide at this hour. We have had a hard day and we are both hungry.'

'Lamb chops?' asked Mrs. Crandall.

'Lamb chops?' inquired the Dean of his guest.

'Lamb chops,' said Barbara.

'And anything else that is promptly available, Mrs. Crandall,' added the Dean. 'You're agreed, Miss Breckenridge?'

'Yes — everything else. Thank you.' They all grinned a little at that, and Mrs. Crandall retired.

'Honestly — this is the first time I've felt like myself for days, Dean Harcourt,' confided Barbara. 'I've had this dreadful duty hanging over me — Grandma ordering me out here to listen to a sermon. It nearly lost me my mind. I was so frightened today. And then you told me — right before all those thousands and millions of people — that I couldn't ever know whether I had one real friend in the whole world.'

'Well——' said the Dean, consolingly, 'you have at least one.'

'Meaning you — maybe; for my Grandma's sake?'

'For your own sake. You're very good stuff.'

'What makes you think so?'

'Because you're here,' said the Dean, gently.

'You thought I would come; didn't you?'

'I hoped you might. If you had not, I fear I should have spent a sleepless night. You see, Barbara, I had only one chance at you. I had to make the medicine pretty strong. And if you had gone back home, angry and sore, it would have meant that——'

'— that I couldn't take it,' assisted Barbara, when he hesitated.

'Either that, or it would have meant that I had bungled my job. It was a rather ticklish experiment.'

A great bell high up in the Cathedral tower slowly tolled five, each stroke followed by vibrations that shook the air as if some living spirit filled the room. Then — after a pause — the carillon in the tower resonantly boomed the tune of a stately hymn. They sat in silence, with meditative eyes, until it was finished.

'What was that?' asked Barbara, her voice seeming very small after the surge of sound.

'We call it Trinity's theme-song,' explained Dean Harcourt. 'Every afternoon at five, for many years, it has been played; in all weathers, in peace time and war time. It is very stirring; don't you think?'

Barbara nodded soberly. 'There are words to it?' she asked.

'Yes. It begins, "Oh, God, Our Help in Ages Past; Our Hope for Years to Come." It has quite a steadying effect, and is useful especially to people in trouble.'

'Makes one feel awfully insignificant; doesn't it?' reflected Barbara.

'At least it makes one's trifling little personal worries seem insignificant,' agreed the Dean.

'It must be wonderful to live in this atmosphere,' said Barbara, dreamily. 'Why, those bells were just like a hard storm that swept the air clean of dust — and germs — and ——'

'And anxieties. The bells hammer at your heart with a loud challenge, too.' The Dean's voice had deepened impressively.

'I think I know what you mean,' said Barbara, softly. 'If you're being pounded full of the Help of Ages Past —

and the Hope of Years to Come — you can't remember how inconvenient it was for you to postpone the house-party at Hyannis.'

'Very well spoken, my dear,' smiled the Dean. 'You are making nice progress. If the Help and the Hope seem bigger than the house-party, that's a pretty good start. . . . Well — here comes our tea.'

'This is a high tea, wouldn't you say?' observed Barbara, rising to let her big chair be moved. 'Am I to come around on your side, Dean Harcourt?'

After Mrs. Crandall and the maid had disposed the assortment of dishes on the desk before them, and had closed the door, the Dean bowed his head and Barbara closed her eyes. They suddenly stung and flooded.

'Gracious Lord,' invoked the Dean, 'be Thou our Guest. Amen.' He raised his head, smiled paternally into Barbara's swimming eyes, and began serving her plate. There was something very mysterious about this vasty room and its churchly appointments. Perhaps one's consciousness that it was part of this big, solemn Cathedral may have had a great deal to do with it. Dean Harcourt had confidently called in another Guest, and you had a queer feeling that the invitation had been accepted. Barbara ventured to express the thought, her voice sounding a bit husky.

'But you aren't afraid, are you?' The Dean searched her eyes.

'Not while you're here,' she replied. 'But — I wouldn't stay five minutes in this room alone — not for five thousand dollars.'

'Nor would I,' said the Dean — 'on such terms. . . . But — leaving the high wages out of it — you wouldn't be frightened. Funny thing about that.... One never feels alone in here.'

'You mean — it's always here?' whispered Barbara.

'You mustn't say "it,"' admonished the Dean. 'There's nothing an "it" can do.... Now — you see if you can't destroy those lamb chops while they're hot.' He took up his silver and began setting her an example. 'And then we will talk some more about this new sensation of yours. Nothing to worry about. You're just coming alive, that's all; and you're a bit bewildered.... Remember about Galatea, Barbara? It must have been an odd feeling — that first empowering, warming heart-beat when she was changed from an ivory statue and stepped down from her cold pedestal.'

'I expect Pygmalion was surprised, too,' rejoined Barbara, with a sly little smile.

'And delighted!' agreed the Dean. 'Seeing statues come to life is a sight that never loses its novelty for the sculptor.'

'I suppose many have come alive — right here — in this room,' murmured Barbara.

'Yes — my dear.' Dean Harcourt's pain-scarred eyes were reminiscent. 'And some of them have gone out to bring other statues to life. Every Galatea wants to become a sculptor — just to show gratitude for her own release.... You know, Barbara, that is the greatest achievement and the highest joy possible in human experience — making things come to life.... We will talk about that, presently.'

'And we haven't talked at all about what I came here to ask you, Dean Harcourt. I wanted you to tell me how I could find out whether I had any sincere friends; and, if not, how I could make some. And — you said, this morning, that the greatest joy in human experience was devoted friendship — and now you say it's making things come to life.' Barbara had put down her fork and was facing the Dean with earnest eyes. He smiled indulgently and nodded his head quickly.

'It's all the same thing,' he said. 'Inviting people to come alive, and making them your devoted friends for life — it's all the same thing.'

There was quite a little interval of silence before Barbara said, confidingly, 'Is that why I feel that you are the best friend I ever had in the world, Dean Harcourt? . . . For I really do!'

'Of course. . . . Won't you have another scone?'

'But — I know I can't ever do — for anyone else — what you are doing for me,' said Barbara, pensively.

'Well — that remains to be seen.'

The tea things had been removed and Barbara was back in the big chair, with her legs folded under her, waiting for Dean Harcourt to resume their conversation. There was a faint sound of distant music.

'Listen!' She held up an outspread hand. 'They're singing — in the Cathedral.'

'Vespers,' explained the Dean.

'Don't you have to go?' asked Barbara, anxiously shaking her head. 'I haven't detained you?'

'No, Barbara. They are all competently served, in there. Mr. Talbot is seeing to it.'

'But you usually attend?'

'If there is nothing more important to do — yes.'

Barbara involuntarily drew a quick little intake of breath, and felt suddenly weighted with a solemn responsibility.

What was happening to her was of more importance than the service in the Cathedral. She felt she should do something about it; make some sacrifice.

'You must see many, many people, Dean Harcourt,' she said, 'who need things to relieve their worries. I should be glad to give some money to be used that way — by the Cathedral.'

'That's a very generous thought, Barbara. Donations of money can always be put to good use,' rejoined the Dean, absently. 'Now — let us get back to your little problem — and see what can be done about it. Whenever anyone starts out to bring some cold, useless thing to life — whether it be a block of ivory or an undeveloped personality — one chooses one's tools. But no tools are effective unless they are employed by loving hands. Pygmalion's apparent tools were his mallet and chisel, but they were used with immeasurable patience, devotion, and personal sacrifice. I don't believe that Pygmalion could have made Galatea come alive by writing a check in favor of the Athens Institute of Fine Arts.'

So — that started them off toward a lengthy talk on the ways and means whereby Miss Barbara Breckenridge might make some friends — for herself alone — preferably by an honest demonstration of her interest in their welfare.

'How would it be, Dean Harcourt,' wondered Barbara, suddenly brightening, 'if I went out some place all alone, where nobody knew me? Wouldn't that be fun?' Her eyes sparkled.

'Getting ready to do it might be fun,' observed the Dean, cautiously. 'Everyone likes the idea of doing a bit of masquerading. That part of it would be quite amusing. But the task of finding out what you want to know is pretty serious business and might take a long time. It would be unfortunate if you went into such an adventure and presently gave it up as a wild-goose chase.'

'You don't want me to try it?' doubted Barbara, disappointedly.

'I did not say that,' responded the Dean. 'But I hope you will consider the cost and avoid disillusionment. Your idea, I think, is to go out alone, perhaps under another name, and live among a different type of people than those who may have valued you chiefly for your inheritance. You think you would like to try living among the poor. Now, this isn't as easy as it sounds.' Dean Harcourt leaned forward, folded his arms, rested his elbows on the desk, and continued in a tone of reminiscence. 'There is a tradition that the poor constitute a simple-hearted, grateful, take-it-as-it-comes section of humanity, and you may have a notion that all you need do, to win their loyal friendship, is to show yourself attentive to their pressing needs. This is a false assumption. You will find that the ugliness of greed, jealousy, duplicity, and downright cruelty hasn't bunched up much in any one class of society. Poverty doesn't, of necessity, make anyone kind or good or grateful. There's a lot of wear and tear on the nerves of the poor that the well-to-do know nothing about. To win friends among them, you will have to live with them, share their work, their discomforts, their anxieties. I am not saying it isn't worth what it may cost, but you should go into it with your eyes open.'

There was a very quiet moment after the Dean had finished his lengthy speech, and through that silence they heard the melody of a hymn. Dean Harcourt reclined in his chair, closed his eyes, and softly recited the words as they were being sung. Barbara's eyes were intent on his lips.

'I was not ever thus — nor prayed that Thou — shouldst lead me on. . . . I loved to choose — and see my path; but now — lead Thou me on.'

After a long minute the distant music died away. Barbara slowly came to her feet, went to the little dressing-room, reappeared with her hat and coat on, and walked toward the desk.

'I mean to try it,' she said, steadily.

'You are a brave girl, Barbara,' declared the Dean. 'But I think it might be more prudent if you deferred your decision until tomorrow. Sleep on it. As you have noticed, the atmosphere of this place is saturated with a mystical element. Costly braveries and tragic martyrdoms make a strong appeal here. The symbols of many stirring legends are leaded into these Gothic windows, carved into the furniture, woven into the tapestries, and carried on the wings of ancient songs. You are under this spell. Reserve your decision, my dear, until you can confirm it in the sunlight and in the racket of traffic.'

'But isn't that what these inspiring things are for' — asked Barbara — 'to challenge people into making decisions?'

The Dean shook his head.

'We've had far too much of that,' he declared, almost sternly. 'Decisions impulsively arrived at on occasions of emotional stampede are not worth very much in broad daylight.'

'Then what *are* they for?' asked Barbara, reasonably enough, she thought.

Dean Harcourt smiled into the artless eyes.

'They're to buck you up,' he said, 'after you've got yourself into it. . . . Run along, now. If you take this other door and follow the hallway, it will bring you out into the Cathedral — in a transept where your arrival will not be conspicuous. You can slip in there quietly — just in time for the benediction. I think you might like that.'

'I'd much rather you did it,' said Barbara, softly.

'Very well . . . Come here.'

She went around the big desk and stood at Dean Harcourt's side, tugging off her little straw toque. He signed to her to kneel by his chair and laid his hand on her bowed head. It was a tender moment and the Dean's voice was very gentle as he said, 'The Lord bless and keep you, dear child. Amen.'

Barbara knew they wouldn't worry about her at home. On receipt of her telegram saying she had decided to remain for a few days, her busy mother would assume that she was visiting Aunt Vic. And she would be glad, for Aunt Vic was a lonesome old thing in spite of her mileage and gallant display of autumnal colors.

It had been a wakeful night, but by no means an unpleasant one. Once she had made up her mind, there were many practical details to consider. Presently her mother would be sailing for Europe. Communication, for a few weeks, would be slowed up. She would not be expected to give a precise account of herself until September, at the earliest. That was fortunate. It would save a great deal of explaining. At eight, Barbara breakfasted in her room with a road-map spread open on the table. She had decided to take to the open country. Everybody she had read about, who had attempted a social experiment, in-

variably went slumming in town, got a job in a stuffy factory, lived in a dirty kennel, and came back at length to
write sour pieces for discontented magazines. Nothing was
farther from her thought than a sociological excursion of
that sort. She was going out to look for sincere friendship.
If the people who might be disposed to like her were
healthy, happy, and clean, there could be no serious
objection to that.

At ten o'clock, Barbara was down in the basement of the
biggest department store, outfitting herself for the adventure. Having arrived early, she was not required to buck
the line for meager gains and engage in fierce scrimmages
at congested crossings, but there was already a good deal
of confusion and clatter. The sales-girls, however, with an
emotional control resembling apathy, quietly defied the
place to drive them crazy.

'Three ninety-nine,' remarked the sales-girl, indifferently,
when Barbara pointed to the pink gingham. 'Reduced
from four fifty,' she added, without warmth. 'Sale on
them, today. Very good merchandise. Bargain. How big
is she?' She held the top of the dress level with her own
shapely shoulders.

'It's the right size,' said Barbara. 'It's for me, you know.'
The sulky eyes cleared a little and were almost pretty.

'You don't want that rag,' she said, scornfully. 'The
nice ginghams are on the fourth floor. You'd look a sight!'

'I expect so,' agreed Barbara, with a little sigh. 'But
this is just what I need. And I'll take the blue one, too,
please. . . . Now, where do I go to find a cute little straw
hat for about seventy-five cents?'

'Say,' drawled the girl, '*wouldn't* that be a cute little hat?
What is this — a hay-ride? Hick stuff?' She seemed to

be getting the idea now, and grinned understandingly. Her mouth didn't seem quite so hard.

'Something like that,' admitted Barbara, casually. 'And I must find a cheap suitcase. I don't suppose you could go along with me, and show me where things are ——'

'No — I couldn't.' The nicely modeled brows were raised a little, indicating that her customer's request was out of order. The tony young lady, who clearly wasn't in the habit of shopping in the basement, ought to know that weekly wages depended on amount of sales. It certainly took a lot of crust to ask a girl to leave her post and go trotting about just to accommodate some helpless Flossie.

'Sorry,' said Barbara, contritely, realizing the situation. 'I shouldn't have asked you to do that.'

The girl turned to a fellow-clerk and, after a brief conference, came around from behind the counter, giving Barbara a faint wisp of a smile.

'Okay,' she said. 'I'll go with you.' It was quite a pleasant voice, if it wanted to be.

Barbara murmured an embarrassed protest to which the girl, with the athletic figure much like her own, made no reply as she led the way to a dreadful clutter of cheap luggage.

'There's a nice little model,' scoffed Barbara's guide. 'That slate-colored one. Dollar sixty-four. But don't leave it out in the rain.... The lady,' she announced, 'wants an inexpensive suitcase.... No — not that one. The hasps are no good. She wants one that will hold together till she gets out of the store.'

The tour was full of interest, the shopping guide making no bones about defending her client. Barbara followed

along, feeling about six years old, while they dickered for
cotton stockings and serviceable shoes — 'Your pretty feet
will be surprised,' the girl had muttered while the shoe-
clerk was loosening the laces.

'You won't be wanting any cheap underthings, I suppose,' wondered the girl, adding, 'We don't call it lingerie,
down here. It's just underthings — and it's a good thing
they're under, where nobody can see 'em, for they're
dreadful.'

Barbara considered this suggestion for a moment and
replied, 'Thanks for reminding me.' She hoped she wasn't
overlooking anything. One could easily give oneself away
if some article of attire was inconsistent. So — they found
the 'underthings'; and, having agreed that the whole
outfit was now complete, returned to the spot where they
had started.

'Perhaps I should get some cheap beads,' remarked
Barbara. 'I am used to wearing these, and — I'm afraid
they'll not be — appropriate.'

'I'll say they wouldn't,' muttered the girl, 'not with this
rummy kit you've gathered up. There are some nice ones
today for fifty-nine cents. Just like these.' She fingered
her own beads with a slim, well-kept hand.

'Good! I'll get some,' said Barbara. 'They are really
quite pretty.' Instantly she regretted having said that.
She hadn't meant it to sound patronizing — but it did.

'Oh, yeah?' growled the girl. 'Quite pretty. I'll trade
with you.'

'That's not a bad idea,' said Barbara, recklessly. Something warned her that she was committing an imprudence
but she was already into it. Raising both hands to the back
of her neck, she fumbled at the diamond clasp. 'Here,'

she said. 'Take them — and wear them — until I come back. . . . And I'll wear yours.'

The sales-girl's eyes suddenly sobered and retreated.

'Say, sister,' she snarled, 'if you're in a mess, that's just too bad, but don't think I'm sap enough to let you frame me.' She leaned forward, while a slow flush of embarrassment crept up Barbara's cheeks, and muttered, 'Don't look so scared. I won't tell. It's none of my business. . . . But I don't see why you had to pick on *me!* I've done you no harm.'

There was no suitable explanation at hand. When Barbara tried to speak her mouth was dry.

'It was — I was — terribly thoughtless,' she stammered, her heart pounding hard. 'It's just that I can't wear my beads — for some time — and I thought you might enjoy them. Better than having them locked up, somewhere.'

'Yeah — or having *you* locked up somewhere,' assisted the girl, savagely.

Barbara shook her head, helplessly, almost on the point of tears, and said, thickly, 'I'm sorry you have misunderstood. I know what you suspect — but — it isn't so.'

The girl searched Barbara's face critically.

'Say — you don't look a bit crooked,' she announced in a tone of perplexity, 'but — what the hell are you up to?'

Barbara looked steadily into the inquiring eyes, and thought fast. A nice predicament, indeed! Starting out bravely in quest of friends, and finding yourself — within an hour — about to slink out of a shop, under suspicion of theft. Well — you couldn't let it stand this way.

'If you will have lunch with me, today, in some quiet place where we can talk, I'll tell you,' she said, companionably. Her self-assurance slightly restored, Barbara ventured to smile.

'Very well,' decided the girl. 'I'll take a chance. I go out at twelve-forty-five. You meet me here. My name is Sally — in case you have to inquire. What's yours?'

Barbara hesitated for only a split second, but it was too long. Sally's mouth tipped up on one end, knowingly.

'You don't want to wear your beads, and now you don't want to wear your name. What would you like to have me think about you?'

'My name is Barbara.'

'Yeah — I notice there's a B on your handbag. But why were you stalling? You're making this pretty hard, you know.'

'I'll tell you all about it, Sally,' confided Barbara.

'All right — and the story'd better be good. I'll take those beads now.' Sally held out her hand. 'If you come back, you may have them. If you don't' — she deepened one of her dimples, not very prettily, and tossed her head in the direction of the frock-coated department manager — 'I'll turn them over to that monkey with the long tail and the big, bright eyes.'

Barbara chuckled a little, partly from amusement, partly from relief. She had never met anyone like Sally before. Sally, she thought, was pretty hard-boiled, but probably worth knowing.

'And here,' went on Sally, in a tone of elaborate sarcasm, as she unfastened her own beads, 'is my valuable jewelry, which you may take with you — as security.' Her eyes were cold blue steel as she touched off this bitter drollery.

Barbara soberly took the beads, ignoring the sour jest, and deliberately put them on, Sally's eyes following her hands with interest.

'Thank you, Sally,' she said, softly. 'I shall like wearing

them.' She smiled. 'They're still warm. Perhaps you'll
find that mine are, too. May I fasten them for you? It's
a funny sort of clasp.' They were very close together now,
the even black fringe on Sally's forehead brushing Barbara's shoulder as she bent forward. Waiting until the
beads had been adjusted, she straightened, smiled, unfastened them — and put them into her well-worn handbag.

'I mustn't wear them now,' she explained. 'People would
ask questions.'

Barbara picked up the impossible suitcase. They both
giggled.

'Leave it here,' suggested Sally. 'You can't go down the
street looking like a boob.'

'I want to put it in my car,' said Barbara.

'Where is it?' Sally inquired.

'Haven't got it yet,' admitted Barbara. 'I'm going out
to buy one now.'

'Huh! Just like that!' said Sally. 'Going out to buy a
car — between now and lunch time.'

'Why not?' It shouldn't take long. A little roadster.
Second-hand one, maybe.'

'Okay,' capitulated Sally, shaking her head. 'I thought
I knew all the answers — but I see I don't. . . . Anyhow,'
she added, with determination, 'you can't go out of here
with that thing; for I won't let you!'

Barbara gave in with a meek little 'Very well,' and turned
to leave.

'Good-bye, Sally — until twelve-forty-five.'

''Bye, Barbara,' said Sally. 'Be seeing you. Maybe. I
hope.'

It was not an easy story to tell, and Sally didn't offer

much help; just sat there in her corner of the cramped little
booth and listened with an absurdly vacuous expression of
bewilderment, occasionally mumbling through the delicious
creamed shrimps such unencouraging comments as 'Well —
for the lova Mike!... Whatcha know!... Well — for cryin'
out loud!... I'll be a dirty dawg!'

These fragmentary observations, Barbara felt, were not
ejected from the depth of Sally's mind. They were the small
coin of conversation in her social circle, no doubt, and so long
as they conveyed her general attitude these picturesque tid-
bits of speech were as serviceable as any other kind of talk.

One thing had to be said for Sally, without hesitation:
she was smart. She wasn't much of a stylist in her manner
of speaking, but she knew how to wear her inexpensive
clothes with distinction. She had the figure to do it; walked
with an effortless grace, with no defensive swagger, no
affectation, no self-consciousness. Barbara had no occasion
to feel apologetic on behalf of her pretty guest's manners
or appearance. Of course, Sally's uncouth slang gave her
away, but this was probably a superficial accomplishment
that might be easily rubbed off if anyone should go to the
bother of taking the attractive girl in hand. Any really
capable sculptor could chip away the few defacing adher-
ences and encrustations that kept Sally from being admir-
able. Her cheap lingo, for example; or was it so cheap?
It might be costing her as much as twenty-five dollars a
week to talk like an alley-rat. She might get a good job if
she mended her speech.

'Um-hum,' umhummed Sally, when Barbara launched
upon her queer experience at the Cathedral. 'I've heard of
him. He's the crippled preacher. Gosh — I wouldn't go
up there and talk with him like that — not for a hundred

dollars!' Aware that this was mere boasting, she hastened to retract the extravagance. 'Oh, yes, I would, too,' she confessed with a childish shrug. 'There isn't anything I wouldn't do for a hundred dollars.'

So — there you were, reflected Barbara; Sally's heart crying out for money to buy the pretty things she wanted, while she herself was trying to escape from her money long enough to discover what sort of person she really was — without it. She was tempted to say as much to Sally, in response to the startling candor of her recent declaration, but felt the time wasn't ripe for it, and continued with her strange narrative.

'I think you're very silly, Barbara, if you ask me,' observed Sally, upon arrival at the narrow bottom of her tall parfait glass. 'Why — anybody would like you! Even I like you — without knowing you — and there's almost no one that I really care for.'

'Your family, of course,' interposed Barbara, not quite satisfied with having said that, for it sounded a bit smug, she feared.

'My family — pooh!' muttered Sally, with frank disgust. 'If I hadn't had a family draped around my neck, maybe I could have gone to school longer.'

'To college — you mean?'

'Well — business school, anyway. I'm sick of what I'm doing. I could stay there till I'm a hundred, without a raise. No future in it.'

'Ever think of marriage?' risked Barbara.

'Yeah — and what I think of it wouldn't go through the mail! No, siree! Got enough people to look after now without taking on some lazy lizard for a husband.' Sally's passionate outburst hinted that there might have been some such motion before the house.

'But you like him, anyway, I think,' inferred Barbara, 'or you wouldn't care whether he was a lizard or a lion.'

'Yeah — I guess so,' admitted Sally, sullenly. 'Wish I could go away.'

'To do what?' inquired Barbara.

'If I told you, you'd think I was crazy.' She glanced at her cheap wrist-watch on the worn leather strap. 'Well — it's time for the dumbbell to get back to the gymnasium. Gosh — how I hate it!... And you — running away from a ritzy house-party! Boy! — if that was me! Say — I wouldn't be climbing into any rusty old jalopy — to go out into the sticks and look for somebody to like me. If that isn't the wackiest thing that ever happened, I must have missed some bad ones.' She got out her compact, made herself a new mouth with amazing dexterity, and returned her tackle to the shabby handbag, which she closed with a decisive snap. 'Thanks for the nice lunch, Barbara,' she said, graciously. 'You're coming with me, aren't you, to get your pretties? I wonder if we'll ever see each other again?'

'Of course,' said Barbara. 'We have a great deal more to talk about. I was hoping we might have dinner together, this evening.'

'You've done enough,' said Sally, shaking her head.

'Very well,' nodded Barbara, disappointedly. 'If you don't care to, I won't urge you.'

'But — gosh — Barbara!' protested Sally, impulsively. 'I thought you were just doing it — you know — to show me a good time. I didn't suppose you really wanted me to. I'd love it!'

It was nearly midnight when Sally, head in the clouds,

left the hotel to go home, after giving Barbara a bear hug at the door of the elevator.

After a leisurely dinner, they had gone up to Barbara's room. For a couple of hours there had been a serious discussion of ways and means for a little liberation in Sally's life. Adroitly manipulating the conversation, Barbara tried to discover what it was that Sally so passionately — but so hopelessly — wanted to do with herself. 'You'd think I was goofy,' repeated Sally. So — they had got back on firmer ground and talked about a course in stenography and bookkeeping. If Sally thought that such training would help her to a better position, it could be easily arranged. At that juncture, Sally's pride staged a brief fight. Then there were tears — and smiles — and exclamations of joy.

Barbara's emotions had never been put through so many paces as during the past thirty-eight hours. Sally, sensing that a little relief was in order, suggested that Barbara try on the new outfit and see how she looked.

'No — you put it on,' said Barbara. 'I'll get a better idea of how I'm going to look, that way.'

'Okay,' agreed Sally, enthusiastically, tugging her dress over her head. 'This,' she declared, archly, 'is going to be good — and I don't mean mebbe.'

It was not only good; it was superb! It was theater! For a little while, Barbara saw only the utterly devastating ludicrousness of the performance, and then it began to dawn on her that she was witnessing a really great show.

Cocking the gallant little hat at a rakish tilt, and swinging the pink gingham skirt from undulating hips — with a hand outspread against her sinuous ribs and her elbow preceding her at a defiant angle, Sally strode up and down before the cheval glass, chewing an enormous wad of imaginary gum. Without the trace of a smile, she regarded herself approvingly in the mirror.

Barbara, sprawled on the bed, watching the ridiculous pantomime, laughed until her side hurt. But Sally was quite unmoved by this appreciation; stood before the tall glass, soberly loving herself, experimenting with fresh postures and new grimaces, poking a fingertip into her cheek to dislodge the fictitious gum, seductively thrusting forward a shoulder, mincingly retreating a few steps and advancing again with an enticing smirk. Barbara sat up — and stared.

Entirely disregarding her audience, Sally shouldered and hipped herself across to the vanity table, sat down, and became immediately transfigured into an incredible primness. Barbara, watching the image in the mirror, was amazed to see the complete change in Sally's face as she pushed up the black fringe off her forehead and settled the hat squarely on the severely disciplined head. Then she rose, and walked toward the door with all the dignity of a Victorian duchess. As an exhibition of impoverished but unlicked nobility, Sally's cold, self-possessed hauteur was almost unbelievably perfect.

'Wonderful!' murmured Barbara, soberly. 'Absolutely marvelous! Sally! How do you do it?'

Sally walked toward the bed where Barbara sat, leaning back on her hands, and stood before her. Looking her squarely in the eyes, and without the faintest suspicion of humor, she said, 'Marie, we will wear the blue gown instead.' Barbara grinned and swallowed dryly, wanting to play up, but hardly knowing what was expected of her. 'Well?' Sally's brows lifted imperiously. 'What are you waiting for?'... Then — instantly — she tugged off the hat, tossed it into a chair, shook her bangs down, smiled companionably, and tumbled down on the bed beside Barbara. After a moment of silence she murmured, deep in her throat, '*That's* what I want to do.'

'And it's what you ought to do,' agreed Barbara, with conviction. After a considerable pause, during which her thoughts were busy, she added, 'I think I can help you.'

'Barbara!' Sally raised up on one elbow, wide-eyed. 'Could you?'

At that, Barbara began thinking aloud. Tim had asked her to join his dramatic workshop in Provincetown during July and August. Her present plans would prevent that. Why shouldn't Sally go in her place? Tim would gladly consent to take her if Barbara insisted.

'I shall write to Juliet, my maid, to send you my summer clothes,' Barbara went on, half to herself, 'for I'll not be needing them, and you may as well have them.'

Sally burrowed her face into the crook of Barbara's arm, and gave a childish little sob.

'You are to plan on that, dear,' continued Barbara. 'I'll see you through. I'll love doing it.'

When Sally had gone, Barbara went to her desk and began a night letter to Tim. It was difficult to compose. Her real reason for not returning to the Cape for the summer defied any sensible explanation. No reason at all would be ever so much better than the real one. Of course, Tim would simply have to consent to Sally's coming. Barbara's promise to help subsidize the expenses of the Playhouse gave weight to her suggestions, no matter how unexpected and bewildering they might be.

When the telegram was finished, and Barbara re-read it, she had an entertaining vision of Tim's squinted-up face, upon receipt of it, and the probable nature of his incredulous remarks. But the message was the best she could do, so she phoned down for a boy to come and get it.

Then she began slowly undressing, her thoughts busy with the stirring events of the past two days. Life had suddenly become a very important affair. She previewed an imaginary picture of the house-party that wasn't going to take place in the big old summer home at Hyannis, and dismissed it with a shrug and a flick of the fingers. She had never been so completely happy before. Sally's friendship was the most exciting sensation she had ever experienced.

In the face of this new heart-warming bond, what she was planning to do seemed unnecessary, inexcusable, silly. What was the good of it? She hadn't quite realized what an idiotic thing it was until she had sat down to tell Tim. Confidential as they had been, she couldn't tell Tim; not so he would understand.

Seated at the open window, in her pajamas and dressing-gown, Barbara tried to recapitulate. She needed, she felt, to reorganize her thoughts a little. If she was getting ready to do something that was so wacky she couldn't confide it to one of her closest friends, maybe her plan should be overhauled.

She didn't have to drive away tomorrow in that battered little teapot; didn't have to lose herself in the hinterland, hunting for friends who might love her in spite of the dowdy clothes. Her friends were genuine enough. Tim; for instance. Of course — Tim needed her support of his pet project. You couldn't be too sure about the sincerity of Tim's devotion.

But — take Sally!

Barbara's brows contracted a little. What would Sally's affection amount to, if she hadn't been promised a chance to do what she had always wanted to do? How much of Sally's sweet tenderness was sheer gratitude? Was Sally loving her for herself — or for what she was going to get? How could one know?

She went to sleep, at last, with a troubled heart. The adventure she had planned seemed now to be more urgent than before. She knew she would never be happy again, until she had made this experiment.

At eight-thirty she was wakened by the arrival of a telegram from Tim.

> OF COURSE WE WILL TAKE SALLY. SEND HER ON. BUT WHAT IS THIS BIG MYSTERY? WHERE ARE YOU GOING AND WHAT FOR? STAND BY FOR TELEPHONE CALL AT NOON. VERY ANXIOUS ABOUT YOU.

The threat of this telephone conversation was a troublesome thought, the prospect of talking with Tim about her plans seeming much more disturbing than the dilemma of composing a telegram. Sally's arrival, at ten, cleared away this difficulty.

'That's easy enough,' said Sally. 'You don't have to be here at noon.'

'Yes — but what will he think?'

Sally dismissed this problem with an overhand gesture.

'Why should you care what he thinks? He's not your nurse.'

Sally did have the most efficient techniques for disposing

of anxieties. Barbara felt that this accomplishment must have been achieved only by long practice. 'What they don't know,' according to one of Sally's favorite maxims, 'won't hurt 'em.'

Not quite satisfied that this was the proper way to treat Tim, but yielding to the seasoned advice she had received, Barbara went down town with Sally and accompanied her to the store, where she collected her wages to date, and notified Mr. Wood that she was leaving. Barbara, standing a little way apart, could not help hearing this conversation. Mr. Wood was gracious enough, but inquisitive.

'Are you,' he asked, 'taking a position in some other store?'

'No, Mr. Wood.' Sally's tone was decently respectful, but it hinted at a recent convalescence from tonsillitis. Barbara turned her face away and grinned, wishing she had the brass to watch Mr. Wood's expression. 'I've had an offer,' continued Sally, 'to join a company of players in Provincetown.'

'You don't tell me!' said Mr. Wood, sincerely amazed. 'I didn't know you'd ever done any acting.'

'I haven't — very much,' confessed Sally, modestly. 'But now I've a chance to — and I want to try.'

'Can't blame you, I'm sure. And I wish you luck.' Mr. Wood followed along, as Sally turned away.

'Meet my friend, Miss — Miss Brown,' said Sally. 'This is Mr. Wood, Barbara.' They bowed and smiled briefly.

'Miss Brown's responsible for my going east,' explained Sally.

'Are you an actress?' inquired Mr. Wood, deferentially.

'Just an amateur,' deprecated Barbara.

Mr. Wood's eyes shifted rather reluctantly to his departing sales-girl.

'Whenever you are in town, Sally, drop in and see us. I don't imagine you will ever be looking for a job again — in a store' — he chuckled a little over the absurdity of what he was saying — 'but if you should, we'll try to find a place for you.'

Sally thanked him prettily. It pleased Barbara that she didn't turn up her nose at this friendly remark. After all, reflected Barbara, as they threaded their way through the crowded aisles, Sally did possess something like an inherent refinement.

'My gosh!' said Sally, as they reached the outer air. 'I never realized how awful that place stinks.'

'Smells,' corrected Barbara, incorrectly.

Returning to the hotel, and having had luncheon, they reorganized their equipment. With many misgivings — for Barbara looked a different person in her new rig — Sally assisted in this metamorphosis of her generous friend. At Barbara's insistence, she packed the modish clothes in the expensive bags with the understanding that she was to keep them and use them as her own.

Then they went to the hotel garage. Nobody there seemed to take much interest in Barbara's appearance which comported nicely with her battered roadster. The well-dressed Sally and her impressive luggage, on the other hand, excited curiosity and attention. The bell-hop fluttered about her, eager to be of service. When the bags were stowed away in the back deck, Barbara tipped him a dollar. As they drove out, the boy stared at them with eyes squinted and mouth slightly ajar. They noted his perplexity and laughed.

Not much was said on the way to Sally's home — a dingy, fourth-rate apartment house in a noisy, untidy street a few

blocks south of the Loop. There Sally disembarked, and
good-byes were said.

'You'll write, then,' repeated Sally. 'Soon as you get
there.'

'Tell me everything,' said Barbara. 'And tell them
nothing.'

Slogging along through lumbersome traffic in the dank
shadow of the shrieking elevated railroad, Barbara eventually escaped into the sunlight, made better time to the
Boulevard, and drove north to the Cathedral, parking the
old rattler in front of the Dean's Mansion. Mr. Talbot,
to whom she had telephoned in the morning, opened the
door and greeted her with a slightly confused smile of
recognition. It was apparent that the absent-minded curate
was unable to define his perplexity, but equally evident
that something had happened to their lovely client since
her last visit. Having stared at her, myopically, until her
own face reflected Mr. Talbot's anxiety, he thought to put
Barbara at her ease by telling her it was a beautiful morning, though it was now a quarter past three.

'I must look dreadful,' reflected Barbara, 'to have
frightened the poor lamb, that way.'

Yes, he said, Dean Harcourt was expecting her, and she
should go in, at once. Preceding her to the library, he
opened the door and departed. Barbara went in and took
the big chair where she had sat in conference for several
hours, only the day before yesterday. It seemed much
longer ago. A lot of things had happened.

The Dean put down his pen, polished his glasses, and
smiled.

'Pretty hat, Barbara,' he observed, dryly.

'A dollar.' She lifted it off, preciously.

'They overcharged you. . . . Well — are you off now?'

'Yes. Have you time to hear what I've been doing?'

'I haven't time for anything else,' said the Dean. 'And please don't hurry.'

With this encouragement, Barbara curled up in the ponderous chair and gave a full report of Sally. When at last she had come to the end of it, Dean Harcourt sat for a while quietly tapping one open hand with the back of the other, deep in thought.

'So — you're going to put her on the stage,' he said.

Barbara nodded, and said she hoped and believed that Sally had it in her.

'I suppose you have carefully considered that you're going to be responsible for whatever may happen to her in this new life with which she is unacquainted,' warned the Dean, soberly. 'When you chop people out of the ivory, and invite them to come to life, it's your duty to see that they make the most of it.'

'Do you feel that way toward me?' asked Barbara, just above a whisper. 'For you brought me to life, you know.'

'Yes — I feel that way toward you, and now I shall be feeling a measure of responsibility for Sally, too. You see, my dear, there's no end to the obligation resting upon a creator.' The crisscross lines encircling the Dean's eyes deepened. 'Bringing people out into larger opportunities is not a mere hobby that may be regarded lightly; taken up and put down; played with, for an hour, and tossed aside. Pygmalion mustn't say to the inexperienced Galatea, after his last chisel-stroke and her first heart-beat, "There you are, my young friend. Run along — and have yourself a good time. I've a date to go fishing."'

'You mean — that if Sally' — Barbara's eyes were full

of anxiety — 'if Sally should get into trouble, it will be my fault?'

'Not your fault, perhaps, but unquestionably your responsibility. This thing you are doing — and the other things you are likely to be doing — glorious things — noble things — are very serious. It is dangerous business to tinker with other people's lives. Even when you think you are doing them an immense favor, it is dangerous.'

'Perhaps it might have been better for Sally,' murmured Barbara, 'if I had left her where she was.'

'No,' declared the Dean. 'I don't mean that. You have done a fine thing for Sally. But now the new Sally is your property to insure and defend. And if — sometime — she encounters a problem too big for her to solve, in the life to which you invited her, you dare not say, with a sigh of dismissal, that you thought you were doing the right thing; and it's too bad; for she really had a lot of natural talent; but that's the way it goes when you try to help anybody — and you'll bid four no-trump.'

Barbara winced.

'I'm laying this on, dear girl, with a pretty heavy hand; but I want you to avoid the mistake that many people make when, on impulse, they decide to wave a wand and order a carriage for Cinderella. You've made a new creature of Sally. Keep it in mind that you have not been dressing a doll. Oh — I see a plenty of this sort of thing. Lady Bountiful has a notoriously short memory.'

'I know,' agreed Barbara. 'I've seen it happen. I never thought much about it before.'

'There's a great exultation,' said the Dean, 'rewarding an act of such stunning and unexpected generosity that the recipient is introduced to a new way of life. To see that this high benefit is conserved may turn out to be pretty tiresome business.'

Barbara nodded slowly and remarked that it gave you quite a little thrill when Fido licked your hand, in gratitude for the candy: but you're willing that Celeste should have the thrill of washing him.

'Barbara,' said the Dean, warningly, 'you're maturing fast. That piece of cynicism was worthy of a woman of fifty.'

'One of our professors — a sour old curmudgeon — said one day, "If the Social Agencies kept track of their clients with the zeal of the Tail-Waggers Association, there wouldn't be so many boys in jail."' Barbara rose, went to the Dean's side, and took his hands in both of hers. 'I'm going now,' she said. 'You've been very good to me.'

'You'll write?'

'Promptly! Everything! Pages and reams!'

'Decided on a name?'

'Brown — Barbara Brown.'

'Does Sally know all about your plans?'

Barbara nodded.

'And I trust her fully,' she added. 'I took the liberty of asking her to come and talk with you before she leaves.'

'Will she?'

'I'm not sure. She didn't promise. Perhaps she might if you invited her. Would you?' Barbara's eyes entreated.

'No; that's not the way,' objected the Dean. 'She will come, I think.'

'Because I asked her?'

'That's a good enough reason.'

Barbara walked to the door, opened it, and said good-bye with her lips only. The Dean regarded her with a tender smile, and her eyes suddenly swam. He shook his head, still smiling; and Barbara, dashing the tears out of her eyes, smiled, too.

'Barbara!' called the Dean, as the door was closing behind her. She turned a pensive face toward him, inquiringly.

'As hats go,' he said, comfortingly, 'I've seen worse.'

When two weeks had passed with no word from Barbara, and the Dean was beginning to be anxious about her, a bulky letter arrived postmarked at Axton, Nebraska. He made haste to read it.

> Dear Dean Harcourt (wrote Barbara): On my way west I saw an advertisement in the *Omaha Bee* asking for help with the wheat harvest on a big farm. 'High-school graduate only,' it said. That interested me. I had no notion of applying for that kind of work, but it seemed to me that if they employed many men surely there would have to be a lot of people to feed them.
>
> Mr. Wendell is a tall, tanned, kind, shrewd, not very talkative man of forty, who could be made up to pass for Lincoln if he had a short beard and a long, black coat in need of pressing. He is a graduate of an agricultural college. There are a thousand acres in wheat and two hundred in pasture for the dairy. I asked him how many cows and he spent some time making a mental count. Then he shook his head and grinned and said, 'Too many.' The cows are Guernseys. I asked him if the Guernsey was the finest make of cattle and he said, 'Yes — if that's the kind you happen to own.'
>
> Everybody calls Mrs. Wendell Midge. I think they must have begun calling her that a long time ago. She plays the accordion skilfully; says she wishes her arms were a little longer. She also is a graduate Aggie. She doesn't talk about

Gershwin or John Dewey but knows more chemistry than I do, and speaks chummily of the characters in a dozen contemporary novels that I haven't bothered to read. The Wendells have no children. This is fortunate for the nine girls who work here in the kitchen and dining-room; for they get a lot of mothering that Midge wouldn't have time to give them if she had a few moppets of her own.

The girls are all from Nebraska towns; all high-school graduates of this year's class. Andy Wendell employs a new cast of waiters each season. Midge says, 'We always get them fresh from school, but don't want them *too* fresh.' As the only college graduate, and a little older, I am directing the dining-room service. My position has the flavor of a cabinet office, where the Secretary of the Navy doesn't actually need to know a cruiser from a catboat.

We are quite a large family; twelve men from the dairy farm, twenty in the wheat; at present an additional dozen helping with harvest. Most of the men are in their twenties and thirties; all high-school alumni but five foremen who are Ag School graduates. There are five or six older men; one keeps books. Andy Wendell says that's the chief trouble on a good many farms: they never know what they've got or what they can afford to buy; pay $130 for a new reaper to cut a crop worth $150. So — old Mr. Blosser keeps the books, draws the pay-checks, watches the markets. We have a nice little printing-press, and get out our own promotion bulletins, for we sell a lot of dairy products done up in flossy packaging. (Haven't I learned a great deal in a short time? We have a patter of our own, same as any other trade.) Andy Wendell dislikes the word 'stuff.' Some farmers call every product 'stuff' — chickens are 'stuff,' turkeys, alfalfa, no matter what; to them it's all 'stuff.' Andy says 'stuff' has been discarded by everybody but the out-and-out hicks. I mention this to show that we are stylists, in good and regular standing.

The venerable Mr. MacLeod is our printer. He always

preaches Sunday mornings at the church in Axton, and almost everybody goes. Preaching is part of Mr. MacLeod's duty as an employee of Andy Wendell. Andy says churches mostly cost too much; have to do so much talking about money there's no time left to talk about religion; says Mr. MacLeod keeps them all sweet — no matter what their creed — because his Scotch burr makes it all sound simple and honest. I said, 'Does Mr. MacLeod preach the old-time religion?' And Andy said, 'Hellyes! — good old Mac believes that Jonah swallowed the ark — or whatever that story was. And so do I, when he rumbles it in his throat.' I like Mr. Wendell very much.

There are no rules and regulations for our conduct. Midge says if they had rules they would have to enforce them, which would be a time-wasting nuisance, and keep everybody at loggerheads. 'No,' says Midge, 'we just let their own common sense tell them how to behave themselves. Once in a while somebody runs out of bounds, and Andy pays him off and quietly scoots him away when nobody's looking. . . . Andy,' adds Midge, 'is a great believer in human frailty.' I think this is funny; don't you? Midge says, 'Andy Wendell wouldn't give a nickel a dozen for people who had to be managed like a lot of grade-school kids. Andy's a little more lenient, that way, than I am,' Midge admitted. Then she lowered her voice and confided, 'Couple of years ago, I had to spank a girl. Pretty nearly tired us both out. I won't do that any more. My hand was hot and swollen for a week.' . . . 'How did the girl feel?' I couldn't help asking, and Midge said she guessed the girl was quite a bit annoyed by it.

We have several rather tepid little romances in progress. It's amusing to see how they are developing. But apparently it has to be undertaken craftily. If a girl shows special attention to the young fellow who has been caught winking at her, she has to be careful about bringing him an outsize dessert, or a low humming begins to gather volume around the busy table; a tune I had never heard before, but seems familiar to everybody else here. The text of the song — which they do not actually sing, aware that the melody will be sufficient — runs, 'Oh you must be a lover of the landlady's daughter or you won't get the biggest piece of pie.' When the tune is hummed, with all eyes intent upon the dessert, and every fork active, and every face innocent, it takes a lot of brass for a girl to continue her campaign. (Does this bore you to death, dear Dean?)

I think I may truthfully say they like me here. At least they are kind and warm-hearted and tell me their little secrets. I feel dreadfully old. Saturday afternoons almost everyone goes down to Axton, our nearest town of any size. Population 850. Andy Wendell says it's plenty big enough. 'Try to make a city of Axton,' drawls Andy, 'and pretty soon you've got to have waterworks, and higher taxes; and soon as the taxes are big enough to tempt office-seekers, then you've got a lot of lazy bums and cheap grafters running your town.' I haven't heard anyone offer a comment about Andy that wasn't enthusiastically loyal and friendly, but I fear he is a bit of a martinet. He is Axton's best customer, and I think he has a good deal to say about things. I don't know: I'm just guessing. Midge told me a couple of men from some wacky little sect came to Axton, last summer, and wanted to organize a church; and they were advised to see Andy about it. They told Andy, when he asked them what sort of religion they taught, that they had had 'a second blessing.' He asked them what they worked at, between church services, and they said they'd been on Relief. And — according to Midge — Andy drawled, 'Well — instead of having two blessings — and expecting the government to furnish the food, I think it's better doctrine to have just one blessing over victuals that you've earned.' Isn't Andy funny? You'd like him, I think. He is very much like you. I mean — you never know what he's going to say next.

I went to town, last Saturday evening, with three of the

girls. My car is not roomy, but it held us all. I offered to treat them to ice cream. There were ten-cent dishes and five-cent cones. They all took cones because I hadn't been working long enough to accumulate any money. I thought that was rather sweet of them; don't you?

Will you have time to write me a wee letter, telling me how you are, dear Dean? Of course, you've seen the news in the papers about what's happened to Sally! Isn't that the oddest thing you ever heard of? Just fancy! — Sally in Hollywood!

Love and Gratitude,

Barbara Brown

And *am* I *brown?* You ought to see me!

II. Flood

It HAD been raining, almost without pause, for sixty hours; raining opaque oyster-white sheets evenly unrolled from an invisible mid-February ceiling; raining pitchforks, cats and dogs.

Young Richardson apathetically turned his swivel-chair halfway round until its Spanish leather back chafed the Spanish leather front of the Manager's desk in Uncle Earnest's suburban bank, laced his long fingers behind his close-cropped blondish hair, and through the spacious window viewed the late afternoon deluge with a scowl.

As a youngster on his unlucky father's farm in northeastern Ohio, Lee had always enjoyed the rain. He remembered it best as an early summer pageant, preceded by fireworks and bowling in a blue-black sky; rain that began with warm splashes on your faded shirtsleeves and drove you dripping into the old barn while the flat-backed horses, on their own, trotted with jingling trace-chains to their snuggery below. Then you and the older boys drew up some empty feed-boxes to the wide doorway and sat watching the slanting downpour with the clear conscience of work-haters loafing with a good excuse.

Much as he had despised the monotonous drudgery of the farm, there was much to be said for such enchanted moments; the tang of sun-baked earth pounded by sprawling raindrops, the heady aroma of new clover in the mows, the sense of security from the storm: it was ever so much better than what he was doing now. Even the pungent reek of the stables: he would have been glad to sniff it again.

June rainstorms in Ohio had personality. They briefly terrorized you, but they liked comedy, too, thinking it fun to catch you out and pelt you with handfuls of hailstones — an occasional bewildered fishworm tossed in for good measure. They tried to scare you with rockets and growls, and then the sun (which, at such moments — according to Lee's politically minded father — resembled the beaming face of William Howard Taft) would come sneaking slyly around the corner of a dark curtain, pretending that nothing had happened.

It was different here in Southern California where the infrequent rain was as grim and glum as a realtor with an overdraft. This California rain had no imagination. Some bleak afternoon it would begin to rain. Spiritlessly, and without any promotional build-up, it would begin to pour as if it had always been pouring. It would continue to pour until the enormous concrete reservoirs in the high hills were full and slopping over, and the usually dusty arroyos were mad and menacing rivers — wide, witless, heartless Frankensteins that went plunging drunkenly and with many a devastating short-cut toward the sea, with buckled bridges on their shoulders, battered bungalows under their arms, and melting gardens in their muddy hands.

'After all,' squeaked old man Crenshaw, from the adjacent cashier's cage, addressing the dejected back of his young boss, 'we've got to have rain, you know. Makes things grow. This country can't live without water.'

'I know,' muttered Lee, sullenly, without turning his head.

'You'd better go now,' advised Crenshaw, after an extended silence. 'You've quite a drive — and it isn't going to get any better.'

'I promised Worthington I would see him here at half-past four — about that renewal.' Lee swung slowly around and fumbled through the sheaf of memoranda that the Lyons person had laid on his desk before she left.

'Well — I can talk to Worthington,' rasped old Crenshaw. 'He'll have to dig up half of it this time — and no foolin'.'

'His wife has been in the hospital, he tells me,' commented Lee.

'That,' snapped Crenshaw, 'isn't the fault of the Citrus Trust and Savings Bank. Somebody's always sick at Worthington's. Somebody's always owing him money he can't collect until the tenth; tenth of what, he doesn't say. You hop into your car and get home while you can. Your Aunt Patty will be worrying about you.'

'I want to talk to Worthington, myself,' persisted Lee. 'I'll telephone home.' He drew the instrument toward him and lifted the receiver.

'You can't,' cackled Crenshaw. 'There's been no phone service for an hour. Worthington won't show up. The rain will be a good enough alibi for him. You'll be waiting for nothing.'

'I said I'd wait,' growled Lee, 'and I mean to.'

'Then I'll go. No need our both staying. You know how I feel about that old note.' Crenshaw made much ado over tugging on his slicker and stomping into his rubbers, impatiently shook his umbrella, stalked to the front door, and dove into the downpour.

Lee looked up at the clock. It was four-ten. Crenshaw was probably right about poor, debt-bedeviled Worthington. He wouldn't come. Lee hoped he wouldn't. This was one of the things about the banking business that he loathed. Every day he was expected to sit here, in the rôle of Old Scrooge, listening — frosty and fish-eyed — to the distressful whimpers of cornered men, some of them old enough to be his father. Their shame embarrassed him. He hated the job as he would have hated the job of pulling the switch in the death-house. In eight months, the remorseless grind of it had eaten through his lining and down to the hard metal.

He knew, of course, that Crenshaw — mean old penny-pincher that he was — had plenty of justice and common sense on his side when he maintained that this was a bank; not a Salvation Army post. It was a bank, and it couldn't do business respectably by renewing inadequately secured notes for people like Worthington. But if Crenshaw were thirty-five, instead of sixty-five, he would have got himself socked on the chin for his cold-blooded avarice. Lee had the spot picked out — a little patch of gray stubble that the old buzzard usually missed when shaving.

Nor did he like the lanky Lyons female any better. She and Crenshaw had been with the bank from the beginning. The pair of them were of one small mind. Their joint contempt for his inexperience and chicken-heartedness was so thinly veiled that they might as well have reviled him to his face. And there was nothing to be done about it. They knew he knew that Uncle Earnest would keep them on as long as either of them was able to stand up.

He drew a block of sketching-paper toward him, took out a soft pencil, and began idly drawing free-hand lines.

He might not be much of a success as a banker, but he knew how to draw cartoons. Lyons and Crenshaw, in a huddle over a ledger, were rapidly taking on form and unmistakable identity. Lee grinned sourly, and polished them off. You couldn't exaggerate this sketch if you tried. Any attempt at a comic valentine would turn out to be an accurate photograph. He carefully tore up the caricature and tossed the scraps into the waste-basket. If old Crenshaw were to happen upon such a portrait of himself, he would be much annoyed. Lyons would have a fit.

He looked at his watch. It was four-twenty now. Aunt Patty would be fretting. He leaned back in his chair and frowned darkly. What an ingrate he was! Everyone but himself kept saying that he was indeed a fortunate young fellow; a bank manager at twenty-two; heir apparent to Uncle Earnest's estate; steeped in luxury: with a lovely girl, already picked out for him by Aunt Patty. A very lucky fellow. Lee wished he could feel grateful.

This alleged good fortune had begun to accrue to him when Lee was slightly past seventeen. When his hapless father died, in time to miss the humiliation of a threatened foreclosure on the decrepit farm, Uncle Earnest — previously a legendary figure — had come on for the funeral; had come by air, an adventure then important enough to share space in the local paper reporting his brother's farther flight. It was the first time Lee had ever seen his wealthy uncle, and he was much impressed. Uncle Earnest was not only a handsome, self-possessed man of the world: he was a good egg. And Lee liked him, followed him about, hung on his words.

Mellowed by the nostalgic sights, sounds, and scents of the old homestead, and the gaunt waxen face of his dead brother, the forceful Californian had made a swift and successful effort to put things to rights. He couldn't help noticing the undisguised admiration that shone in Lee's eyes while all this business was afoot. Three days after the funeral, the Ohio Richardsons were in a fair way to sustain themselves, their future practically secure. Jim and Roy, detesting school, were overjoyed to remain with Mother on the redeemed farm. And how easy it had been for Uncle Earnest to dispose of the mortgage that had haunted them for years. Lee had driven him into town, in the old Model T, and leaned against the railing that fenced the bank president's desk while Uncle Earnest conferred with the great man. It had made his inexperienced young heart bump with family pride, the way Uncle Earnest unbuttoned his checkbook and licked the old mortgage as casually as if he might be buying a cigar. On the way back to the country, Uncle Earnest had said, 'So you don't like farming, eh? Well — I think I'll take you back with me to California, and we'll see if there's anything you do like. Want to?'

Lee wanted to so badly that his voice was shaky when he said, 'Oh — yes, sir!'

'Better turn around then and we'll go back to town and get you some suitable clothes. We will start west tomorrow morning.'

That was the way Uncle Earnest did things. No grass grew under his feet. It had been quite an experience, going out to the Coast on fast trains, sleeping in a Pullman, eating in a dining-car with Uncle Earnest, who excused his own extravagances by declaring that when he couldn't travel first-class, by Golly, he wouldn't travel at all.

Aunt Patty, childless and restless, had taken Lee under

her wing immediately upon his arrival in Santa Claudia.
His uncle, he discovered, was under the other wing. It was
amusing. In Ohio, Uncle Earnest had been so capable, so
decisive, so dynamic. At home, he spoke his mind in-
frequently, tentatively, always with a cautious glance at
Aunt Patty who regarded him with the brooding anxiety
of a perplexed mother gently disciplining a not very bright
child. Lee's position in her esteem was slightly better than
Uncle Earnest's. As a youth and a dependent, his prompt
and complete obedience to Aunt Patty's whims was to be
expected. He had no dignity to lose.

Aunt Patty was dainty and petite, but she had the re-
lentless energy of a Diesel engine. Doctor Throckton —
according to an unexpected outburst of confidence on the
part of Uncle Earnest — had said it was thyroid; too much
thyroid, or too little: Uncle Earnest had forgotten which.
But however Aunt Patty's pathology was to be accounted
for, Uncle Earnest could not keep up with it, and Lee
divined that whatever the future might hold for him, his
immediate job was to attend Aunt Patty.

It was not at first an irksome occupation. She showed
him all Southern California, himself at the wheel of her
smart twelve-cylinder coupé. She took him to a swanky
tailor in Beverly Hills, told him which fabrics he liked
best, and sat by while they took his measure. She bought
him a spirited horse and a three-hundred-dollar saddle,
gave a high-keyed garden party for him, and mothered
him to suffocation. She would have held him on her
lap and rocked him to sleep if he hadn't been six feet
long.

Aunt Patty had an authentic talent for planning, down
to the last detail, how her family and friends should engage

in the pursuit of happiness. It had to be conceded that she did a very good job. You couldn't put your finger on any one item of the program she made for you, and denounce it as an obnoxious and insufferable imposition; but you knew she was strangling the life out of you.

Sometimes, at the dinner table, she would get herself going on a monologue of plans so far-reaching and comprehensive that you were ready to burst with laughter. But you retained your serious expression of interest and approval while she prattled on. Uncle Earnest was only fifty-four, physically sound, up to his neck in all manner of business enterprises, had no thought of retirement; but Aunt Patty would forecast the eventuality of his decline, coupled with the consoling thought that Lee would be prepared to take over as Uncle Earnest sought the peace and comfort of a wheel-chair in a sunny corner of the patio.

Uncle Earnest's contribution to such embarrassing nonsense was usually restricted to brief grins, mirthless chuckles and perfunctory nods, with an occasional sly self-defensive wink in Lee's direction; but it was a pretty grim form of entertainment, for the good old boy's experience must have warned him that his wife's predictions had a dismaying habit of coming to pass, with the inexorable accuracy of astronomical calculations.

As for Lee's future, Aunt Patty had been plotting and mapping it without delay. There was to be, 'of course,' a year in an exclusive prep school, 'near home, darling, so you can bring your school friends here for week ends.' This would be followed by four years in college, 'where — naturally — you will want to specialize in banking and business administration.' Then Lee was to come home and relieve Uncle Earnest who, by that time, would be wanting to retire but not yet too old to enjoy the two-year tour around the world 'which we have been planning on for a long, long time; haven't we, Earnest?' Uncle Earnest would shift his cigar to the other corner and rattle his paper and say he supposed so.

'Of course we will hope,' she had said, on one occasion, 'that Lee will have found some sweet girl whom we can all love. They can have the whole west wing for their little nest — and she can do over that part of the house to suit her heart's desire. I hope you won't think me foolishly forehanded, Earnest, but I was looking at some perfectly exquisite drapes today; exactly the thing for their sun-parlor, when the time comes. She will adore them!'

'Patty!' Uncle Earnest had shouted, unexpectedly. 'For Mercy's Sake! Have you decided yet how many children they are to have, and what they are to do with themselves when they grow up?'

'Let's not make a joke of this, Earnest,' Aunt Patty had replied, fervently. 'I'm sure I don't know what might have become of us, if we hadn't planned a few things — as we went along.'

It was quarter to five now. He would wait for Worthington until the clock struck, and then he would go home. Caroline would be there. Aunt Patty had invited her over for the week end. He would have to do something, pretty soon, about Caroline.

Really — it had been almost uncanny, the way Aunt Patty had engineered her plans for him. Everything had come out as she had ordained.

It had even seemed that his mother's death, on the day he was starting west for his summer vacation at the end of his Junior year, had been timed so as to interrupt as briefly as possible the schedule of events arranged for him. He needed only to drop off, en route, and attend the obsequies. Jim had married a neighbor girl. The old place would carry on. Lee felt himself superfluous, and was glad to resume his journey.

He had taken Aunt Patty's orders without debating them; had graduated last June at Columbia; had returned to Santa Claudia; had let them ease him gently into the Manager's chair at the Citrus Trust and Savings. In almost every particular he had obeyed Aunt Patty's wishes. Lee had not bothered to inform her that his Saturdays, during his last two years in the university, had been spent in art classes at the Metropolitan; for it would have disturbed her to know that his mind was not wholly devoted to preparation for a business career. He knew it would break her heart if he confessed that he hadn't the slightest interest in banking, and wanted only — above all things — to paint. She would have been still further distressed if she had seen some of his impressionistic sketches.

Uncle Earnest and Aunt Patty had come on to New York for the Commencement ceremonies. That night, after making sure they were in bed, Lee had slipped out of the hotel to attend a farewell party given for him by his arty friends, down in the Village. He would be back soon, they all told him. It was flat against nature and sense, what he was going to do. You couldn't make a sow's ear out of a silk purse, they said. They all drank a good deal of cheap sherry, and a couple of the girls cried. Altogether — it was a sad leave-taking.

'And Uncle Earnest and I have something very pretty to show you when we get home,' Aunt Patty had said, mysteriously, when they were comfortably settled in the train, next day.

This very pretty something had turned out to be Caroline Brooks, a recent discovery of Aunt Patty's. Caroline's family had come out from Massachusetts to make their home in Los Angeles. No time had been wasted in promoting this acquaintance. Aunt Patty had not deceived him. Caroline was indeed a pretty girl, perhaps a little lacking in vivacity, but — as Aunt Patty said — 'a most agreeable young woman.' And, of course, she would have to be agreeable — in the sense of being willing to agree to anything and everything — if she hoped to live in peace with Aunt Patty. Lee wondered whether it was much of a compliment to say of a person, 'He is agreeable.' Why should you want other people to be 'agreeable,' unless you hoped to fashion them into mere tools and playthings?

Lee wasn't sure that he wanted an 'agreeable' wife. His instinct warned him that to get this insured agreeableness you had to reconcile yourself to the idea that it would be found in an inevitable combination with a flock of incipient phantoms and fears.

Take Caroline — for instance: Aunt Patty was always referring to the girl as 'so *spirituelle*.' Well — that might mean that she was unusually refined, meditative, ethereal; or it might mean only that she had a tendency toward pulmonary tuberculosis. There were so many things Caroline did not do, because she was afraid of them. She didn't know how to swim, and was unhappy on the beach. She rode with the inflexibility of a clothespin — apprehension staring from her lovely, sky-blue eyes — because she was afraid of the horse; and the horse — however unintelligent about everything else — guessed that she was scared, and decided to help her find some good reason for it. She was ever ready to play golf, but it wasn't much fun either for her or the others, seeing she was always either hunting her ball in the high weeds, or trying to scoop it out of the mud. But Caroline was sweet, and had a trick of looking at you with an unabashed adoration that made you feel small and ungrateful if you failed to take immediate steps toward some gesture of appreciation.

Aunt Patty had seen to it that Lee and Caroline had plenty of opportunities to develop their friendship. Indeed, the dear old lady's match-making campaign had been pursued with such resolute vigor that it had become ludicrous. He and Caroline had even ventured to joke about it, on the sly; though it was easy to see, in Caroline's childishly perplexed eyes, a slightly hurt look. It was funny, but Caroline didn't want it to seem an utter farce.

Ever since Christmas, when Aunt Patty had been almost ruthless with her comments on the privileges granted by mistletoe (sprays of it dangling from every open doorway in the house), Lee had observed her mounting impatience. The long-planned trip around the world was to push off in April. Aunt Patty couldn't bear to leave, she said, until she could feel that Lee was going to be contented during their absence. In short, she had demanded, why didn't he ask Caroline, and be done with it? He expected to; didn't he? Well — what was he waiting for? Why didn't they have the wedding at once — 'so Uncle Earnest can set his mind at rest about this whole matter.' This silly remark had made Uncle Earnest laugh until it had brought on an attack of his asthma. But Aunt Patty hadn't thought it a bit funny.

As Lee left the house, this morning, she had walked with him to the door, her arm hugging his. 'I expect to improve your uncle's cribbage game, after dinner tonight,' she said, in a confidential tone. 'It will give you and Caroline a chance to have a nice quiet talk.' Lee had grinned, and patted her hand, without promising.

'I quite insist, Lee,' she had added, meaningly.

The clock struck five, deliberately, firmly, as befitted a statement by a bank clock. Banks always kept the correct time. When a thirty-day note was due, they knew it.

Lee rose, stretched his long arms to full torsion, and gave an audible sigh. He would go now and face the inevitable. It couldn't be postponed another hour. After all, Caroline was a dear girl. She would be a good wife. They wouldn't quarrel. Caroline and Aunt Patty would get along together comfortably, which was something to be considered. It would be disastrous to marry a girl with any spunk.

Bidding good night to the old watchman, Lee splashed down through the alley — almost curb-deep with a yellow stream, popped into Bryson's garage, agreed with Bryson that it was nice weather for ducks, spun his engine, and rolled his sport roadster toward the street. There were very few cars on the road and these few were proceeding with caution. Ocean Boulevard was wide but the river that overflowed it was wider. You had to look sharp to find the pavement. There were no street lights.

As he neared Cuyahoga Canyon, where the beautiful new bridge spanned the arroyo, Lee could hear the roar of water pouring down through the deep cut in the palisades. He slowed the roadster almost to a stop as his headlights showed huge piles of débris straining against the concrete balustrade. The car behind overtook and passed him, hurling a great dirty wave that showered his windows.

Lee decided that if the bridge was safe for the other fellow, there was no reason for him to hesitate. He slipped into second gear and started across.

For many months after that, he would wake in the night with a start and re-experience that first demoralizing sensation when the bridge collapsed. With a grinding crash it parted in the middle like the big gates of a canal-lock, and then slowly toppled. The memory of what happened during the next few minutes was to remain for a long time as painful as a physical wound, a confusion of swift and suffocating events over which you had no more control than a basket spinning in a whirlpool.

He had had just enough presence of mind left to turn off the ignition as the roadster was swept from the broken bridge and into the current. After that, his movements were not directed by his reason: it was simply a blind, strangling, drowning struggle to escape from his trap. He was never able to remember how many times the car rolled over. The windows broke and the river poured through. Glass from the shattered windshield slashed his forehead. Something metallic — perhaps a heavy chunk of road machinery embedded in the river — pierced through the fabric of the top while the car was upside down, and cut a gash in his scalp. He clawed at the door-handle, and pushed with the strength of desperation, his lungs bursting, his brain spinning. Presently the door let go and was torn off. He rolled out into the roaring flood, and the roadster went bumping on, end over end.

Lee couldn't recall much of what happened from then on; just a succession of hard buffetings by wreckage careening down stream. Something huge — it looked like the twisted verandah of a wooden cottage — bore down on him and he grabbed at it as it swept by. Round and round it whirled until one corner of it stuck in the muddy embankment and paused for an instant before dislodging to resume its drunken journey to the sea. In that brief moment, Lee let go his hold and tried to swim, his breath coming in agonizing wheezes. Then, as his torn and bruised hands clutched at the slippery embankment, he realized that his muscles were relaxing. His consciousness was leaving him. Some piece of flotsam banged him on the head, and roused him to a final struggle. The sense of abject terror, that had left him momentarily, returned to inspire the fight for life. Digging his numbed fingers, elbows, knees, feet into the embankment, he dragged himself out of the savage river, and lay — sick and spent — in the mud.

He could only guess how long it was until his mind had cleared enough to prompt further action. Wearily struggling to his feet, he plodded, stumbled, often falling to his knees, on a wide, circuitous route back to the boulevard. Even in his utter exhaustion, he grinned a little when at last he reached the road. It had been a rough trip across Cuyahoga Canyon, but he had crossed it. Dim lights glowed near the pier of the broken bridge where a dozen cars were huddled at a safe distance. He had a notion to walk over to them, but there was nothing they could do for him. Toreador Pass would be just as badly flooded as the Canyon road. It was silly to think of trying to get back home tonight.

Temporarily forgetting that telephone service was disrupted, he trudged south, with the water churning in his shoes, resolved to find the gasoline station which he knew was not far away. When he found it, the place was abandoned and pitch dark.

There was nothing to be gained by standing still, for he

was chilled to the bone. Doggedly he resumed his purpose-less plodding southward. San Benito was only five miles and on much higher ground. Perhaps he could find some-one who would put him up. He wondered where his roadster was, by now; probably mired some place far out in the bay, broken up beyond hope of salvage, no doubt. He tried to imagine what he would look like, about this time, if he hadn't been lucky enough to force his way out. Lee shud-dered. But for that little spot of good fortune, he would now be dead as cold mutton.

A mile or more farther on, he came upon a little cluster of tourists' cottages by the roadside which he identified as a motor court. There were no lights visible. Lee tried the door of the nearest cottage and found it unlocked. Groping about, he discovered a candle on the table and lighted it. The little cubicle was furnished simply with a bed and a couple of chairs. There was a diminutive gas stove and a toy bath-room adjacent. He stripped off his muddy clothes, draped them over the chairs in front of the heater, treated himself to a shower, wrapped up in the blankets, and gradually relaxed. But not to sleep. His nerves had been too savagely tortured to permit an immediate restoration of his mental stability.

In the morning, reflected Lee, rescue crews would prob-ably find his car. Uncle Earnest would be making every effort to get news of him. Aunt Patty would be in a grand state of hysteria. If he didn't show up or send some mes-sage, within a few hours, he would be given up for lost. For the present, he was the same as dead. It was an odd sensation — to be the same as dead. He didn't have to go back, at all, if he didn't want to. He could let them think he was dead. It would certainly solve a lot of problems. For the next two hours, he drowsed, roused, dreamed, half deliriously toying with this idea. The temptation to run away, change his name, and live his own life, was not a pretty thing to contemplate; quite too fantastic; perhaps impossible. Eventually someone would recognize him and there would be a shocking scandal, and that wouldn't be fair to Uncle Earnest and Aunt Patty. But it would be almost worth the risk — to escape from further life with Aunt Patty. No — it was silly even to speculate on such a wild project; but it had its points: no doubt of that. At length he slept, fatigued to complete exhaustion.

At the first hint of dawn, Lee shook the dirt out of his clothing and distastefully tugged it on. His shoes were still damp, but the loathsome clothes had dried out fairly well. Peering into the cheap little mirror he examined the gash in his forehead. It had been deep but not long or ragged: it would heal without attention. His hair was matted over the scalp-wound, and he decided to let well enough alone for the present.

The rain had stopped and the sky was clear. It was going to be a bright day. He stepped out of the cottage but saw no sign of life. There was no reason why he should tarry. Laying three one-dollar bills on the little table — Lee felt this would be ample — he was pleased to note that he still had a little over a hundred in his soggy wallet. The diamond ring they had given him for Christmas — he hadn't wanted it; always felt like a sissy, wearing it — had survived the night's rough experience. The watch, he assumed, was ruined. It wasn't running.

He decided he would walk until he came to San Benito and make an effort to communicate with his people. If the telephones were working again, he would call up the house and they would send Spratt for him. Jack would probably have to detour around through Santa Ana, or some place over there.

The sun was coming up brightly now; and, in spite of his extreme discomfort, Lee was almost gay. He was going to have at least two hours more of freedom, the first he had had for a half-dozen years. There was a certain exhilaration of independence, he reflected, that nobody could realize but a tramp. The meadowlarks were calling. They seemed hilarious about something; their liberty, maybe.

At the outskirts of San Benito, Lee found a little 'quick-and-dirty' open for business. He mounted a tall stool at the counter and ordered ham and eggs. Screwed to the greasy wooden wall, at the rear of the dingy room, was a toll-telephone.

'Phones still out?' called Lee, to the owner-manager-cook.

'Nope; she's O.K., now, cap'n.'

While the ham sizzled, Lee sat eyeing the telephone. All he had to do now was to deposit a quarter and resume his chains. He thought he would eat his breakfast first, which he did — ravenously. Then he paid his check, punched a vending machine for a package of cigarettes, lighted one, and strolled out. He wasn't ready to call up yet.

San Benito was waking up. More people were appearing on the street. Shop doors were opening. Lee sauntered on through the business district into the residential zone. When the houses began to thin out, his steps slowed. If he was going to telephone from San Benito, he had better go back to the little hotel on the corner, and do it. As he stood, debating, a big, ugly oil tank lumbered past him, slackened to a stop, and a friendly young voice sang out, 'Want a lift, buddy?'

Lee climbed up beside his benefactor and offered him a cigarette.

'Thanks for taking me on,' he said. 'Much better than walking. Very good of you.'

'I'm going through to San Diego,' said the driver.

'That's good,' Lee heard himself saying. 'So am I.'

He couldn't blame people for glancing at him with disapproval as he sauntered through the smart shopping district of San Diego. He was, he felt, a disreputable-looking creature: too dirty and unkempt, in fact, to go home, regardless of the reasons for his untidiness. They would surely forgive his delay in returning when he explained that it was necessary to recondition himself. As for his tardiness about telephoning to relieve their anxiety, well — he could say he thought the phones weren't working. He had often lied to Aunt Patty. There was no moral law requiring slaves to tell the truth.

Turning in at the first attractive men's furnishings shop, he outfitted himself with fresh linen, a new pair of shoes, a hat, and a ready-made gabardine suit, some toilet articles; packed his purchases in an inexpensive bag, and registered at a second-rate hotel. On the point of writing his name, it occurred to him that the papers had probably reported him lost, and he didn't want his people at home to learn of his self-rescue until he could tell them. His name on the hotel register might be identified by some reporter. So — he wrote 'Lawrence Runyan,' and gave his address as Seattle.

He was glad he had retained his initials when, a few minutes later, he called a boy to take his clothes out to a cleaner, for his suit was marked with them. After he had shaved and arrayed himself in his new kit, he felt a different man. Hungry again, he devoured with relish an Irish stew in the hotel's coffee shop. The meat was decidedly second-class, but he liked it.

Lee hadn't been out in Exposition Park since his first summer in California; had driven Aunt Patty down to Coronado, and they had gone through the park. He had wanted to stop at the zoo, but the smell of animal cages always made Aunt Patty sick. Now that he had some free time on his hands, it would be pleasant to stroll through the zoo. He had never had a chance before.

A long yellow streetcar whip-cracked around a few down-town corners and laboriously ground up the long hill. Arriving in the park, Lee heard music and leisurely pursued it. An organ recital was in progress, relayed by strong amplifiers to the beautifully landscaped plaza. He sat down on a green bench in the shade to listen. Tourists, by couples and families, were sauntering about; or, like him-self, lounged on the benches. It was not the most suitable spot for serious thinking. He had promised himself that he would settle everything, out here, and dispose utterly of his indefensible urge to prolong his freedom. One fact was crystal clear: if he was going back to Uncle Earnest and Aunt Patty and Caroline — and old Crenshaw and the sulky Lyons woman — and the Spanish leather chair in the Citrus Trust and Savings, he would have to do it very soon.

But the afternoon sunshine was sedative, the graceful eucalyptus trees were at peace, the tourists had nothing important on their minds, the formal beds of stock and snapdragons and primula and pansies were not excited about anything, and Schubert's 'Unfinished Symphony' bore him effortlessly along, its subjunctive mood condoning his irresolution.

Somebody had left a paper on the bench. The headlines were tall, broad, black, and a bit noisier than usual. Flood news. Lee didn't take up the paper; just leaned apathetically in its direction, and looked at the pictures. There was a large one of himself on his roan mare Cynthia. It was, he reflected, very good of Cynthia. Anyone who knew her would recognize her. He was pleased to observe that his own picture would not be so easily identifiable. His face had been shadowed.

After the organ program was over, Lee strolled down into the ravine and looked at the polar bears. They were sitting up, smilingly soliciting peanuts; an acquired taste, probably; not many peanuts being raised in the Arctic Circle. He lazily meditated on this for a while. You take a polar bear, now — he was saying to himself; cart him away from his natural habitat, build a commodious home for him, complete with den, rocks, and a nice swimming-pool: order his life for him; give him the toys to play with that you think you would like if you were a polar bear. Pretty soon he surrenders to circumstances and gives up trying to be a polar bear, and shares your peanuts with you, feeling that you expect him to show his gratitude for the fine big cage by liking the things you like. Some people said that caged animals usually lost their minds. These polar bears had not lost their minds. Indeed it was rather clever of them to accept their plight so suavely. But there was no doubt that they had lost their souls. Eating peanuts was, for them, an exhibition of gross immorality. The question was: shall the polar bear sulk and refuse to eat peanuts, and thereby be true to his nature — or shall he pretend to be happy in his pretty prison? But — suppose you were to open the big iron gate and let him out? What would he do then? Go back to the Arctic? And if he did, would he sometimes reflect that he was a fool for wanting his liberty? Perhaps he might even hanker for peanuts, up there where there aren't any peanuts.

Feeling that he had paid enough attention to the bears, and a little disgusted with them, Lee proceeded farther down the road, induced by a finger-board that said, 'To the Swans.'

A bareheaded, florid, stocky man of fifty was seated on a campstool, before an easel, facing the pond. Lee paused and the artist glanced up over his shoulder. They exchanged nods.

After a little, Lee said:

'Rather difficult subject, I should say. Don't they ever sit still?'

'Sometimes,' replied the other, absently, 'when it's very warm and they've just been fed. They're unusually restless, today. I'm not trying to do anything about them, you'll notice.'

Lee thought this was an invitation to look at the canvas, so he drew closer.

'I see,' he said. 'It's the pleached tree-shadows on the pool that you're after, today. You'll do the swans later.'

'You paint?' mumbled the artist, without very much interest.

'A little,' Lee confessed. 'But not this sort of thing. It takes a special aptitude, I think, to do lights and shadows on still water. You've certainly got it — if you don't mind my impertinence.'

'A pleasant remark,' said the artist, without looking up,

'is never an impertinence — if it's addressed to anyone but a damn fool.'

'Well — my judgment of such things doesn't amount to much, I'm afraid, but I think what you're doing is every way as good as the work of this Chicago fellow, Trowman. Of course you know his swan pictures.'

'Yes, I know them. You like them?'

'They're excellent! The picture I like best of the lot is the one Trowman did in Jackson Park. I never saw the original. It's in the Chicago Art Institute; isn't it? You've seen it, no doubt.'

The artist dipped his brush again and touched the canvas lightly before replying. Then he glanced up, and smiled companionably.

'I'm Trowman,' he said. 'I'm rather partial to swans.'

'I wouldn't give it another serious thought, Richardson. You've only one life to live and — the Good Lord knows, and said so — the life is more than meat, just as a head is more important than a hat. You've been offered your freedom. You'd better take it.'

It was nearing midnight. They had had dinner together, repairing afterward to Trowman's room to continue their talk. Lee, in grave need of confiding his problem to someone, and much attracted to the artist, had told him the whole story, feeling it was safe in his custody.

'I'm not sure' — continued Trowman, contemplating a procession of smoke-rings — 'I'm not sure but it's your duty. What are you going to be, in your luxurious cage, but a damned hypocrite? You despise the banking business; therefore you will not do it very well. You'll probably bust the bank, and that won't be fair to your Uncle Earnest.

You'll secretly despise your Aunt Patty, and sooner or later the old lady will realize it; probably have her heart broken. And I think it's a dirty trick to ask a girl to marry you for any other reason than that you love her. Here you chatter along about the sacrifice you would be making if you went back and resumed the old burden — for their sakes! Hell! — your sacrifice would be nothing compared to all the forbearance they would have to practice, in trying to live with you. They'll hate you, boy!'

Lee nodded, stamped the fire out of his cigarette in the ash-tray, rose, and took up his hat.

'I think you're right,' he said, wearily. 'I know you're right. It was a godsend for me to have someone like you at hand to help me to a decision.'

Trowman came to his feet and offered Lee his hand.

'You'll be ready to go with me, then, starting early Sunday morning. I'll enjoy having you share the driving. We should make it to Chicago in a week, that way.'

'And you think you can find me something to do, in the way of commercial art?' asked Lee, realizing it was a tiresome question, for they had gone over all this with care.

'Of course, of course,' sighed Trowman. 'I won't let you get into any trouble. You can earn your expenses, and have plenty of time left over for drawing lessons. Now, you pop along to bed, Richardson. You've had a hard day.'

Lee paused at the door, grinned rather self-consciously, and said, 'By the way, Mr. Trowman, perhaps you'd better get into the habit of calling me Runyan. Mustn't let my name slip out, you know. It's too risky.'

'Good point,' agreed Trowman. 'You're Runyan now. Lawrence Runyan. You must begin at once to feel you're Lawrence Runyan, so that you can make an immediate response to your name. Your people would probably have called you Larry. I shall call you that, if you're agreeable. This Lee Richardson is dead, and you're not to think about him, any more, Larry. There's nothing you can do for him.'

Within a week after their arrival in Chicago, Larry was growing restless in Tony Trowman's classes. He had reasons for thinking that several of his fellow students felt the same way. Most of them were younger than he. All of them had respect for — at least curiosity about — the modernistic schools of painting. Tony was invincibly, irascibly orthodox. He had no patience with modernism in any of its manifestations; wore an old-fashioned flannelette nightgown; polished his own shoes; looked as if he cut his own hair.

But you had to take Tony seriously. He was a sound workman. He knew his swans, his dappled sunshine on still water, his highlights on dim interiors. He was an artist of the classic school, uncompromising in his demand for his students' adherence to formal subjects, academically treated.

'The trouble with you young squirts,' Tony would snarl, 'you want to paint before you can draw. That's all that your precious realism comes to. Your so-called realist is too damn lazy to learn the rudiments of drawing, so he pretends to be pioneering a new field. And then he has the brass to say that anyone who doesn't appreciate his senseless smears is lacking in imagination. Bah! The hell with it!'

One morning, flushed with annoyance over Trowman's contemptuous comments on this subject, Larry blurted out, 'But you wouldn't say that Manet and Monet and Renoir didn't know how to draw; would you, sir?'

Immediately he regretted his impulsive speech. Trowman had done a great deal for him at a time when he was in serious need of friendship. This was a poor way to repay him. Tony made no rejoinder; gave him a long, searching look as to say, 'That — from you!' — scowled, shrugged a shoulder, and walked out of the room. After that, their relationship never regained its former status, though they worked together in harmony, and were scrupulously considerate of each other's feelings; much too considerate.

Now that this constraint had damaged the only important friendship he had left, Larry began to realize his isolation. It had not yet depressed him seriously, for his days — and evenings, too — were fully occupied. His work with the advertising concern was being received favorably, his wages were ample to permit his living comfortably in a fairly good apartment, and his drawing technique was rapidly improving under Trowman's attentive criticism.

But the Saturday half-holiday and the Sunday leisure were hard to take. They brought on a previously unexperienced type of loneliness, a loneliness that sapped your vitality, dulled your mind, and destroyed your appetite.

It was a lucky thing for Larry when he and Roger Price became close friends. Roger had graduated in Architecture at Cornell, last June, and had found a not very promising job with a firm of architects that had been immensely prosperous until building operations everywhere had come to a standstill. With a good deal of idle time on his hands, Roger had been studying with Tony Trowman who had insisted on his familiarizing himself with the Gothic.

'When these bad times are over,' Trowman had said, 'there'll be some new churches to build — and college chapels — and things like that. And nobody will know how but you! All the rest of 'em won't be able to build anything but big, ugly, square warehouses, made of cement and plate-glass framed in chromium.' Feeling that he still had something left to say about this, Tony had added, venomously, 'And the walls of the lobbies covered with deformed giraffes hitched to bathtubs on wheels — and misshapen nudes with their arms full of snakes.' Roger had taken Tony's advice without enthusiasm, for he wasn't specially interested in ecclesiastical architecture; but it would be excellent practice. If you could draw good Gothic, you could draw anything. Presently he found himself absorbed by it, working late in the evenings when most of the others, but Larry, had gone home.

By early May, they were spending their Sundays to-gether, usually on long hikes into the open country, after an hour on a north-bound train. Sometimes Larry was invited to the Price home in Evanston for Sunday dinner. He had not confided his story to Roger, nor had he suffered any misgivings about that, but he always felt unworthy of Mrs. Price's warm friendship. Her attitude toward him was almost maternal, and when she greeted him as 'Larry,' he sincerely wished that was his name; wished he had nothing to hide; wished it was easier to look squarely into those honest blue eyes. Roger's sister Jean lived at home and attended Northwestern. She was a very attractive girl and Larry could easily have taken an interest in her, had it not been for a little incident, at their first meeting, which made him thereafter uncomfortable in her presence.

It had happened at their dinner table. They had been talking about inept, unusual, fantastic names that people had given to their pets. Mrs. Price knew a woman with a cat named Nebuchadnezzar. Doctor Price knew a successful young surgeon in Cleveland, Doctor Paige, who had once owned a valuable red Irish setter named Sylvia.

'And that young banker who was drowned, a few weeks ago, in a California flood,' said Jean, 'had a horse named Sybil.'

'Cynthia,' corrected Larry, automatically.

'That's right; it was Cynthia,' consented Jean. 'Did you see the picture? What a dreadful thing to have happened to him!'

'It almost killed his aunt, who idolized him, the paper said,' added Mrs. Price. 'They were about to leave on a long voyage, but had given it up.'

'I should have thought that a good reason for going,' put in Doctor Price.

The conversation shifted, but it was some time before Larry felt at ease. It had been a pretty close call. Jean had seen his picture. He found himself reluctant to meet her eyes, and realized that she had noted his altered mood as she gave him another quizzical glance. After that their relationship was amiable enough, but it could never be anything closer, even when the time came that he felt quite assured she had no suspicions about his identity.

In July, the Price family went to their summer cottage in Wisconsin, and Roger engaged a small suite in the bachelor apartment house where Larry lived. Through those days, they were practically inseparable. One Sunday morning, with no definite destination, they were strolling north on Lake Shore Boulevard.

'What's all the hubbub?' drawled Larry. 'Where's everybody bound for — all of a sudden?'

'Trinity Cathedral,' replied Roger. 'Very popular preacher in there. It's the thing, now, to hear Dean Harcourt on Sunday morning.'

'Odd fad,' commented Larry. 'What does he talk about that's so interesting?'

'Dunno,' mumbled Roger. 'Never heard him. By the way' — brightening — 'that's one of the finest examples of English Gothic in this country; follows the general lines of York Minster. The windows are superb! I've done some sketching up here. How would you like to go in — so long as we're this close?'

'We'd have to stay; wouldn't we? Couldn't just look around, and walk out, while the thing's going on.'

'It might be interesting to hear what the old duffer's got to say. Want to?'

It was a huge crowd and a serious one; nice-looking people, too; not at all the sort who would go galloping about in search of a sensational harangue. Larry, entering with indifference, was immediately impressed. It was indeed a very beautiful church. The great nave was rapidly filling. The organ was playing. It was a restful atmosphere. If you were worried or on a tension, this was the place for you. Your little frets didn't stack up very high under this vasty, vaulted roof. Nor you: you didn't stack up very high, either: about the size of a grain of sand on the seashore.

The place made you dreamy. Everywhere the bright young radicals were denouncing religion as a sedative offered to numb your ambition. Well — it was a sedative, all right. No doubt about that. You could feel it in the air, slowing you down. Maybe that was what this scurrying, stampeded, anxious, envious, pushful, fretful generation needed — a sedative. Wherever they went, there were plenty of stimulants. The keen young philosophers apparently saw nothing menacing in stimulants, goads, and irritants for these jittery people. It was the sedatives that they were down on. Mustn't take anything that might quiet your nerves: you might form a habit. It didn't matter if you formed a habit of taking stimulants, until you couldn't live without a deafening din around you; had to have drums, had to have cymbals, had to have confusion. Religion should be abolished by law, thought the bright ones; for it was nothing but a sedative.

The preliminary ceremonies, hymns, and prayers were over now. Larry had been barely aware of them; too busy with his own reflections. The famous preacher was being led into his pulpit by two assistants, for he was a cripple. It was a striking face, deeply lined, thoughtful, testifying to a wisdom that was just, a justice that was kind, a kindness that was courageous, a courage that was patient. The voice was of a peculiar resonance. It had an intimate quality, as if it spoke to a small circle rather than a congregation of two thousand. The Dean wasn't addressing a crowd: he was talking to you.

'Every normal person,' began Dean Harcourt, 'is incurably provincial. No matter how much he knows about geography or how widely he has traveled, the meridian lines of latitude and longitude cross where he is standing. The true north is always north of him.

'He sets his watch backward or forward as he journeys, and the time he keeps is the correct time. Others may speak of Greenwich Time, Central Time, Tokio Time, but his time is the Right Time; and when the sun goes down it is difficult for him to imagine daylight persisting anywhere else. The focal point of world interest is wherever he happens to be.

'In his opinion, the men of ages past lived bewildered lives, making mistakes in dealing with the forces of nature and menaced by ignorant fears. They doubtless did the best they could, he admits, though it is hard to understand how the wisest of them missed seeing so many obvious facts that ten-year-old boys take for granted.

'Men of the future, he surmises, may improve the practical adaptation of our discoveries, but the most important period of world development is now. He grins when he thinks of his great-grandfather's manner of life; and, in respect to his great-grandson, he has no thoughts at all. The world was hardly worth living in, when his great-grandfather was here, and it may have come to an end before his great-grandson arrives. In other words — if I am of normal mind, the best place to live is here and the best time to live is now. The world centers in me. The most important fact in the world is myself. The Master referred to this personal conception of the world as "the kingdom."'

Larry had heard much such ideas presented, but not quite in this way. They seemed to mean more than they had ever meant before. Perhaps the solemn atmosphere of the Cathedral made them impressive; perhaps it was the curiously pervasive quality of this man's voice. The words had the flavor of authority. They had weight, height, depth. They had size.

'Of course,' the Dean was saying, 'not everyone is of normal mind. Something upsets the orderly processes of a man's thinking, and then it begins to appear to him that the kingdom is some place else than where he is, and some time other than today. Some say the kingdom was here, and is gone: some say it has not been here, but is coming. The Master said, "The kingdom is now; it is here; it is yours. It is within you."'

Larry found his attention divided between the things the

Dean was saying and the thoughts they suggested. It made no difference where you went, you took your kingdom along. You viewed the whole universe from the windows of that kingdom. If the world was running down, it was because your kingdom was growing shabby. If the world was en route to better things, that was because things were looking up in your kingdom. If there was wholesale confusion in the world, it was because your kingdom was confused. You carried a replica of your world inside your heart. If the big world outside seemed about to go to smash, that was because your kingdom was breaking up.

That was why it was so important to your happiness and your success and influence that your kingdom should be unencumbered, unafraid, and unashamed. 'All other problems will settle themselves,' said the Dean, 'when you have set things right — in your kingdom.'

There was a little more, after that, but Larry did not hear it. He stirred from his dismaying reverie when the Dean raised his hand and the people stood. Mechanically he rose and stood with them. After a while the closing ceremonies were ended, and they all slowly funneled through the great front doors.

'You've got to give it to the old boy,' said Roger, when they were out in the sunshine. 'He makes you listen. His stuff sounds as if it came from headquarters. Want to wait a little, until the crowd clears out, and look at the windows?'

'Some other time,' said Larry, absently.

'How about a spot of lunch?'

'I'm not hungry. If you don't mind, I believe I'll go back. I've some letters to write.'

'No — it is not a new or strange story, Mr. Richardson,'

Dean Harcourt was saying. 'Sometimes people do a great deal of damage in exercising a possessive love; do it with the very best of intentions. I daresay your Aunt Patty never realized that she was making something of you that you didn't want to be.'

It had not been difficult to arrange for an interview with the Dean. Larry had returned to his apartment on Sunday very much depressed. Nothing had been said at the Cathedral that touched his problem specifically, but the Dean's words had searched and scorched him. He had indeed made a dreadful mess of his life. Sitting down at his desk, he had tried to write to Uncle Earnest and Aunt Patty; had made a dozen starts; had torn up many half-finished pages, beginning again and again. Then he had given it up, and had impulsively written a note to Dean Harcourt. Could he have a private talk with the Dean? He was in trouble; needed counsel. Would the Dean be so kind?

And now he had finished telling Dean Harcourt all about it. He had not found it hard to do, once he had begun. Occasionally the Dean had interrupted with a brief question or a laconic comment, but had encouraged his guest to proceed to the end. At length Larry made a little gesture of laying the whole thing outspread on the big mahogany desk, and relaxed into the massive Gothic chair.

'Of course,' continued the Dean, thoughtfully, 'you have not come to ask me whether you have done the wrong thing. You know the answer to that question. I have no reproaches for you, for I assume you have attended to all that yourself, and have probably done a good job. It is a mistake, I think, to rebuke anyone who has rebuked himself. It puts him on the defensive, and that destroys the work he has already done on the subject.'

Larry grinned. He had never heard it put this way before, but it sounded like good sense.

'The thing now is to find the best way out, which may or may not be the quick way,' the Dean went on. 'We must proceed carefully. You're dead — so there's no hurry. By the way — in discussing your case, I suppose we'd better think of you as Larry. Right?'

Larry nodded.

'Let us talk first about your Aunt Patty. Here is an example of misdirected devotion. Love, like any other tremendous energy, can work evil as well as good. It's like fire, water, ink, electricity: it has to be used properly. Do you remember the story of Pygmalion?'

'And Galatea?' remembered Larry.

'The same. Pygmalion could have made anything he pleased of that valuable block of ivory; could have carved a Grecian athlete or an angel or a martyr. The Athenians would have admired his skill, but the statue might not have breathed. Pygmalion carved out an ideal that he loved so dearly that she came to life; but it was his love, rather than his genius, that brought her alive.'

'Lucky for both of them,' drawled Larry, 'that she liked herself well enough to like him.'

'Maybe she didn't,' rejoined the Dean, half to himself. 'Perhaps she just pretended — out of gratitude. There's a lot of that sort of thing. You would have done that, yourself, but for the flood. These Pygmalions, who undertake to bring things to life — in their own image or according to their own ideas — ought to divide the blame if the job turns out badly.'

'I wish Aunt Patty could hear you saying that, sir.' After a moment's pause, Larry went on. 'If I wrote them

I was here in Chicago, they wouldn't wait for me to come. They would hop on a plane. And when they arrived, you could talk with them. Would you, Dean Harcourt?'

'If I know my Aunt Patties,' said the Dean, smiling reminiscently, 'that wouldn't do much good. Perhaps more could be accomplished by a letter.'

'Will you write to them, sir?' Larry's voice was unsteady.

'If you like. I shall state the case as fairly as I can, pointing out that it would be unwise to ask your return to conditions so intolerable that you ran away from them. I shall tell them that you want to be an artist, not a banker; that you want the privilege of selecting your own wife; that you want to live free of their supervision. I shall not say where you are or what your present name is.'

Larry's face was illumined.

'That will be wonderful of you, Dean Harcourt,' he exclaimed. 'You have been very good — and I'm afraid I have taken a lot of your time. I'll go now. Here's their address.'

'Just a moment.' The Dean signed for Larry to sit down again. 'Now — I have told you what I shall be saying to Uncle Earnest and Aunt Patty. But I've a few things to say to you. While it is true that your Aunt Patty has been injudicious, she and your uncle have given you many valuable benefits. Your university education, for example: have you any plans for repaying that debt?'

'I hadn't given it a thought, Dean Harcourt, but I believe they would be hurt if I said I would send back the money.'

'I agree that they would not want the money. But the debt should be discharged somehow — in money or service. You can't settle that university debt by refunding to your

uncle and aunt. Tuition fees do not support universities.
You're in debt to society. It's a debt that can be discharged
only through your contribution to the public welfare. Now
you are hoping to make painting your life work. What
kind of painting? Will it benefit society? Can you pay
your social debt with it? Will your pictures make anyone
a better citizen? Will they inspire people to be more courageous, more kind, more patriotic?'

'I doubt it,' confessed Larry, without looking up.

'So do I,' said the Dean. 'From what you have told me
of the sort of art in which you are mainly interested, I
gather that you will not be in a position to pay your debt.
Now — you run along and think that over, Larry.'

Saturday afternoon, in prompt response to a telephone
message from the Cathedral, Larry took a taxi to the Dean's
house. Evidently some word had been received from Uncle
Earnest or Aunt Patty. A great deal depended on their attitude toward him. Larry was almost sure they would want
to conciliate, but he had done them a grave wrong and they
couldn't be blamed if they reproached him.

He was met at the door by an arrestingly beautiful woman
of thirty-eight to forty. She was smartly gowned in street
clothes. Her carriage and manner identified her as a
sophisticated, socially experienced person, hardly the type
one expected to meet in these solemn precincts.

Larry gave her his name. She smiled graciously and said
the Dean was expecting him. As he followed her down the
long hall, he thought she was one of the most superb crea-
tures he had ever seen; so pronounced a brunette that she
seemed to be of Latin origin; something decidedly exotic.

Opening the library door, she stood aside, with a comradely look into Larry's eyes, and signed him to enter. Dean Harcourt detained her to say, 'We will not want to be disturbed for an hour, Sonia. If there is anyone else wait- ing ——'

'Mrs. Tucker.'

'Oh — the one who just lost her daughter. Well — you talk to her, Sonia. Take her for a walk in the garden. Take her for a drive up the lake shore. You know better what to say to her than I do. Tell Talbot to look after the reception parlor.'

Without making any reply she softly closed the door be- hind her. Advancing to the massive Gothic chair he had occupied before, Larry couldn't help saying, 'Pardon my asking, Dean Harcourt; but is that lady your secretary?'

The Dean laid aside the bulky letter he had been reading, polished his glasses, and glanced toward the closed door with a tender smile.

'No,' he said, after a reflective pause, 'that lady is an ex-officio, part time, volunteer assistant. Several years ago, facing a little dilemma, Sonia came here to talk about it and accidentally collided with someone else who was fretting over a much more serious problem. She discovered that the best way to ease her own mind was by offering sympathy and substantial aid to other people in distress. So — ever since — that has been her occupation. To pay expenses, she operates an exclusive gown-shop.'

'She's certainly lovely!' said Larry.

'Yes,' murmured the Dean. 'And wise — and sound — and good.' He took up the letter. 'Well — we have heard from our Aunt Patty. It is addressed to me, and it is some- what lengthy. And here is a briefer one from Uncle Earnest, addressed to you.'

Then the Dean proceeded deliberately to read aloud
the letter from Aunt Patty. It had been written in bed
and was somewhat incoherent in spots. The joyful news
had disorganized Aunt Patty. Lee could have anything
he wanted; he could do anything he wanted. He would
never have to think of that silly old bank again. He was to
pick his own friends, live where he pleased, spend his time
painting — 'if that's what he likes.' It was a complete
capitulation. Lee was alive! Nothing else mattered.

Uncle Earnest's note was to the same purpose, only
more steady.

'Your usual allowance,' said the letter, in closing, 'will
be at your disposal. Tell me where to send it.'

'They are very fine people,' said the Dean, gently, 'and
these are very fine letters.'

Larry nodded — too deeply moved to say anything.

'But an affection like that,' continued the Dean, 'in-
creases your obligation. You'll have to do something very
important, my boy, to justify their feeling toward you.'

'Have you any suggestions, sir?'

The Dean leaned back in his tall chair and meditated for
a moment before replying.

'A few days ago, I had an interesting letter from a friend
who feels very deeply that the public should have its attention called to the advantages of life in the country. The
men and women who established our republic were mostly
farmer-folk. In recent days, thousands of their children
have crowded into the factory centers where most of them
live cramped, artificial, discontented lives.

'Now — this letter goes on to say that we have latterly
glorified everything but the farm. We have extolled our
industrial progress, bragged about our big cities, covered

the walls of our great office buildings with pictures of der-
ricks, and hoisting-cranes, and shipyards, and ——'

'I think I see what you mean!' exclaimed Larry. 'You
want me to paint pictures of life in the country.'

'Well — why not? Wouldn't that delight your Uncle
Earnest, who was brought up on the farm? And you were
a farmer boy. You would know where the lure is. Practice
the appeal of the Navy. Its pictures say, "Come with us
and see the world: see the faraway places." Why don't you
portray the country so attractively that men will long for
its freedom?'

'I can try,' said Larry.

The Dean took up his pen and wrote an address.

'They're threshing on that thousand-acre farm in
Nebraska, next week, according to my correspondent.
Go out there with your artist's tackle, and see what you
can do.... This Mr. Wendell will be looking for you.
He will welcome you. Shall I tell him you are coming?'

'Yes, sir.'

'And — one more thing, Larry. I suggest that if you
want to find these farm hands at their best, go as an itinerant, vagabondish fellow, simply dressed, living off the
country. Don't be toplofty or remote. Live their life,
speak their language. You have done it and you can do it
again. Did you ever chew tobacco?'

'Once,' remembered Larry, gulping. 'Do I have to?'

'No — you won't have to. But if it is offered to you,
don't reply that you never learned to eat it.' The Dean
held out his hand. 'Be on your way. Let me know how
it goes. Give my regards to Mr. Wendell. I'm glad to see
you making repairs in your kingdom, Larry.'

The time had gone by so quickly that Larry was amazed
and chagrined when he glanced at his watch.

'I beg your pardon, sir,' he stammered. 'It must be well past your dinner hour. I am sorry.'

'I hadn't noticed,' said the Dean. 'Is it dinner time? How about staying with us? You might enjoy knowing my curates; bright fellows.'

There was a tap on the door, and Simpson came in with the wheel-chair. The Dean introduced them.

'Mr. Runyan will be with us for dinner,' he added. 'Come along, Larry. You may push me, and Simpson will inform Mrs. Crandall to put a little more water in the soup.'

Larry had a queer sensation, trundling the Dean down the long hall. It was, he felt, very precious freight. A curious warmth suffused him. He was proud of his assignment.

At dinner there were many diverting stories told. Talbot was an accomplished raconteur, Simpson provided the dry chaff that Talbot pretended to find bothersome, the Dean teased them both. It was an event that sparkled; and Larry, having neglected to eat properly for a couple of days because of his distraught mind, found the dinner immensely satisfactory. Mrs. Crandall, as hostess that night, was delighted by the practical compliments he bestowed upon the table.

'I was hungry,' he remarked to her, unnecessarily, when she gave him the second piece of lemon pie.

'You're a big man,' she said, comfortingly. 'But don't hint for any more pie. That's the last of it.'

The little town of Axton was only five miles from the Wendell Farm. Arriving on a local train at four, with a battered canvas suitcase containing a few changes of linen and his painting equipment, Larry walked the distance along a graveled road, feeling that the dust and the heat would put the finishing touches on his make-up as a nomad.

All the Wendells knew about him they had learned from Dean Harcourt's letter which had briefly introduced him as an amateur painter who wanted to do some sketching in the country. He could pay for his board, thought the Dean; but perhaps Mr. Wendell, in need of extra help, might let him work part of the day to cover his food and lodging.

Andy Wendell was sitting out on the lawn under a tree when Larry appeared, hot and dusty.

'I expect your name is Runyan,' greeted Andy, cordially. They shook hands, and Larry sat down on the grass. 'You'll want to wash up for supper. We're pretty full here. They've rigged some cots in the big haybarn. And there's plenty of running water, out there. So — you get acquainted with the boys and they'll find you everything you need. And we'll look for you at six.'

'Are you expecting me to work,' asked Larry, 'or am I a boarder?'

'Well — I think you might enjoy working, part time, just enough to pay for your keep. That'll get you a little closer to the people, and you'll enjoy yourself more. Suppose you plan to go out with the other boys in the morning and work until about ten. Then you go anywhere you like — and paint. I'll let 'em know that you're doing the pictures at my order.'

Larry came to his feet and took up his cheap luggage.

'One more thing, Runyan. Dean Harcourt wrote me that he thought it would be just as well if our people here believed that this little deal hadn't been planned very far

in advance; almost as if you'd just dropped in, like. So —
maybe you'd better not tell anybody he sent you to me.
Is that all right?'

He wasn't a stranger very long. The farm hands were
changing from their soaked field-garments and taking turns
under a shower that had been wind-pumped from a one-
hundred-and-ninety-foot well. It was cold. Larry liked it,
and stayed under it until somebody shouted, 'There's the
lad that can take it!' When he opened his bag to fish out
clean clothing, inquisitive eyes noted that his kit was very
modest indeed. One of his neighbors sighted the paints and
brushes.

'You an artist?' he asked, while several others gathered
around.

'No — I just daub a little — for fun.'

'What kind of painting?' asked another, with a wink
at the bystanders. 'Pictures — or signs — or barns?'

'Yes,' said Larry, looking up with an amiable grin.
'Everything like that. Pictures — and signs — and barns.'

'Got any pictures along?' someone wanted to know.

'No. Sorry,' said Larry.

'I expect he sells 'em as fast as he can paint 'em,' observed one of the older men, struggling into his shirt.

'Yeah — faster than that,' said Larry. 'Sometimes they
buy 'em from me before they're half done.'

Everybody thought this was pretty good. The new fellow wasn't going to get sore if they teased him a little.
And, while he might be a painter, he wasn't a sissy. There
wasn't a man of the lot who had his physique. So — by
unspoken consent — they took him in. And presently the
supper-bell rang.

He was given a seat at the end of one of the two long

tables. There was very little conversation for the first fifteen minutes. Every man had burned up an amazing quantity of calories, since noon, and nobody was ashamed of his appetite. The stewed chicken and noodles and mashed potatoes and gravy and candied yams and corn on the cob arrived in such astounding profusion that you wondered what the Wendells would do with the food left over — but it vanished as if by some elaborate conjuring trick.

Nine girls served the tables. They were all bright; some of them were pretty. The girl who seemed to be directing the others immediately attracted Larry's interest. She was a blonde with a beautiful figure and a graceful posture. She was not aloof, but she was superbly self-contained. Larry wondered whether she might be a member of the Wendell household, but immediately gave that up. Mrs. Wendell was a motherly, roly-poly, chubby, short, warm, chatty person who couldn't possibly have been related to this head-waitress.

Larry ventured a little longer glance at the girl and their eyes met. She smiled a little, as if to make him feel less a stranger, and turned away to perform some errand. He wanted to look at her again, but didn't care to risk showing too much interest. After a while, the earnest feeders became somewhat less savage, and laconic conversations became epidemic.

'One thing you've got to say for the Wendells,' remarked a young fellow on Larry's right. 'They give you enough to eat — and they bring it to you fast.'

'Seem to have plenty of help,' rejoined Larry, for something to say.

'Yeah — and they know their business. The head-

waitress hasn't been here very long; but she's the best one
we've had since I'm working here. Easy to look at, too.'

Larry nodded. He would have liked to ask some more
questions, but decided not to pursue the subject. It was
possible that his tablemate had noticed the attention he
had paid her, and wanted to appraise it.

Now the girls were removing the dinner plates and
coming with the strawberry shortcake. The head-waitress
was occupied with her duties. Larry felt safe in looking
her way. He liked the way she stood; liked the curls on
her temples; liked her slim hands; liked her disciplined
vivacity. She was adorable, he thought.

They did not tarry long after dessert. As Larry neared
the doorway, the girl stepped forward, smiled, and said:

'You've just come; haven't you?' And when Larry admitted it, she asked, 'Did they give you enough to eat?'

'A gorge!' said Larry. 'Thank you. This is a good place
to be.'

She smiled again, quizzing his eyes, as if there might be
a question or two she wanted to ask; and turned to make
some pleasant comment to the young fellow who followed
in line. Larry felt reluctant to leave. He was very curious
to know more about her.

As a half-grown youth he had never liked the farm in
Ohio. There was too much worry and fret. You had a
feeling — generated by the family's habitual failure to
make ends meet — that no matter how hard you worked
there would be little to show for it. If there was anything
left, after harvest, the mortgage and the tax-collector got it.

It was a new sensation to work on a farm where nobody
was groaning about a mortgage. Maybe Andy Wendell

had his worries; but, if so, he kept them to himself. Out in these dazzlingly yellow wheatfields, you didn't have a care. You thrust the shining prongs of your long-handled fork into a man-sized sheaf and tossed it high onto the wagon, rejoicing in your strength. This kind of toil was invigorating.

They had turned out early. The poultry yards were putting on a concert in which the guinea section outsquawked the rest of the orchestra. Scores of hens were boasting that they had already done their day's work.

Soft, because of insufficient outdoor exercise, Larry's five miles through the dust and heat of a hot afternoon had made him quite willing to roll into his cot at eight-thirty, too weary to chat or smoke. The clean aroma of the freshly filled haybarn was sweetly sedative. He had slept like a child, and wakened with a clear head. Customarily, the first thing he did in the morning was to light a cigarette; but not so today. He didn't want one; didn't think about it.

They took turns dancing under the cold shower and went to breakfast with rampant appetites. Apparently the Wendells didn't care how much you ate. There was an extensive pig farm beyond the dairy, a half-mile away, where Andy Wendell grew his hams and bacon and sausage.

'You don't get any of this new-fangled tenderized ham here,' observed one of Larry's table companions. 'Andy doesn't believe in putting his hogs through a chemical laboratory. This ham tastes like ham!'

'Andy has good eggs, too,' mumbled another, with his mouth full. 'My pa always said that a cooped-up hen couldn't lay a fresh egg, no matter what you fed her.'

Larry couldn't remember when he had eaten three fried

eggs in a row, but the buxom waitress had shoveled them onto his plate and they were too good to resist; especially with this huge slab of ham, and the biscuits and honey.

The tall blonde — who didn't seem quite naturalized — had not appeared yet. Maybe she was in the kitchen. Ah — here she came, assisting with the serving. The pink gingham dress was simple, and probably cheap, but it brought out the color in her cheeks. The short white apron that defined her curves came up over her shapely shoulders. She had been in the kitchen where it was plenty hot, and the little yellow curls that framed her face had rolled tightly of their own accord.

Larry caught her eyes and she tipped back her head a little and smiled a recognition, almost as if he and she were companions, almost as if they were fellow aliens. He nodded a smiling salutation. His heart raced. They were going to be friends. It was the first time that a woman had so completely captivated him. He had never taken any stock in love at first sight, but he knew he wanted this girl and had a feeling that she belonged to him.

She was standing near the door as they filed out. Almost every man had something to say to her. It was apparent that she was popular. One of the older men inquired, 'Did you make the biscuits?'

'Were they good?' she countered.

'Grand!'

'Then I'll say I made them,' she confided, 'but you mustn't tell Midge I said so.'

And who was Midge? Larry hadn't seen anyone yet who deserved this title. He was nearing the doorway. The girl confronted him with smiling eyes and parted lips. She seemed prepared to say something as he passed, but at that instant someone had called to her. Barbara was a pretty name, Larry thought.

After the midday dinner, Larry did not return with the men to work. Tucking a canvas under one arm and a camp-stool and collapsible easel under the other, he sauntered out to the orchard where the harvest apples were ripening. The limbs bent with their weight. Selecting a spot at the corner of the orchard where it met a wheatfield set with precise rows of stacked sheaves, he unfolded his easel in the dense shade. Then he walked over to the nearest shock of sheaves and pushed it over, tossing some of the sheaves onto the yellow stubble to break up the primness of his middle background.

It was an absorbing and rewarding task under a cloudless sky in an unvarying light. For two hours he carried on so diligently that he was not conscious of the muscular strain. Then the sense of fatigue arrived. He rubbed his arms and flexed his fingers, paced about for a few moments; and lounging on the grass, filled and lighted his pipe.

He was thinking about her when she appeared; had been so occupied with his day-dreaming that she was quite near before her footsteps on the grass brought him to attention. She was still in the pink dress and carried a small stone jug.

'Mrs. Wendell asked me to bring you this,' said Barbara. 'It is iced pineapple juice. She thought you might be thirsty.'

Larry rose and took the jug from her hand. The hand was well entitled to be reproduced in a studio, he thought, wondering how she could have taken such excellent care of it while doing housework.

'Very thoughtful of Mrs. Wendell,' said Larry, 'and

very kind of you to bring it. I think everyone is friendly here. Don't you?' The tone of his question implied that the two of them could view the Wendell establishment from a spectator angle. Barbara gave him a quick, wide-eyed glance, and then sobered a little.

'Thank you for thinking so,' she said. 'We try to make people feel at home here. Everyone seems contented.'

'You've been here for some time?' asked Larry.

'Oh, yes — ever so long.' Barbara stretched out her superbly modeled arms to measure the time, glanced alternately at each hand, and gave Larry a half-teasing smile.

'Would you like to sit down?' he asked, pointing to the campstool.

She nodded, and sat before the easel, with her back toward him, regarding the canvas with interest. Larry liked the shape of her head; the small, close-set ears. 'Patrician,' he said to himself.

'It must be nice to draw lovely things like that,' she murmured, naïvely. 'You must be very fond of apple trees, to make them seem so real.' Then, half turning, she went on — while he sat admiring her almost classic profile, 'I don't suppose you could do a very good job if you tried to paint something you didn't like.'

'That's so. The more you like a thing, the better picture you can make.' Larry had resumed his seat on the ground, with his back against a tree. He wondered if she had a natural aptitude for drawing. Her comments had been childish enough, perhaps by intent. He wished he knew where to place her. 'There is an old, old story,' he continued — 'a fable — about a sculptor, who carved a girl out of marble.' He paused to give her a chance to comment or query.

'I remember,' said Barbara, who had turned again toward Larry's canvas. 'We had it in school. She came to life. But it wasn't marble: it was ivory.'

'You're right,' agreed Larry. 'It was ivory. An interesting story, in any case. Pretty dangerous business; bringing things to life. They might not like what you made of them.'

Barbara slowly turned and gazed down at him over her shoulder, her eyes quizzical.

'Galatea must have been quite lonely, at first,' she remarked, 'and dazed, too; not knowing anything about anything.'

'I never thought about that before,' admitted Larry, trying to make his voice sound casual in spite of his mounting curiosity about her mental equipment. 'Perhaps Pygmalion took her by the hand and led her about in Athens. Maybe he took her down to one of the nice little gownshops first; for, of course, she would be interested in pretty clothes.'

Barbara nodded, and drew a tight-lipped, enigmatic smile. Then she shook her head, apparently arriving at an obstacle to this pleasant idea.

'That wouldn't have been very kind,' she said. 'Pygmalion was poor. He wouldn't have shown her pretty dresses — when he wasn't able to buy her anything.'

'Well — he had her on his hands,' said Larry. 'What do you suppose he did with her?'

'Took her home,' replied Barbara, practically, 'getting more and more anxious as they neared the house, for he didn't know how the family would take it; and ——' She paused for a moment, and added, 'Now you go on with it.'

Larry was rejoicing in the whimsical mood of this girl whose case, he felt, was almost as problematical as Galatea's.

'So — Pygmalion led her into the living-room where his sweet, gray-haired mother sat darning his socks ——'

'Make it a tunic,' suggested Barbara. 'He didn't wear socks.'

'Mending his best tunic, then,' amended Larry. 'And his mother looked up, and said ——' He chuckled. 'Now it's your turn.'

'His mother looked up,' continued Barbara, measuring her words, 'and didn't say anything. She just put down the tunic she was mending, and looked up at Galatea, and held her spectacles close to her eyes with both hands, and looked at Galatea — and then she looked at Pygmalion. But she didn't say anything.'

Larry couldn't carry it off soberly for another instant. It was too good. He laughed delightedly, and urged Barbara to go on. She was momentarily thoughtful; then obligingly continued.

'After a pretty long silence, Pygmalion said, "Mamma, I made this out of a block of ivory. She can't talk yet because she doesn't know any language but the one they speak in ——"'

'In Ivory,' assisted Larry.

'And besides — she wouldn't talk because she doesn't know anything. But you'll like her when you get used to her, Mamma. She's pretty; don't you think?'

Larry was hilarious and told Barbara she was being wasted in her present occupation.

'And then,' Barbara went on, indifferent to Larry's amusement, 'Pygmalion's mother spoke for the first time. ... What did she say? You've got to help, you know.'

'His mother replied' — Larry's brows knitted studiously — 'His mother said, "Yes; she's pretty enough. But what

can she do?" And Pygmalion sighed and said, "I don't
know. You ask her."'

Barbara shook her head.

'No,' she objected, 'his mother wouldn't say that. She
knew Galatea couldn't do anything; not if she didn't know
anything. I think his mother said, "You'd better take her
right back where you got her, and see if you can't persuade
her to be ivory again."'

'I gather that Pygmalion's mother wasn't much of an
idealist,' commented Larry.

'Yes — but you said, yourself,' challenged Barbara, 'that
it was dangerous business, bringing things to life.' She
rose and said she must go back to her work. 'We've had
a lot of fun,' she added.

'We'll have to talk about that old legend again,' declared
Larry. 'There's more to it than meets the eye.'

'I often think about it,' said Barbara, soberly. 'There's
only one other story that covers as much ground: *Alice in
Wonderland.*'

'Do you know — it's an odd thing' — Larry's voice was
puzzled — 'I hadn't thought about that old Pygmalion
story for years; probably not since high school; and this
is the second time in a week that I've talked with someone
about it.'

Barbara studied his eyes for a moment, and turned to go.

'It's time we were introduced, don't you think?' said
Larry. 'My name is Runyan — Lawrence Runyan —
Larry, to my friends. I know your name is Barbara.'

'Brown. You may call me Barbara, if you like. Everyone does. We're not very formal here. 'Bye. Time for you
to get back to your apples.'

The days passed too swiftly. Larry worked with the

field-hands in the forenoons; sketched in the afternoons; sauntered down the lane with Barbara in the evening after the supper work was done. It was a wonder, he thought, that they were not openly teased. Apparently the local contingent felt it was natural for them to pair off. They were both alien, and everybody knew it; couldn't help knowing it.

On several occasions, Larry had asked leading questions, giving her abundant opportunity to talk about herself; but she had firmly rejected these offers to clear up the mystery. Once they were leafing through a magazine together and came upon the picture of a yacht and Barbara remarked, 'She has a lovely suit of sails.' Larry grinned. No landlubber would speak of a 'suit' of sails. That phrase was used only by people who knew their ropes. But he didn't say anything. Perhaps she would want to confide, sometime.

And why didn't he take the initiative, Larry sometimes asked himself. Barbara knew he had been something other than a tramp painter. She was quite too bright to accept him at face value. Maybe, if she had been as inquisitive about him as he had been about her, he would have told her. *Maybe* he would. He wasn't sure about that. She might resent it if he confessed that he was not as poor as he had pretended to be. They had been willfully reticent, but there was one thing they shared — their poverty. They had made no bones about that. Perhaps Barbara had come from a prosperous family that had lost everything: she had decided not to attempt a brave front among her well-to-do friends: this accounted for her seeking employment where she wasn't known. Larry contrived a flock of explanations — all in the same key — to account for Barbara.

He had plenty of misgivings. On the second Saturday evening — it was customary for everybody to go over to Axton, on Saturday afternoon and evening — he and Barbara had driven 'to town' in her dilapidated jalopy. She had suggested it herself and had asked him if he wanted to drive. In keeping with the rather ironical jokes they often exchanged about their poverty, Larry said, as they rattled across the bridge over Yellow Creek, 'Where did you get this Rolls Royce, Barbara?' to which she replied, 'It was a birthday present.'

'When you were six?' he inquired.

'You're just envious,' she retorted.

'Maybe it's a family heirloom,' he suggested.

'I'll give it to you,' she said, 'if you'll show me how to draw.'

'Then I'd have to buy it gasoline,' Larry muttered, dismally. 'But,' he added, companionably, 'I'll tell you everything I know about drawing. It won't take long.'

'You're always running yourself down, Larry,' she had remarked, gently. 'You shouldn't do that. It's a bad habit. Besides — it isn't true. You know you're good. And you could be a really important painter, if you tried.'

They had parked on a side street, for the town was full, and had sauntered down to the most brightly lighted corner where the popular drugstore was doing a thriving fountain business.

Pausing before the congested doorway, Larry said, 'I'd buy you a dish of ice cream, Barbara, but I really ought to have my hair trimmed.'

'Your hair's exactly right,' said Barbara, glancing up with a look that was so intimate it was almost a caress. It set Larry's heart up to the speed limit. And then she raised on tiptoe to say, in a half-whisper, 'Let's have cones. They're only a nickel. I want a chocolate one.'

'Well, all right,' he had consented. 'But if I don't get my hair cut, I can buy you a standard-sized dish.'

'No,' she insisted. 'I'll be quite satisfied with a cone.' And he had been foolish enough to let her have her way; and that, too, in face of the fact that he had a check for five thousand dollars in his pocket that Dean Harcourt had relayed to him from Uncle Earnest with the remark that it was 'back pay on your allowance.'

The incident was trivial, but it touched him. He was not only ashamed; he was hurt; his heart ached for this gallant creature who had been obliged to practice petty frugalities until the difference between a nickel and a dime deserved serious consideration.

But he couldn't tell her. He had kept his secret too long. If he tried to explain now, she would unquestionably resent his continued deceptions. Some day he would tell her, when he had thought of a plausible way to do it.

When they were out on the street again, Barbara took his arm. He pressed hers close against him, and was thrilled by a little tightening of her hand.

'Larry,' she said, confidentially, 'if you really think you should have your hair trimmed, and haven't the money, I can let you have a dime. You can pay it back. I'd like to.'

'You said I didn't need it,' he replied.

'You don't,' she said. 'I like it — that way. So dis-tinguished.'

It gave him a tightness in the throat. Barbara — work-ing for a pittance more than her keep; counting pennies; having to wear cheap clothing. And now trying to lend him a dime to piece out the half-dollar it would cost to

send him to the barber. It was a shabby way to treat her.
He hated himself for his deceit.

And he didn't have the impudence to tell her — in words
— how much he cared for her. If she had any sense, at all
— and she did — Barbara would consider it a doubtful
compliment to be told that he loved her, when there was
nothing he could honorably do about it.

That night they had strolled up the only business street,
on one side, and had come back on the other; saying little.
Then they climbed into the decrepit roadster and drove
home. It was moonlight. Barbara sat close to him.

'Thank you for taking me, Larry,' she said, softly, as
they drove slowly into the lane. He looked down into her
upturned face and smiled. Her eyes were serious.

'It was sweet of you,' he replied, a bit unsteadily, 'to
let me go with you.' He could have kissed her, at that
moment. They both knew it. And each knew the other
knew it.

Nothing more was said until the roadster rolled to a
stop in the open shed beside the one-story barracks where
the girls lived.

'You have been very kind to me, Barbara,' said Larry.

She made no reply; smiled absently, drew a little sigh,
and stepped out of the car.

'If you will join me, tomorrow afternoon,' he said, 'I'll
have a sketching-block for you — and we'll see what you
can do.'

'Well — perhaps,' she replied, after a little hesitation.
'If there isn't too much to do here. . . . Good night.'

He was unable to interpret her altered mood. Something
had dampened her spirit. Perhaps she thought there was
another girl, somewhere, to whom he was committed.

There had been one little moment when it seemed that he should have given some expression to his feeling for her. Barbara couldn't help knowing how he felt. And his failure to admit it must have convinced her that something stood in the way; a girl, doubtless. Or, perhaps she may have suspected that he was a fugitive from something; too sportsmanly to entangle her in his dilemmas. Whatever it was, Barbara left him in a sorry state of bewilderment. He wanted to call to her and tell her that there wasn't anybody else; that there never would be anybody else.

He was a long time going to sleep, that night. Only a couple of the older men were in their beds, diligently sawing their slumber into precise lengths. Wide-eyed and worried, Larry debated what to do. One by one, the men returned until the cots were all occupied. Tomorrow, if he had an hour alone with Barbara, he would tell her that he loved her. If she was willing to listen to that, he would ask her to marry him — if and when he got on his feet, in a position to support her. If she consented to wait, their relations would be cleared up. Then he could cast about for some practical method of easing her into the truth about himself. But the more he thought about that, the less promising it seemed. Barbara had too much common sense to tie herself up — for life — to a tramp, no matter how much she cared.

The next afternoon, Larry was in the shade of a tall sycamore, doing a sketch of the green pasture. It was not going very well. He had lost interest. It was nearing four o'clock, and he had given Barbara up. If she was coming, she would have been here by this time. A slow tide of distaste for his occupation was creeping up. Fine way for a man to spend his time; painting the corner of a pasture.

That cow, beyond the fence, had some business there, and
could give a good account of herself. But what he was
doing had no justification, at all. He was nothing but a
loafer, and not even enjoying his own indolence.

Now his depression magically lifted. He waved his hand.
It was easy to see that their comradeship was back on the
old basis. Barbara was beaming; almost running, as she
drew nearer.

'And you brought an extra stool for me,' she exclaimed,
happily. 'And a sketching-block! How nice! Now I shall
be an artist!'

'Right!' said Larry, warmly. 'And you won't have to
feed people any more. You will paint pictures, and they
will be hung in the Metropolitan.'

'I expect you've been there,' she ventured.

He nodded absently, his attention focused on the pencil
he was sharpening. After he had produced a point that
satisfied him, Larry snapped his pocket-knife shut, and,
with elaborate casualness, asked, 'Have you?'

'Yes,' said Barbara, promptly, 'many times.'

'Want to talk about it?' he inquired, out of the corner
of his mouth, as if anxious not to be overheard.

She leaned toward him, matching his rather furtive air,
and shielding her lips with her open hand, replied, in a
stage whisper, 'No.' And they both laughed — but not
merrily — after which Larry formally moved to abandon
the thin ice. 'So that,' he said, with finality, 'is that.'

'I should have been here sooner, Larry, but just as I
was leaving the house, one of the girls wanted me to see
something in today's paper. Do you ever read the Hollywood news?'

'Not very often. I go to the movies, sometimes, but I

don't try to keep up with the movements among the stars. I never know who has married whom until long after they're both married to other people.'

Barbara laughed, and told Larry he should be better informed.

'The reason I wanted to see the paper,' she went on, 'a few days ago the girls were chattering about their favorite movie people and asked me what actress I liked best. I said my favorite was Sally Singley, because I'm acquainted with her. She used to work in a department store in Chicago.'

'Did you ever live in Chicago?' Larry inquired.

'No — but I happened to be there; and that's how I came to know Sally. She had a lot of natural talent as an impersonator. She went east to a dramatic school. And not very long ago, she was taken to Hollywood to work on a picture. They gave her a good part, too. Well — today there was a whole page of Sally, and the girls wanted me to see it. But when they went to look for it, somebody had carried it off. And I had to drive to Axton to get one.'

'You certainly were interested in Sally,' remarked Larry.

'It's too long a story to tell,' said Barbara, 'and I'm not going to bore you with it. But I had a little something to do with Sally's getting into this business. There she was, dissatisfied and grumpy, in that basement store.'

'Was that where you knew her?'

'Yes — but I didn't work there. I went there to buy things, because they were cheap. And Sally told me about herself, and I coaxed her to try for the stage. Maybe she never would have taken the risk if I hadn't practically dared her to do it.'

'So — now she's getting on all right?' asked Larry, trying to seem interested.

'You'd think so from the amount of attention they're giving her. There must be a half-dozen pictures of her — in night clubs and at the races and — almost everywhere. I hope she will be able to keep her head. She's a mere child, so far as experience goes. It worries me, more than a little.'

'Sounds like another Pygmalion problem,' remarked Larry. 'You brought Sally up out of the basement, and now you're wondering what's going to become of her.'

He was a little surprised when Barbara, with sober eyes, nodded her head; for it wasn't like her to accent the importance of anything she had ever done. And surely she couldn't have done very much for Sally; unless, of course, she had made some investment in her before the family went broke. Larry couldn't get it out of his head that Barbara had once enjoyed unusual opportunities. However penniless she might be, today, there had been a time when she was much better off.

'The trouble is' — Barbara was frankly talking to herself now — 'Sally Singley has no background; hasn't a thing to hang on to. She loves praise — and will go to almost any lengths to get it.'

'She's probably an exhibitionist by nature,' commented Larry. 'Some people can't get enough publicity; have to have ink on their corn flakes at breakfast.'

'It's a detestable frailty,' agreed Barbara, 'and yet ——' she added, reluctantly, 'I'm very, very fond of Sally. It would hurt me dreadfully if anything happened to her.'

'Well — cheer up! Maybe she'll see it through.... Now — let's find out how much you know about drawing. You must keep it in mind that this sheet of drawing-paper has only two dimensions; height and width. And your picture must have three; height, width, and depth. Now — it's easy enough to draw that wire fence; but to put that cow in the picture, so that she won't seem to be a part of the fence, is the task — dear pupil — that lies before us.'

'Will the cow stay where she is?' asked Barbara.

'This cow,' replied Larry, soberly, 'may or may not stay where she is. If she remains, we will have one cow. If she moves about, and lies down somewhere else, we will draw her again; and have two cows. Did you ever draw a cow, Barbara?'

'No.'

'Did you ever *milk* a cow?'

'No; did you?'

'Thousands of times.'

Barbara looked squarely into his eyes, shaking her head.

'Larry,' she said, solemnly, 'I can't figure you out, at all.'

'Nor can I place *you*, Barbara. Shall we tell?'

Barbara's eyes grew misty.

'I can't, Larry,' she said, thickly. 'I'm sorry.'

III. Rocket

Quietly letting herself into their third-floor-walk-up apartment, Sally was relieved to find that her mother was out.

She put down the heavy luggage, carefully laid Barbara's expensive hat on the table, patted her moist forehead with the back of her hand, and drew a deep breath which she exhaled with a prolonged and comforting 'Woo!'

All the way up the steep stairs she had plainly heard what her mother was going to say: 'Sally Singley! What on earth are you doin' home this time o' day? And where have you been and a-goin' with that swell baggage? And who paid for that suit you got on — I'd like to know?'

In the face of these inevitable questions, Sally was going to make short work of her explanations. She had given earnest thought to the fabrication of a lie that might seem a little more credible than the actual facts; but, nothing plausible having occurred to her, she had resolved to tell the truth, however preposterous it might sound.

She was going to say that shortly after the store opened, yesterday morning, a beautiful and attractively dressed girl of her own age had come down to the basement to outfit herself in the rummiest sort of cheap clothes, had taken her out for lunch and dinner, had explained that she didn't know whether anyone liked her — except for her money — and was going away where nobody knew her, to see if she could make some friends on her own account.

And if her mother broke in to exclaim — as she undoubtedly would — that she had never in all her born days heard of anything so crazy, Sally intended to agree with her on that, and proceed to finish the story, to wit: this strange and splendid creature had given her all of her exquisite clothes, and was sending her east — with full expenses paid — to study for the stage. Sally had decided not to add (though it was an enormous temptation) that she was carrying, in this smart new handbag, a pearl necklace that had cost more than the apartment house they lived in. Her story was certainly a lily — and it wouldn't be improved by any such gilding.

It pleased Sally that she would not now be required to dash at once into her fantastic tale. In her mother's absence — she had probably gone around the corner to the Cash-and-Carry — Sally would get out of this lovely blue silk suit, hide the alligator cases under her bed, and at her leisure break the astounding news in a manner less likely to bring on a stroke.

She smiled happily as she undressed. Without planning it, she had picked an opportune time to come home. Lola and Bennie would not be back from high school for a couple of hours. Dad wouldn't show up until half-past six, if he showed up for supper at all. Sally wouldn't have to confide in any of them but Mother. Thursday morning, after they had all cleared out — but Mother — she would go to her train. And when she was safely out of town, Mother could tell them whatever she thought would satisfy their curiosity. It was all going to come off without much excitement. Mother would have a fit, but she would get over it. She wasn't a bad sport, when all was said and done, making no bones about her wish that Sally's life had a little more happiness in it. Of course, Mother had her scratchy spells, especially when raising all hell with Dad for spending so much money in the bars. Some nights, when he puffed and staggered in, she would nag and nag at the poor old thing until he would get to shouting that if she objected to a man's having an occasional glass of beer she hadn't any business marrying a linotyper. Dad was a fairly good egg. You couldn't help pitying him. But it certainly was disgusting the way he drank everything up until the milkman wouldn't leave any more unless he was paid, and the iceman — they couldn't afford an electric refrigerator — wouldn't stop; and Sally, who was already giving Mother half of her wages, would have to shell out the rest of it — or the gas would be turned off, and the lights too.

She wasn't going to say a word to Lester; and — boy! — would he be sore! Lester would come drifting in, after supper tonight, with that smarty grin and that slow, slinky gait, pausing at each step to teeter on his toes, acting as if he owned the place, not even bothering to take off his hat. He would probably suggest that they go to a movie, and then remember, on the way — if they went, which they wouldn't — not this time — that he hadn't any change. (Change for what? I ask you!) It would be a treat to see Lester's face, Thursday night, when he came smoothly skating in, and they told him she had gone away. Sally had been trying to make up her mind to give that bird the air for all of two years. It was going to be easy to do now. Gosh! — it would be fun to see it. Lester would sit down, with his hat on the back of his head, and wait awhile; then he would go snaking about, looking for a cigarette. Then he would say, 'Where's Sally?' And Mother, who was all fed up with him, would say, 'Oh — didn't she remember to tell you, Lester? Sally has gone away out to Provincetown — to study for the stage.' And Lester would wrinkle up his nose and say, 'Hunnh?' with a little jerk of his spine as if somebody had jabbed him with a pin.

Only one thing worried Sally now. She had half promised Barbara that she would go up to Trinity Cathedral and see this Dean Harcourt. Of course she didn't positively have to do it — and she certainly didn't want to; but it really wasn't decent to refuse when Barbara had asked her. Well — if she was going to do it at all it would have to be tomorrow. She would telephone, as Barbara had suggested, and try to make an appointment. Perhaps she had better do this at once, before Mother got home.

Going to the telephone, which was on top of the radio which was on top of the battered old buffet in the dining-room, Sally dialed the number, and was talking primly to a Mr. Simpson when her mother arrived in time to hear her saying, with elaborate dignity, 'If it is at all convenient, I should like to see Dean Harcourt tomorrow afternoon, for I am leaving town Thursday and may not be back for several months.' Becoming aware of her mother's presence in the doorway, Sally turned to face her, still talking; 'Thank you very much. Yes — that's right — Miss Singley. Five o'clock? That will be fine. Thank you.' She hung up the receiver. Her mother had sagged into a chair, holding the basket of groceries on her lap, her face twisted into a baffled grimace that wasn't either laughing or crying.

'Sally,' she muttered, 'what have you went and done now?'

And Sally told her.

With ten minutes to spare, she left the bus directly across

the street from the Cathedral. Sally had often passed this famous edifice without actually seeing it. Now that she had an errand here, she was amazed at the height of the massive towers. The Cathedral occupied the whole block. How little and low the steps seemed that led up to the three great entrance doors. But when Sally had crossed the wide boulevard and began to ascend the steps, she found them of normal size. It was a tremendously big place; so big it almost frightened her when, coming in from the sunshine, she found herself in this vast, heavily shadowed forest of stone pillars reaching up and up into the darkness.

The only lights were two tall candles on the high altar, far away. They flickered; not in nervous little sputters but with a sort of steady beat, like a pulse — like breathing. The great windows, catching the western sun, glowed with rich colors, almost as if the figures in them were alive. The place was quiet, but not dead. Sally stood there for a long time in the broad central aisle, looking at the gorgeous windows, at the distant altar, at the carved timbers high aloft. Presently she became aware of organ music. It sounded from far off, seeming to come at you in little wisps and then in long waves. And then it swelled into big rolling breakers that almost took your breath. And then the tide slowly went out until nothing was left of it but little ripples and soft whispers.

As her eyes became accustomed to the dim light, Sally saw the bent figure of an old woman bobbing among the pews, dusting the cushions.

'Will you tell me where I should go to find Dean Harcourt?' she asked.

'Oh — that's away over on Marlborough Street, Miss,'

said the old woman, pointing her brush over her shoulder.

'I thought he lived in the Cathedral,' said Sally.

'Well — yes,' conceded the old woman, 'the Dean's House is all a part of the Cathedral, as you might say. But you go into it around on Marlborough, unless' — she straightened and pointed into a far, dark corner — 'if you aren't afraid of getting lost, there's a door, to the right of that big pulpit. Follow the hall — and keep going — a long way. And then you'd better ask somebody.'

Sally decided to make this adventure. Proceeding through long rows of pews and across aisles, she reached the cloistered wall; then groped down that aisle until she was under the very shadow of the great pulpit where she paused and listened intently. In the gloom she heard the muffled sound of someone sobbing. In the front pew there was a girl crouched on her knees with only the back of her head and shoulders visible, her face buried in her folded arms.

Aware of her own heart-beats, Sally stood for a moment, wondering whether she shouldn't go back to the old woman and inform her that somebody ought to do something; but, after an interval of indecision, thought she had better attend to her own appointment without further delay.

The hall was dimly lighted and she walked slowly for a long distance before she came to an unmarked door. Tapping timidly, she listened. Hearing nothing, she turned the knob and opened the door a little way. It was a huge library. Sally pushed the door farther and had a view of the whole room. In the corner, directly across, sat a white-haired man behind the largest and most beautifully carved desk she had ever seen. The man glanced up, smiled, and said, 'Come on in.'

Sally crossed the room and sat down in the big chair to which the man had pointed. She knew now — from Barbara's description — that this was Dean Harcourt.

'I'm afraid I came in the wrong way,' she said, a little flustered.

'It's no matter,' said the Dean. 'You're here. Perhaps you are Barbara's Sally. I was expecting her — about now.'

Admitting her identity, Sally settled back farther into the big chair, reassured by the Dean's friendly attitude.

'Barbara wanted me to come and talk to you,' she said.

'Very well.' The Dean leaned forward, folded his arms, and smiled encouragingly.

'I — I mean,' stammered Sally, 'Barbara wanted me to come and have a talk with you.'

'What would you like to talk about?'

'Oh — I don't know.' Sally inspected her red fingernails, and felt that she wasn't giving a very good account of herself. This man certainly wasn't helping much. It was his turn to talk. Then, impetuously, she said, 'The only thing that's really on my mind, just now, is a girl I saw, out there, crying fit to break her heart. I thought maybe someone should see what it's about.'

'Out in the Cathedral?'

'Kneeling down — in one of the seats.'

'What seemed to be the trouble?'

'I don't know. I didn't inquire. It really wasn't any of my business.'

'All alone — was she?'

'Yes, sir.'

'And crying.'

'Yes, sir.'

'And you didn't stop.'

'No, sir.' Sally's voice was growing smaller.

The Dean sighed and shook his head a little.

'Barbara told me that you wanted to be an actress.'

'Yes, sir,' replied Sally, brightening. She was glad they were through talking about the girl.

'To be a really good actress, Sally,' said the Dean, slowly, 'a woman should have an immense capacity for sympathetic understanding. Do you think you have that?'

'Why — I don't know, sir. I'm afraid I never thought much about it.'

'It's very important. You cannot interpret life unless you are keenly sensitive to all sorts of human dilemmas; responsive to other people's wants and hurts.'

There was a constrained little pause before Sally said, 'You think I should have tried to find out what the trouble was?'

'Don't you think so, too?' countered the Dean, gently.

'Shall I go back — now?' Sally slipped forward in her chair.

'Why not?'

She rose and started toward the door where she tarried to inquire, 'What shall I do with her?'

'I don't know,' replied the Dean. 'She's your discovery.'

'You mean — finders keepers?'

A broad smile spread over Dean Harcourt's deep-lined face as he nodded approval.

'I never heard it put just that way before, Sally,' he said, 'but that's what it comes to. If you find it's something you can't handle, bring her in here; but it will be better for both of you if you can deal with her problem yourself.'

'All right,' agreed Sally, in a tone that made them almost the same age. 'I'll try.' After she had closed the door, she swung it open again to ask, 'Will you be here when I come back?'

'It depends on when that is,' drawled the Dean. 'We have dinner here at seven, and I usually go to bed about midnight.' He waved her on her way. 'Good luck, my dear.'

The girl — she seemed to be about nineteen or twenty — had stopped crying and was slumped down into a pathetic little crumple of despair. Sally edged her way into the pew and sat down close beside her. When the girl did not look up or give any sign of acknowledging this friendly attention, Sally slipped an arm around her and said, quietly, 'What's gone wrong, kid?'

This brought forth a fresh flood of tears. Sally waited patiently until the little storm subsided, and the girl had reached out a hand to be held.

'Come on, now,' coaxed Sally. 'Let's have it. You can't stay here any longer. We lock up at six.'

'Can't I sleep here?' asked the girl, thickly.

'Of course not!'

'I did — last night.'

'Weren't you afraid?'

'Yes.'

'Well — you can't — any more,' declared Sally. 'Better tell me all about it.'

It wasn't a very exciting story. Mary Ellen hadn't run off from a cruel stepmother, or the threat of a marriage with some rich old buzzard who held a mortgage on their house. She hadn't stolen anything, or kidnapped anybody, and she wasn't going to have a baby. Mary Ellen had had a row with her boy friend and had left home — and her office job in Kankakee — to make her own way in Chicago. She had never been here but once, with her parents and two small brothers, when she was fourteen. They had come up to see the Fair. That was all she knew about Chicago until a week ago last Tuesday. No — her folks didn't know where she was. They had sided in with Warren. That's why she had left, really. They were all against her. Yes — she supposed they were about half-crazy with worry. It had been in the papers, a couple of times — and on the radio.

'It's a wonder you weren't picked up,' remarked Sally.

'I was afraid of that,' admitted Mary Ellen. 'Maybe that's why I couldn't find a job. I was scared and nervous — and felt like a criminal.'

The rest of the story was simple enough. Nobody wanted to have anything to do with her. She had completely lost her self-confidence, and had a furtive air. Her money was all gone. She had been locked out of her room, last night, at the cheap lodging-house, because her week was up, and she couldn't pay in advance.

'When did you eat last?' asked Sally.

'Yesterday noon — a hamburger and a glass of milk.' Mary Ellen drew a long, shuddering sigh.

'Well — you ought to be glad,' said Sally, 'that you're not in some kind of a mess. You're hungry and broke — and ashamed to go back home, where you belong. But if that's all there is to it, you're lucky. Come on. Let's go and get some supper. I'm hungry too.'

The tears welled up into the girl's eyes.

'Do you belong to this church?' she asked.

Sally shook her head.

'Never been here before in my life,' she said. They moved out into the aisle.

'Awful big; isn't it?' murmured Mary Ellen.

'I'll say!' Sally shivered. 'And full of spooks.'

'How did you happen to speak to me?'

'Well — if you really have to know,' confided Sally, as they walked down the broad aisle, arm in arm, 'I'm studying to be an actress — and a good actress has to be interested in other people's troubles.'

'And you go around — looking for people in trouble' — Mary Ellen's eyes were wide with disappointment — 'just so you can see the expression on their faces — when they cry?'

'Mmm —no — I'm not quite that bad a brute,' defended Sally.

'I'm glad,' said Mary Ellen, relieved. 'That would be pretty awful: wouldn't it?'

'Yeah,' agreed Sally, mechanically, 'pretty awful.' Plenty of times, she reflected, that was exactly what she had done; watched people's facial contortions when they were hurt, humiliated, scared, snooted, scorned, fired —- without personally caring a hoot — so long as she might capture their painful grimaces. My Gosh! — that *was* pretty awful, when you came to think of it

It was quarter after nine when Sally rang the doorbell at the Dean's House on Marlborough Street. She had spent a busy evening. Mary Ellen had begun to come back to life with the application of hot bouillon, and by the time she had put away a thick T-bone steak, an outsize baked potato, two ears of corn, a crab salad, and a large wedge of berry pie, she was ready to listen to almost any counsel her benefactress might offer.

After that they had gone in a taxi to the shabby lodging-house and disentangled Mary Ellen's personal property from Mrs. Kluck's small claim on it. Sally had competently taken charge of this negotiation, in the course of which she had imparted her unreserved opinions about the treatment Mary Ellen had received. These sentiments had been conveyed by phrases more familiar to seafaring persons than to the stingy and stupid old proprietress of this establishment. Mary Ellen — whose admiration for Sally was now but little short of worship — stood by, grateful but slightly stunned, as her champion poured forth a spume of invective that would have fried a lizard.

Then they had taken another taxi to the Illinois Central where a telegram was sent to Mary Ellen's mother, and a day-coach ticket to Kankakee was bought for a dollar and ten cents. Sally mentally added up the evening's expenses and found that the whole job had been accomplished for only a little over ten dollars. Mary Ellen was going to send it to her, soon as possible.

With all of this business attended to, Sally decided to go about her other affairs without waiting for the departure of Mary Ellen's train. She hadn't felt the least bit sentimental toward this relief job.

'You'll be all right now,' she had said. 'I must run along.'

'Home — maybe?' asked Mary Ellen, still clinging to Sally's arm.

'No — back to the Cathedral. When I found you, I had gone there to see the man that runs it; had an appointment with him. He'll be wondering why I don't show up.'

'Won't he be furious with you?'

'No; he's not that sort. Besides ——' added Sally, airily, 'he is a good friend of mine. He'd wait up all night.'

'Must be a very nice person,' remarked Mary Ellen.

'I'll say,' agreed Sally. She glanced at the clock. 'I'm off now. You've just thirty minutes to wait in this old dump. Better go upstairs and sit down. No — don't kiss me. Lipstick! 'Bye!' They hugged each other, and Mary Ellen cried a little.

The solemn front door at the Dean's House — everything, Sally observed, was sort of churchy; doors, windows, hinges, railings — was promptly opened by a stocky, near-sighted man of forty-plus, with thin pink hair, a long nose, and an unusual number of large teeth. When he spoke, his voice was a squeaky treble and his accent was so bah-jove British that if you'd heard it on the stage you would have booed the ham for overplaying it. At his first word, Sally puckered her mouth into a hard little rosette to keep from laughing.

'Aouw — good night!' said the man. 'Woun't you come in? I fawncy you will be Miss Singley.' He bowed and stood aside as she entered.

'Not forever — I hope,' said Sally, pretending to be shocked by this dismaying forecast.

'Beg pawdon, Miss?' The generous mouth and wide, pale-blue eyes registered perplexity. And when the guest failed to explain her cryptic comment, the funny-looking man said, 'Dean Harcourt is expecting you, Miss.'

'Thag you,' said Sally, ceremoniously, from a constricted throat.

'Aouw — quite!' The man nodded several times. 'I'm Mr. Talbot, you know.'

'Aouw?' responded Sally, respectfully enough, though the intonation made Mr. Talbot blink rapidly.

'Will you be so good as to go upstairs, Miss?' Mr. Talbot was pointing the way. 'The first door, please, at the left of the lift.'

'Aouw,' said the duchess, with much dignity. 'So that is what's left of the lift.' She glanced back over her shoulder at the astonished Mr. Talbot, as she ascended, winked impishly, and immediately ministered to his baffled spirit with a comradely smile. He stood in his tracks and stared.

The door at the left of the lift was open. Dean Harcourt, with a large volume spread open on his knees, sat in his wheel-chair beside a table piled high with books. He was in his conventional clericals, except for a black velvet lounging jacket. Sally paused in the doorway and he motioned her in.

'Fawncy my coming back — at this hour,' she lisped shrilly, with such a faithful imitation of Mr. Talbot's high-pitched voice that the Dean regarded her with silent amazement. My Word! — she even *looked* like Talbot! Same bug-eyed, ingenuous, toothy smile! 'Perhawps I'm too late — quite!' she added as she moved toward the vacant chair.

Dean Harcourt was full of suppressed laughter, and making an effort to compose his face.

'You mustn't do things like that, Sally,' he said, reproachfully, though his voice was unsteady.

'I thought you'd think it was funny,' said Sally, with the repentant air of a mischievous six-year-old.

'And so it was,' admitted the Dean, chuckling deep in his throat. 'but that is the wrong kind of fun.' His voice grew serious. 'You are indeed a gifted mimic, Sally, but you must give a good account of it. You have a very sharp weapon there, my dear, and you should not handle it recklessly. You might hurt someone. You might even cut *yourself* with it.' He paused, lowered his voice, and added, 'I hope he didn't hear you.'

Sally brightened, reassuringly.

'The panda? He wouldn't care. I did it for him — before I came up. I think he rawther enjoyed it.'

'I wouldn't be too sure of that,' cautioned the Dean, 'and I'm almost certain Mr. Talbot wouldn't like being called a panda.'

'They're rawther nice — pandas,' said Sally, thoughtfully. 'Wish I had one.'

'Well — you can't have this one.' Dean Harcourt laid a silk bookmark into the place where he had been reading. Sally took the heavy book from his lap and made room for it on the table. They exchanged smiles.

'Wouldn't you like to take off your hat?' asked the Dean.

'What's the matter with it?' inquired Sally.

Then the Dean laughed aloud, which he almost never did; and Sally, feeling that she had had enough fun, laid her hat and gloves on the table, drew her chair closer, and sighed contentedly. She felt very near to this kind and wise old man, as if she had known him always.

'How did you find your — your patient?' asked the Dean, gently.

'Hungry.'

'You fed her, I suppose.'

'Up to there.' Sally tipped her head back and thumbed a line across her shapely throat. 'Want to hear about it?'

'Did you get her fixed up?' inquired the Dean; and when Sally nodded, he asked, 'Did you have a good time?' And when she nodded again, he said, 'Then you needn't tell me. We will talk about something else.'

'Let's talk about Barbara,' suggested Sally, impulsively. 'Hasn't she been wonderful to me?'

'I don't know,' murmured the Dean, half to himself.

'It's too early to tell. I wish I did know,' he went on, slowly, 'for I feel somewhat responsible. Barbara told you, I think, how she happened to decide to ——'

'Something you said,' broke in Sally, when the Dean hesitated. 'And I loved the story about the sculptor carving the girl out of ivory and she came to life. Barbara said you had done almost the same thing for her — and then she did the same thing for me; and ——'

'And that makes me responsible for both of you.' The Dean's voice deepened impressively. 'Now — you are going away to have your chance. You have wanted to be an actress and the way has been opened. All the circumstances seem favorable; almost too favorable.'

Sally glanced up with surprise.

'Too favorable?'

'Yes. The most risky way to acquire anything is to get it free. Things that cost nothing aren't often worth much more than that. Sometimes they are a liability. I could have wished that your trip east and your expenses at the dramatic school had been provided for by money you had saved out of your wages, money accumulated by many a little sacrifice of personal pleasure. The way it is, you are a bit handicapped by the fact that you have made no investment. You will keep that in mind, won't you, Sally? I want you to do a serious job!'

'Being serious isn't in my alley, Dean Harcourt. If I've got anything — it's comedy.'

'I know, I know,' nodded the Dean. 'You're a comedian — but comedy is a very serious business. More than any other people, we are a fun-loving nation. But we like our farces to be the vehicles for sound common sense. We have relied on our cartoonists, clowns, and ballad-writers to

furnish us with our more valuable opinions. Will Rogers
was one of the most influential voices of our time.' The
Dean paused, smiled, pursed his lips reminiscently, and went
on, Sally attentively following the play of his memories.

'When I was in college, vaudeville was popular: it was
one of our principal diversions. The rating of a troupe was
based on the volume of applause. We discovered that the
very worst act in the show would curtain with a violent
waving of the Stars and Stripes. The poorer the show,
the larger the flag. When they knew they weren't entitled
to any applause on their merit, they fell back on flag-
waving. It has been a long time since anybody has resorted
to the old flag-trick on the stage, though I fear it is still
practiced extensively on public platforms where serious
matters are under discussion.'

'Yeah — I know,' agreed Sally. 'My Dad says whenever
they begin praising Lincoln, you want to hang on to your
pocketbook.'

'Poor Lincoln,' sighed the Dean. 'He has gathered up
a lot of strange friends, for one who — in life — was such
a lonely man.' Shaking loose from his momentary dejec-
tion, he went on. 'I think you get my idea, Sally. Be an
honest comedian. It is a position of trust. Satirize the
things that are fraudulent. Don't make fun of anything
that is good — and sound — and worth keeping. Don't
make jokes about faith. Don't rely on profanity and off-
color wit to raise a laugh. That's as cheap and dishonest
as the old flag-trick.'

'I never thought about that before,' said Sally.

'Well — now's the right time to think about it. Will
you write to me — and tell me how it goes? I shall be
deeply interested.'

'Have you heard anything from Barbara?' asked Sally, reaching for her hat.

'Not yet. But she will write to me, I think.' The Dean held out his hand. Sally took it, but was reluctant to go.

'I'll write to you, Dean Harcourt, soon as I get there,' she said. 'And I'll come to see you, when I am home again — if you'll let me.'

'And you will be nice to Mr. Talbot, on the way out; won't you, Sally?'

'Aouw — quite!' she answered barely above a whisper, her eyes dancing.

Sally did not have time to write to the Dean from Provincetown. By one of those fantastic pranks of Circumstance, which do not occur oftener than once in a blue moon — except in the theatrical field where almost anything can happen at any time — Miss Singley's sojourn in the players' colony on Cape Cod lasted just three days.

But if an analysis were made of all the events contributory to this abrupt alteration of her summer plans, it would be found that there was nothing unusual about any one of them, considered separately.

There was, for instance, nothing extraordinary in the fact that Timothy Wainwright — while a rapidly growing youth — had fallen afoul of a stammer which, by dint of vigorous self-discipline and careful handling on the part of his parents and teachers, had been so effectively cured that only a few small scars remained as a memorial to his infirmity. And what was left of Tim's speech impediment, far from limiting his powers as an actor-director, gave his diction a peculiar charm.

If — to illustrate — he was reading a line of dialogue beginning, 'Yes — but consider what might happen next,' there was likely to be a thoughtful pause before 'but,' and a momentary struggle with 'c-consider.' He didn't really stutter: he just paused for an instant before taking the hurdle. But not always. Sometimes Tim would run along for days without such little detainments. Then, for no reason at all, there would be a brief recurrence of his difficulty.

To the winning of these occasional skirmishes, Tim's technique had been brought to perfection by long practice. Upon arrival at a guttural or any other high-fenced consonant, there would be a mere split-second when he would tightly pinch his eyes, open his mouth, and wrinkle up his nose; particularly when executing such official admonitions as, 'C-continue, please,' and 'K-kindly c-concentrate.' It was almost as if he had met a sneeze, and had been able to divert its attention. Sometimes it was a bit funny, as when he read such a line as, 'Clara — kiss your cousin.' But nobody felt that his eccentricity interfered with this popular director's art. Indeed it was curiously consistent with his habitual deliberateness; and, by the old rule that people are more often loved for their imperfections than their proficiencies, Tim was immensely admired. Sally — for one — knew instantly that she was going to like him.

Nor was there anything unusual about the fact that Dick Veddar, that audacious and successful agent-scout, whose classy organization maintained impressive offices in New York and Hollywood, had made it an annual practice to drop in, for a day or two, and look 'em over. Customarily he prowled around in Provincetown and Dennis, and up in

Vermont, when the season was well advanced. This time he had come early; so early that the new crop of ambitious Thespians had hardly become acquainted with one another, much less resolved themselves into a smoothly working unit.

By virtue of their long-time friendship, plus the fact that Dick's visit was to be brief, Tim had given less than the usual attention to the new arrivals. He had been filled with curiosity to meet the unpredictable girl from Chicago whom Barbara — with the flimsiest of explanations — had sent to take her place; but there had been no opportunity to question her. Barbara's brief note had offered no information beyond the bare statement that Sally was a naturally talented mimic.

That first night at dinner, Tim had made them a friendly little speech and Dick had told some amusing stories about the movies. Then each of the newcomers — this was at Dick's suggestion — stood up for identification. According to their respective gifts of gab and brass, they ventured to be briefly witty in introducing themselves. One young fellow, who made the Easterners giggle by saying he was from Oshkosh, observed that it wasn't any funnier than Pawtucket, which had just reported. One girl assumed a baby-doll voice, winning an appreciative round of applause. Her next neighbor hoarsely muttered her name in a tragic tone, and Tim called across to inquire if she was from Wuthering Heights.

When Sally's turn came, a little hush fell, for nobody knew anything about her, and it would be interesting to see what manner of person she was. All eyes turned in her direction; but Sally, who — with open compact in one hand and lipstick in the other — was reorganizing her mouth, seemed completely oblivious to the fact that it was her turn to rise. The delay lengthened and the silence grew tense. Sally was too deeply absorbed by her task to notice. Dabbing at her upper lip with the scarlet stick, her transfixed eyes intent on her mirror, she executed a series of the most astounding grimaces, ranging all the way from seductive smiles to haughty scowls.

The entire company was rapidly filling up with compressed chuckles, but nobody broke the spell while Sally continued to make faces at herself. Then, suddenly startled by the silence and the realization that everyone was looking at her, she glanced about with abject terror in her eyes, pushed back her chair, scrambled to her feet; and, in an embarrassed little voice, squeaked, 'Silly Sangley — I mean — Sally Singley — Chicago.' She paused for a second, shrugged a shoulder languidly, assumed a hard-boiled expression, tipped back her head, and added, huskily, 'Telephone Magenta 23230.'

The laughter and applause came on tentatively. Their attitude toward her had changed from amusement to pity — and then it had begun to appear that they had been taken in; but now they weren't so sure about that as they watched Sally resume her seat with much self-satisfied preening and shouldering, apparently unaware that she had been putting on a show.

'Looks as if you had something there, old boy,' muttered Dick.

'Dunno,' drawled Tim. 'Can't quite make her out. She's either a great actress or a damn fool.'

'She could be both,' said Dick.

The next evening at dinner Tim announced that they would read a play. Repairing to the little theater, a cast was chosen from among the newcomers and seated in a semicircular row on the stage, the old-timers filing into the orchestra seats, eager for this spot of fun.

Sally had drawn the rôle of a lady's maid. It was not a fat part and offered very little opportunity for drollery, especially when the lines were merely to be read and no 'business' was expected. When the scripts had been distributed, Tim, seated at the end of the row, said he would read the first act through, so that each of them could learn his own relation to the play. It turned out to be one of Mr. Wainwright's occasions for stumbling a little over difficult words. The veterans, sitting in the dark, squeezed one another's hands and ached with silent laughter. The people on the stage were too scared to show signs of amusement.

At length, Tim had finished; and, telling them to proceed now with the reading of their parts, he came down and joined Dick in the second row.

'I wish this Singley had a better chance to let herself go,' whispered Dick. 'She can't do anything with "Yes, madame."'

Sally read her lines without distinction, which was inevitable, for you couldn't spread yourself much over such sapless remarks as, 'Mr. Blossom on the telephone, madame.' It wasn't that she wanted to show off; but her part, she felt, was unforgivably lean.

But at the very end of the act, she gave a performance that by one word changed the whole course of her life. She had the last line. It was addressed to her mistress, who had called to her, presumably from off stage, and all she had to say was, 'Coming.'

When her cue arrived for this final speech — you would

have sworn from her facial expression it was Tim Wainwright — Sally tightly closed both eyes, opened her mobile mouth, wrinkled her nose, hung for a second on the edge of delivery, and then exploded with a maidenly, 'C-c—*choo!*'

It was the most devastatingly silly thing that had ever happened on that stage, and they all laughed until they cried. The only person present who didn't seem to think it was funny was Sally herself, who childishly wiped her nose with an embarrassed finger, and appeared not to understand. This set them off into fresh gales of laughter, which Sally regarded with a baffled, half-frightened little grin. Tim began feeling sorry for her.

'What's the matter with you asses?' he growled, turning to his hilarious neighbors. 'Can't you see that was an accident?'

'Accident — my Aunt!' scoffed Dick, mopping his eyes. 'She's good — I tell you! She's better than good! She's a natural!'

'You mean — you think she did that on purpose?' barked Tim.

'Of course she did!' declared Dick. 'And it was a high-class job!'

Then they all went back to the dining-hall and danced. On the way, Tim contrived to exchange a few words with Sally, making no direct comment on the absurd episode that had unfitted everybody for further work that night, but asking her a few questions about her previous experience. Sally cheerfully confessed that she knew nothing about acting; and, except for a small part in a high-school play, had had no training at all.

'It's just that Barbara found out I could imitate people,' she explained, modestly. Then she glanced up at Tim, and grinned.

'Yes,' he agreed, 'you do that nicely.'

'I hope you'll let me stay,' said Sally. 'I shouldn't blame you if you threw me out. I never did anything — but work in a department store.'

'Is that a secret?'

'I'm not ashamed of it — if that's what you mean.'

Dick joined them as they entered the dining-hall, and was introduced, after which Sally was appropriated by the young gentleman from Oshkosh.

'Well — what is she?' inquired Dick, offering Tim a light.

'Starts at scratch,' said Tim. 'No stage experience. Sales-girl in a store. Naïve as a child. You know — I still think that sneeze was accidental.'

Dick muttered absently, 'You're crazy!' — his eyes following Sally as her new friend led her into the rumba. Then his brows wrinkled studiously and he turned again to Tim. 'Worked in a store, eh? I say, old man, I've got an idea. Tell you about it, later.'

When the phonograph stopped for a change of records, Dick sauntered across the room. 'I'd like to have a moment with you, Miss Singley,' he said, 'if your friend will permit.' They strolled to the corner farthest from the racket and sat down in a wicker divan.

'It's about that seventy-five thousand you have just won in the Irish sweeps,' began Dick, confidentially. 'Of course you will not think of going back to the store. Nobody would, in the circumstances. Have you made any plans yet — or aren't you ready to talk about it?'

There had been a momentary widening of Sally's eyes —
a surprised look that was instantly replaced by a crafty
expression of defense. Half-averting her face and donning
a smarty grin, she slowly began chewing an enormous wad
of imaginary gum. Then, elevating one shoulder, she
asked — with badly impaired articulation, 'Wadda yuh
want to know for?'

'I'm a reporter,' said Dick. 'Wanna get nice little story.'

'Pitcher in your paper, too, mebby?' wondered Sally,
warming slightly.

'Umm-humm. In the store, selling — whatever you sold
— at the goodole stand.'

'Like hell!' snapped Sally. 'If you print a pitcher o' me,
I want one a-sittin' behind the wheel o' my new speed-boat.'

'Oh,' said Dick. 'So you've bought a new speed-boat
already? What kind is it?'

Sally nonchalantly chewed her fictitious gum for a long
moment and replied that it was 'red.' Dick grinned and
asked, 'I mean — what kind of engine?'

'Gasoline,' said Sally.

At this, Dick laughed merrily; and, abandoning their
farce, said, 'Neat recovery.' But Sally looked him squarely
in the eyes and refused to come out of the character he had
assigned to her. This dashed him a little. He smiled sincerely.

'You're pretty good,' he said.

'Oh — yeah?' Sally was stonily cynical.

'Now — I've a little idea.' Dick's tone was genuine.
'One of our studios is getting ready to cast a picture about
a young woman — a store clerk, I believe — who won a
potful of money in a lottery.'

Sally laughed dryly.

'Yeah,' she said, 'I knew it wouldn't be long until they'd be makin' a moom-pitcher just like what's happened to me.'

'Stop it!' growled Dick. 'I'm serious.'

'You can't kid me, big boy!' snarled Sally, grinding her gum. 'First you're a reporter — and now you're De Mille — er somebody. Huh!'

Dick leaned forward and scowled into her face impatiently, and she made an ugly nose at him. He held his open hand under her chin.

'Spit out that gum!' he commanded.

'Not till you ask me nicely,' mumbled Sally, her cheek bulging.

Dick cupped both hands, and in a sickeningly wheedling tone, said, 'Atta nice girl. Pit out nasty big wad of gum for Poppa.'

Sally leaned over and spent a long time ostensibly consolidating the gum, a portion of which seemed to have adhered to her back teeth, requiring her to poke at it with her fingers. She finally accomplished this disengagement, put her lips close to Dick's hands, opened her mouth, and disgorged. He wouldn't have been much surprised — so perfect was the pantomime — if Sally had actually made a deposit. When she raised her head, the expression on her face had completely changed. She smiled companionably.

'What were you saying — about the picture?' she asked, politely.

Dick stared at her.

'There might be just a chance,' he muttered, half to himself.

Sally waited for further explanations.

'It might be worth a trial,' Dick went on. Then, facing her, he said, 'Now — look! I'm making you no promise —

you understand! I don't have it to say who plays in this picture. But they're looking for somebody — and — it might be you!'

'You mean — you want me to go to Hollywood?' Sally's voice was unsteady.

'For a screen test — that's all. And a little talk with the producer. There may be nothing in it for you — but your expenses. And a nice ride on a plane.'

'When?' asked Sally, her eyes shining.

'Sooner the better. Tomorrow. Be ready to get out of here in the morning. Night plane from New York.'

Sally half-closed her eyes and drew a long, luxurious breath through her sensitive nostrils, as if inhaling a delicious fragrance.

'I think I'm dreaming,' she murmured.

Because it was to be rated a 'B' picture, Gigantic Studios had not invested much — either in time, talent, or cash — on the production of *Funny Money*.

The shooting had proceeded with unusual dispatch. Half of the sets were stock shots. And most of the others — Libby learning to drive her swanky new convertible, Libby making a monkey of herself at the exclusive beach club, Libby at the airport, Libby ordering thousands of dollars' worth of sport clothes — were taken on location, requiring only that a 'dolly' be trucked about for a few days.

So it had not been a hair-raising adventure when Gigantic employed the unpredictable Sally Singley to do Libby, the hoydenish shop-girl who had suddenly found herself rolling in riches.

But to Sally, whose previous experience with the motion-picture business had been limited to her occasional patronage of the movies and a sketchy interest in the fan magazines, *Funny Money* was a project of major importance; and, because she had the most conspicuous rôle in this monumental work, she betrayed no feeling of mousiness in defining her relation to the industry that had made Hollywood famous. In short, the thing went to her head.

Perhaps if the people who were immediately associated with her had made a little more allowance for her utter lack of experience in this strange game, they might have viewed Sally with less impatience. But, mistaking her artless ingenuousness for impudence (though she had plenty of that, too, Goodness knew), everybody made capital of her blunders which were indeed many and grievous.

Sally resembled her Maker in at least one particular: she was no respecter of persons. She ignored the high-walled caste system of Hollywood with an unconcern that would have represented the courage of a martyr if it hadn't been a mere case of foolhardiness founded on ignorance. Mr. Manx, for instance, she called Kitty. You weren't supposed to take such liberties with your director. Mr. Upham, the producer, had a tic that went off frequently in a combined squint and sniff. Sally could and did do it as competently as Mr. Upham. The mimicry was enough to make a dog laugh — but it was decidedly unfunny in the opinion of Mr. Upham.

'Wait a minute!' Sally would shout, after a final rehearsal when they were waiting for '*Quiet! Action!*' 'I'd rather do it *this* way, Kitty! Let me show you. It'll be ever so much funnier!' And the maddening fact about these rash impertinences was that Sally, at least four times out of five, proved she was right. When they let her have her own way, it *was* funnier; so funny that it made even the blasé kippers laugh, up on the catwalk. But that wasn't helping Sally much in the esteem of her colleagues.

She ad-libbed so recklessly that nobody else knew what to do or when to do it. Her pantomimes were so superb that she made the rest of the cast look like wooden effigies. She never gave anyone a cue, nor did she care whether she had any co-operation or not. She giggled when they blew up in their lines. Sally was a one-man show, and a very good show, too; but this did not make her popular with the people who had it all to say whether she was to be a star or a meteor. Day by day, the producer and the director and the veterans in the *Funny Money* enterprise mentally forgave and promoted — one by one — all persons who had ever won their disfavor, so that there might be room, at the bottom of their list of acquaintances, for Sally Singley, the lowest form of life.

Dick Veddar, suspecting from the first that his protégé was getting off to a bad start, lectured her with all the frankness of an elderly stepsister, but to no avail. When he grew savage — scowling and growling and cursing — the most he ever got for his pains was a perfect picture of how he looked while in this indignant mood, reflected in the facial contortions of the best mimic in captivity.

'Can't you realize,' Dick would sputter, 'haven't you sense enough to see what you're doing to yourself — and to me, too? Why — Gigantic wouldn't take you on for another picture — not if you were the only woman left in the whole world! Don't you know that everybody in the company is mad at you?'

'Pouf! They're jealous.'

'So much the worse for you! Jealous people can be very

mean. Everybody's talking about you. You're letting me down.'

'I'm building you up, big boy! *Funny Money* is going to be good. You'll see!'

And *Funny Money was* good; so very good that Gigantic made a pile out of it. But its success on the screen arrived too late to spare Sally the grief that Dick had predicted for her.

From the first, she had been utterly stampeded by her good fortune. She had made a few feeble gestures in the direction of her natural obligations; had sent her mother a long telegram while en route west; had wired Dean Harcourt, too, asking him to notify Barbara. And would the Dean be so good as to tell Barbara to write to her in care of 'my agent.' Sally had got quite a wallop out of writing 'my agent,' and enjoyed the idolatrous look on the face of the stewardess when she counted the words. Some people, sighed the stewardess, had all the luck.

In a week, there had been a letter from Barbara, slaving on a Nebraska farm, warmly congratulating Sally on her success and wishing her well, and wanting to hear from her, quickly, fully. And Sally was going to answer Barbara's letter as soon as she could find a leisure moment. Dean Harcourt had written too. Sally was going to answer this one, some time, though it wouldn't be so easy to do. The Dean had said, 'Because I feel somewhat responsible for the circumstances in which you find yourself, please remember what I said to you. Special talents are dangerous. People do not often get into trouble doing the things that they don't know how to do very well. Bunglers don't have many chances to make costly mistakes. It's the experts who make the ruinous blunders. Cold-blooded, unattractive people don't get into messes by chumming with the wrong crowd. It's the lovable, obliging people who encounter tragedies through misplaced confidence and quick friendships. . . . Be sure to keep close to Barbara. Don't outgrow that friendship or forget that obligation. . . . I shall be thinking about you, Sally; fretting a little about you too, I fear.'

Sally's salary was modest as compared to some, but it seemed a lot of money — thirty times as much as she had earned in the store. Dick counseled her to be economical, reciting some sad stories of people who had thrown away their easy money and had gone stony broke.

'If you weren't such a damn fool,' he said, 'you might even learn something from this wacky picture you're making; for you're certainly Libby — to the life! And don't think for a minute that when you're down to your last dime there will be a mass meeting of your new playmates to buy you an annuity. The day you go broke they won't recognize you on the street. It's easy to see why you're doing such a good job as Libby. You *are* Libby!'

It was a fact. As imprudent as Libby, Sally shoveled out her money without stopping to count it. Her handbag bulged with big banknotes. She excitedly entertained people who wanted to interest her in everything from Dusenbergs to kangaroo-farms. She bought a bright red roadster, engaged an expensive apartment, ordered more clothes than she had any use for, and paid a high tuition at the Clover Club for a not very thorough education in roulette.

She came to the lot late in the morning and remained at the tonier restaurants late in the night. Because of her skyrocketing from nothing to everything, the movie chatter-columns played up her Cinderella story until every place she entered buzzed with it. She liked that. Sally wasn't the least bit shy or self-conscious. It was fun to climb up on a tall stool, in one of the popular bars, knowing that a crowd would instantly gather. And it was fun to put on an impromptu show for them.

At length, *Funny Money* was finished — at least as far as Sally had anything to do with it; and, after a few grand and glorious days of celebration with people she hardly knew, she sent for Dick and asked him what she was to do next.

'Don't ask *me!*' he growled. 'You'll have to play the rest of the game with your other friends. I threw in my hand, long ago.'

Sally, who had a headache, cried a little.

'What am I going to do, Dick?' she moaned. 'I haven't any money, and I owe everybody in town.'

'Well — you'd better liquidate. Turn in your car for whatever it will fetch, sell everything that will sell, hock everything that will hock, settle with the people who will try to put you in the calaboose if you don't pay them; and then buy yourself a nice one-way ticket to Chicago. I'm sorry — but you can't say I didn't warn you.'

It wasn't long until everybody knew it. Because news gets about pretty fast in Hollywood, it was only a day or two until the widely syndicated chatter-columns had advised the whole nation that the bright young star, who could imitate anything from a director to an octopus, was now open for engagements with a lot of free time at her disposal.

The sales-girls who had worked with Sally and had followed her vividly publicized career with mixed feelings of astonishment, pride, and envy, gathered in groups to breathe down the backs of the necks of others who had brought their morning papers. 'What'll she do now?' they asked one another, a query which at that moment was of great interest to Sally herself, afraid to answer the door or the phone.

The whole world knew. The Provincetown players heard about it with a buzz of interest and a minimum of sympathy — human nature, unfortunately, being such as it is. Tim Wainwright, sincerely sorry, wired to Dick Veddar asking what was the matter and wasn't Sally any good, to which Dick replied:

SHE WAS TOO TOO GOOD   LETTER FOLLOWS

Lester, jarred out of his reptilian gait, came bounding into the shabby Singley flat, waving a paper; and Mrs. Singley, who despised him, read the fatal tidings, her flabby face distorted and her lips soundlessly shaping the distressing words. Lola, whose social rating at the high school had immeasurably risen until she had begun to limit the list of persons worthy of her society, came home at noon, red-eyed and sullen. Slouching out to the kitchen, she growled, 'I suppose you've heard,' and her mother nodded her head and mumbled, 'I wonder what she done.'

Mrs. Crandall rose suddenly from her rocking-chair in her little parlor at the Dean's House, and proceeded downstairs with the paper, meeting Mr. Talbot on the way. Noting her unusual excitement, he stopped her to inquire, and she showed him.

'My Word!' squeaked Mr. Talbot. 'Too bad! She was a jolly good mimic! Perhaps you'll be telling the Dean?'

Of course she would be telling the Dean. Stilling her agitation, Mrs. Crandall softly opened the door of the library, and laid the paper on Dean Harcourt's desk. She waited silently while he read. Then he handed the paper back to her, drew a deep sigh, and shook his head.

'I was afraid of that,' he said.

Larry Runyan came to supper that evening dispirited. It had become a recognized custom for Barbara to join him, about two o'clock, wherever he was painting, and remain until four. He had confidently expected her today as usual, and she had not come.

It had been a dull and profitless afternoon. From three o'clock on, his eyes were turned more often toward the house than the clump of cottonwoods he was presumably reproducing on his canvas. It made all the difference in the world, Barbara's absence. He realized as he sat there, slumped, apathetic, and glumly desolate, that this enchanting girl had become indispensable to his mental activity — to say nothing of his inner peace.

They hadn't talked of love. By unspoken agreement, that subject was taboo. Their mutual affection had rather taken the course of an intimate comradeship. It was not always easy to maintain. Sometimes, sitting side by side, their hands touched. It occasionally happened that when Barbara leaned over to pick up a pencil or a ruler she had dropped, her curls might lightly brush his bare arm. Once, to indicate a correction — he had been standing behind her campstool — Larry had dropped to one knee and looked over Barbara's shoulder while his arm, under hers, pointed to the spot on her drawing where she had erred. On this occasion of their nearness — to which she had sweetly yielded — he was sorely tempted to tighten his arm about her and say, 'We've had enough of this make-believe, darling! I love you!' But it wouldn't have been fair, he thought; not until he was able to confide that he wasn't the person he seemed to be. To make that confession was to risk losing an endearing friendship. The thing that made his restraint more difficult was Barbara's attitude. She made no overt bid for his tenderness, but it was clear enough that she shared it.

She had been seriously in earnest about her sketching, and Larry was proud of her progress. For the first few days, his commendation had been inspired mostly by his increasing love for her and the pleasure it gave him to have her close by. Her presence stimulated him. But it was not long until he was taking a master's delight in the intelligent dexterity of his bright pupil. He began to have a genuine respect for her workmanship. Perhaps, he thought, it was his sincere admiration of her supple mind that enabled him to discipline his heart.

How long they were going to be able to keep their balance on this emotional tightrope was a problem that Larry was willing to trust to future developments. He had almost stopped fretting about it. Of course it couldn't go on indefinitely. In a month or six weeks the season's heavy work would be completed, and the Wendell Farm crew reduced to a skeleton staff of hardy perennials. It seemed unlikely that Barbara would want to remain through a long and savage winter. Larry had invited her to discuss that question and she had waved it aside with a careless, 'I don't know yet.'

As for himself, it would be absurd to hibernate here in the snow. The Wendells wouldn't want him. No — this delightful association with Barbara was — on its present basis — shortly coming to an end. Until now, he had been accepting his happiness, doled out to him by the day. This afternoon, restlessly waiting for her, the threat of an early separation from Barbara took on alarming proportions. He knew now that he couldn't live without this girl, and his fear that he might lose her depressed him until it was almost as if tangible weights slowed his steps as he slogged across the yellow stubblefield on his way home.

Arriving at the big haybarn, in no mood to join the general chaffing that was inevitable as they cleaned up at the end of the working day, Larry dragged his old suitcase from under his cot; and, tossing his sketching tackle into it, sat down on the bed, inattentively overhearing the conversation among the threshers, scattered about in various stages of undress.

'Yeah — easy come, easy go,' drawled a voice at the end of the row of cots.

'It ain't far from corn-pone to plum-pudding, but it's a long way back,' chattered somebody under the cold shower.

'Bet she wishes she had some o' that kale now that she threw away,' remarked the old man near by who was pulling on his trousers. He glanced at Larry for confirmation of this platitude, nodding his head emphatically; and Larry, feeling that he was expected to make some rejoinder, signified his assent with a humorless nod.

'Who is this unfortunate lady?' he inquired, negligently.

'That Singley girl, in the movies. The papers have been full of her. Don't you keep up with the movie stars; a young feller like you?'

Larry admitted that he had heard of her; and, with more

interest than he cared to reveal, wanted to know what had happened to her. The old man laughed on a tone three lines above the treble clef, hooked up his galluses, and proceeded to explain.

'This girl was nothing but a clerk in a store, and because she knew how to make funny faces they shot her out to Hollywood; and did she cut a swath? Now she's out on her neck, everybody sore at her, flat busted ——'

'You mean "busted flat," Uncle Jim,' yelled one of the youngsters, at which hackneyed sally they all laughed uproariously.

'Well — have it your own way. She's busted, anyhow. No more job 'n' a rabbit. *Sic semper tyrannis!*'

'That isn't what you're trying to say, Uncle,' laughed young Edmunds, who taught high school in the winter. 'You mean, "*Sic transit gloria mundi.*"'

'And what does *that* mean?' inquired old Blosser, the timekeeper.

'Well, loosely translated,' grinned Edmunds, 'it means liquidation on a large scale, such as you get in a cyclone.'

Larry took no interest in this badinage; sat through it with a sober face. When the general merriment subsided, he asked, quietly, 'When did all this come out?'

'Just now — far as we're concerned. Jason was up to the house and got a morning paper.'

Presently they all began straggling toward the dining-room, candidly impatient as a lot of hungry dogs. Larry lagged. He wondered if Barbara knew. She had never confided her exact relation to Sally Singley; but it must have been intimate. Perhaps she had learned the bad news about her friend, early in the afternoon. If so, that might have accounted for her failure to show up.

The supper-bell rang, and they moved into the house with alacrity, slipping into their seats with the effortless ease of seals. Larry couldn't keep his eyes away from the door that led to the kitchen. Barbara hadn't come in yet. He thought he would know instantly, when she should appear, whether she was troubled.

The serving of supper continued. Larry listlessly toyed with his food, and watched the door with nervous impatience. The Swanson girl was directing the service. It took much longer than usual, thought Larry, for these gluttons to wolf their rations. He was anxious to get out. At last, a hundred chair-legs scraped the floor, and they all toothpicked toward the door. Larry had decided to ask Letty Swanson. She would probably giggle, and the other girls might titter; but he would ask her. But he didn't have to; for, as he neared the door, old man Blosser, immediately preceding him, inquired.

'I don't know, Mr. Blosser,' replied Letty, soberly. 'She's not here.'

'Not here! Have you looked for her?'

'Her car is gone,' said Letty. She looked as if she were going to cry, and she wasn't very pretty, anyhow. Larry was ashamed to stare into her ugly little face, with her lips turned wrong side out; but he did so, and pushed forward to learn what he could.

'Do the Wendells have any idea what has become of her?' he demanded, making no concealment of his anxiety.

'Midge says they don't know where she went,' said Letty, sniffling.

Larry strolled aimlessly across the yard and turned down the lane. He thought he knew what had happened. Barbara had learned about Sally's disaster and had impulsively scurried away to see what she could do. It must have bitten pretty deep, he felt, if she was in such haste that there wasn't time even to let him know she was leaving. Maybe she didn't want him to know, for fear explanations would be in order.

He had thought her much better balanced than to rush off in a panic. It was obvious that the poor dear had started for California; for that's where Sally was, according to reports. Driving — to California! In that old crate! By herself! No money! — or, at best, a few dollars saved from her small wages. What could she do for Sally when she got there? Well — you certainly had to give it to her for her loyalty! Larry looked at his watch. Quarter to seven. He wished he had a good car. Unlikely, though, that he could overtake her. She had a long lead of several hours.

But he wasn't going to lie wide awake all night in Wendell's haybarn, worrying himself to death. He would get someone to drive him over to Axton. There he would find a man at the little garage who would drive him to Omaha. He could take the first plane to Los Angeles, and be there when Barbara arrived. This thought promptly crystallized into a decision. He turned abruptly and began to retrace his steps. Andy Wendell was coming to meet him. Larry's heart quickened. Maybe Wendell had some message.

'Guess you heard,' said Andy, quietly. 'Barbara left here in a hurry, a little after two. Said a good friend of hers was in trouble. Midge thinks it's the movie actress that our girls have been chinning about. It seems that Barbara knows her. All sorts of rumors floating around, as you might expect of a lot of silly girls with nothing much to think about. What they don't know, they guess at. One story is that Barbara and this Sally Singley — probably a stage name — are sisters; and by Golly, from the pictures, they *are* about the same height and shape.'

'It's possible,' muttered Larry. 'Anything else make you think there might be something in it?'

'No; can't say as there is.' Andy trudged along, thoughtfully, for a few steps; then came to a stop. 'Of course, Runyan, you and I both know that Barbara is out of her natural element here. Maybe you know all about it. You're fond of each other, as anybody can see, and she may have told you about herself.'

Larry shook his head.

'No, Mr. Wendell,' he declared, with convincing firmness, 'I know nothing about Barbara — other than what we all know about her here. I have no notion what her relation may be to this movie girl, but I know there is a strong attachment. And I believe that Barbara has started for California.'

'That's what Midge thinks,' said Andy. 'Barbara was pretty much upset when she left; said she didn't know how soon she would get back; said we should tell you that she had to go — and to say good-bye to you for her.'

After a long moment, Larry said, 'I don't see how she can get to California in that old car.'

'Well,' drawled Andy, 'it's a pretty tough-looking old vehicle; that's a fact; but the body has had a much worse lickin' than the engine. I figured maybe it was in a wreck, and they had to rebuild the motor; cracked block, maybe. She can go to California if she wants to; and go pretty fast, too.'

'I wonder what she'll use for gas,' queried Larry. 'She didn't have any money; did she?'

'Not much more than enough. She hasn't spent anything since she's here — far as I know. I paid her wages up to today. She wouldn't take any more.'

'Wish I'd known,' growled Larry, imprudently.

'Guess you wouldn't have had much to spare,' grinned Andy. 'And she wouldn't have taken it, even if you had. Midge tried to lend her some.' There was an extended silence.

'I'm afraid I'll have to go now, too, Mr. Wendell.' Larry made this speech at considerable effort. 'I don't believe I could accomplish anything more here; not with her on the road, alone, and practically without funds.'

'Well — that's natural,' said Andy. 'I told Midge you'd probably be restless. How would it be if I drove you over to the highway. I suppose you could hitch-hike. Lots of fellows do.'

'Thanks,' said Larry, brightly. 'I'll appreciate that. I can be ready in ten minutes.'

Luckily, everybody was interested in a horseshoe game, back of the haybarn. It wasn't very cordial to run away without saying good-bye; but they all knew by this time that Barbara had left mysteriously, and it would add up to an exciting total if he departed hard on her heels. He wasn't quite up to brassing it out. So, without making any unnecessary racket, he packed his simple kit and hurried away. Andy was waiting in front of the house with Midge beside him. Larry slipped into the back seat of the sedan, and they were off. Apparently Midge knew everything that Andy knew. She was unobtrusively sympathetic. After they had driven through the main street of Axton, and a block north to the well-traveled thoroughfare, the car stopped and Larry got out.

Midge said, 'I do hope you find her, Larry. I know how much you care for her. And — and you come back — whenever you can.'

'That's right,' said Andy. 'We'll always be glad to see you.'

Larry waited until their car was safely out of sight. Then he walked back to the little garage. Three men, interested in his approach, sat out in front, their grimy chairs tipped back on their hind legs. Larry signed to the one who seemed to be boss, and they stepped inside.

'You're Mr. Maxie?' began Larry.

'I'm Maxie, yeah. Name is Pepper.' Maxie was crisp and suspicious.

'What will you take to drive me to Omaha?' queried Larry.

Maxie looked him over, with sullen disinterest.

'You can go over on a bus in the morning.'

'I'm in a hurry. I want to go now.'

Maxie thrust a thumb under his belt, grinned unpleasantly, and said, 'I wouldn't drive to Omaha tonight — and have to put up at a hotel 'n' all — for less than thirty-five dollars.'

'Very well. Get out your rig.'

'That would be cash, of course; and maybe you'd better let me have it before we start.'

Larry took a bill out of a well-filled wallet. Maxie, sucking a tooth, eyed the wallet with sour respect, and fingered the bill.

'Nothin' smaller than that?' he asked.

'No.'

'Well — you can pay me when we get there. By the way — ain't you this painter fellow that's been out at Andy Wendell's?'

Larry nodded and Maxie's eyes narrowed.

'Didn't you and Andy and the Missus drive by here, little

while ago? I seen 'em come back without you. How come they didn't leave you off here?'

'Because they thought I was going to bum my way.'

'Well — I think I'll just call Andy up. This doesn't look hotsy-totsy to me. They'll be home by now.'

Maxie retreated into his greasy little cubbyhole, and Larry could hear him rumbling his story at some length. Then there was a brief silence, after which the receiver clattered back onto the hook. Maxie came out presently carrying his coat over his arm.

'Okay, Buddy,' he said, a little less ungraciously, 'let's go.'

'I suppose Mr. Wendell satisfied you that I hadn't stolen anything at his farm,' Larry couldn't help saying, as he climbed into the flivver.

'Yeah,' said Maxie, as they turned east toward the highway, adding, deliberately, 'There must 'a' been a lot goin' on out there today. This good-lookin' gal that's been workin' there went a-skitin' through here, in her old bus, about two o'clock. Meggs, the fellow at the station, says she stopped and sent a telegram.'

Larry clenched his teeth to keep from asking a question; but Maxie had all the information and was eager to pass it along.

'Meggs says she wired some fellow in Chicago; told him she'd be with him about noon tomorrow; so anxious to see him, and all that sort o' thing.'

It made Larry sick. Some fellow in Chicago. Some fellow in trouble. His mouth felt dry. Barbara had run away from some fellow in Chicago; some damned, worthless fellow in Chicago. Now he was in a bad mess, and out of loyalty she was going back to him. Larry knew she couldn't be to blame. He was painfully hurt, but his heart went out to her.... Maxie was chattering local gossip, but Larry didn't hear him. Maxie asked him some question, and he didn't reply: didn't hear what Maxie had asked him; didn't tell him to repeat it. His head was blurry. Well, there was still this Sally person to be looked after — by somebody. Barbara had been devoted to her; had worried about her. If his surmise was correct, Barbara had rushed away to face some trouble in Chicago that she was obviously unwilling to confide to anyone. Perhaps he should pursue his intention to aid Sally. He could do that much for Barbara.... Maxie had shut up now, and was moving along steadily at fifty-five.... Larry stared at the darkening road with cloudy eyes.... Some fellow in Chicago; eh?... After a half-hour of silence, Larry cleared his dry throat, huskily, and turned toward the stolid Maxie.

'I don't suppose this gossiping station agent told you the name and address of that — of that Chicago party,' he inquired, half truculently.

'Nope.' Maxie was miffed and sullen. 'Or if he did, I don't remember.' Then, with heavy dignity, ''Twasn't nothin' to me. None o' my business.' Apparently pleased with his own hauteur, he leaned out at the window and accented his indifference with a record-breaking stream of pungent tobacco juice.

Larry said no more, after that; just sat there silently despising Maxie, and wondering what excuse there was for this wild-goose chase to California. He didn't want to go to California. He wasn't interested in Sally. If Barbara heard of it she might be contemptuous of his unsolicited intervention. Barbara would be too occupied with the problems of this fellow in Chicago to give a second thought to Sally — or to himself. He had lost Barbara; that's what it all came to.

And then he gave himself to some day-dreaming about her tenderness, and experienced a little thrill as he remembered — and, for an instant, relived — the enchanted moment when, with his cheek close to her shoulder, and his arm under hers, he had pointed out the necessity for a heavier shading in her sketch; and had been deeply stirred by her magnetic warmth. She had drawn a quick breath. It had brought them closer. Her arm had gently pressed his against her side. There was no forgetting the ecstasy of that experience. Barbara did care for him! No matter what sort of obligation had swept her away from him; back to Chicago on some probably distasteful errand of rescue — Barbara belonged to him, and he would not give her up without a fight. . . . The Nebraska highway was straight as a ruler. But Larry's thoughts traveled a rugged road; now over summits where the air was light and heady, and his heart pounded hard; now down in the valley where the fog was thick.

Dean Harcourt was alone in his library when Barbara arrived at twelve-thirty, tanned and wind-blown. She went swiftly to him, and sat on the edge of his desk, close beside his chair. He took her by both hands and smiled a welcome.

'You made a quick trip, my dear.' His brows knitted anxiously. 'I hope you weren't driving too fast.'

She shook her head — gazing down into his eyes happily.

'It's like getting home,' she said, softly.

'It's like having a daughter,' said the Dean. 'It is fortunate for you, Barbara, that you don't realize how fine you are.'

'I know I'm fortunate in having a place like this to come to,' she murmured.

'You haven't had your luncheon, I hope,' said the Dean, practically; and when she shook her head, and said she was ravenous, he pushed a button. 'I'll tell Mrs. Crandall you are here, and when she remembers how much it takes to fill you up she may want a few minutes to prepare. Meantime' — he surveyed her with a droll expression of dismay — 'why don't you go upstairs and wash your face and comb your hair?'

'Do I look so dreadful?'

'Dreadfully dreadful! Run along now, and hurry back. We have much to talk about. I suppose you're fretting about Sally. And of course you'll have to do something about that.'

'It's what I came to talk about, really,' said Barbara. She rose, took up the Dean's hand and with childlike impulsiveness laid her cheek against the backs of his fingers.

'Away with you!' he demanded, clearing his voice sternly. 'Soap, water, brooms, pumice stone, currycombs!'

Mrs. Crandall put her head in, and when she saw who was there, she entered and gave Barbara a welcoming smile.

'I suppose you're hungry again,' she said, grumpily, as they hugged each other. 'There's only one other person that comes here who seems as hollow as you are.' She turned to the Dean. 'You know who I mean; that handsome, no-account painter — that Larry somebody. He certainly was hard on food.'

Barbara's arm relaxed from around Mrs. Crandall's comfortable girth. Her face sobered, and her inquiring eyes drifted across to Dean Harcourt.

'Larry!' She moved slowly toward the big desk. 'Larry?' Her lips were parted, questingly. 'You don't mean — Larry Runyan!'

'Yes, dear,' replied the Dean.

'Has he been here?'

'Yes.'

'Does he know — about *me?*'

'No; not unless you told him.'

'Did you know that he is out at the Wendell Farm?'

'Yes — I knew that.'

'Well,' said Mrs. Crandall, 'if you'll excuse me, I'll go and see about your lunch.'

Neither Barbara nor the Dean commented on that. Mrs. Crandall closed the door behind her. There was a long moment of thoughtful silence.

'We must talk about that,' murmured Barbara. 'I've deceived him, shamefully. You know — I was pretending to be very poor, and I let him keep on thinking so. And — I know he's awfully fond of me — and' — she lowered her voice to a whisper — 'I may as well tell you — I'm simply mad about him! But he's penniless; with no prospects, at all; just tramping about. And he's proud, too.'

'Well — we will talk it all over,' said the Dean, reassuringly. 'Go, now, and make yourself pretty. And don't worry. If Larry loves you, and you love him, I daresay you'll contrive some plan for solving your problem.'

'I can't help feeling that Larry has been through some very tragic experience. He won't talk about himself. I expect he must have told you.' Barbara's eyes searched the Dean's.

'But he hasn't told you?'

Barbara shook her head.

'And you won't tell me?' she asked, wistfully, unhopefully.

'A question like that, my dear,' said the Dean, gently, 'should be able to answer itself.'

At half-past two, Sonia came in to announce the first caller. The Dean introduced them.

'Sonia knows about you, Barbara,' he said.

Barbara had risen; and Sonia, motioning her back into the big chair, sat on its broad arm.

'You see, Barbara,' explained the Dean, 'I am not as well as I might be. If I should slip away, without giving two weeks' notice, there would be many a problem left half-solved. So — Sonia knows almost everything. And, incidentally, she is very helpful.'

Barbara looked up into Sonia's eyes; and, after a moment's search, her lips parted in a slow smile.

'Sonia.' The Dean's tone was businesslike. 'Let me tell you what is afoot here. Barbara is leaving, Friday morning, driving back to the Wendell Farm. She learned that Sally was in much trouble and came here to consult with me about what she might do to help her. We have agreed that she should go to Hollywood — and see. But, first, she thinks, she should return to Nebraska, and spend a few hours with the good friends she has there; for she left in such a hurry that she had no chance to say good-bye.'

Barbara gave him a grateful look. The Dean — bless him! — was making it appear that this decision was her own, when the fact was that she had decided to go directly to California. She had told him as much and he had shaken his head.

'No, Barbara,' he had protested. 'These people have been very kind to you. And you must remember that you went to them, in the first place, looking for friends who would love you for your own sake. You have satisfied yourself on that point. But the Wendell Farm people are not guinea pigs to be used for experimental purposes. Did

you ever consider what a dangerous weapon a friendly
smile is? You turn the brightness and warmth of it upon
some lonesome, wistful, unprivileged soul, and instantly he
glows and grows. It meant little to you; it meant everything to him. Now if — after giving him that new reason
for thinking life is good — you should neglect him and forget him, you have done him a great deal of damage. . . . In
this instance, while you do have an obligation to Sally
Singley, it mustn't be discharged at the cost of those good
friendships in Nebraska. . . . And — another thing: you will
never be happy again until you have cleared up your misunderstanding with Larry. You'd better tell him all
about it. Don't leave anything untold. In solving a problem of this sort, there's nothing that can take the place
of the truth.' And Barbara had promised; her heart already pounding apprehensively at the thought of what she
would have to say to Larry.

'So —— ' went on the Dean, in a matter-of-fact tone,
'Barbara will go back to Nebraska, see her friends, and
then take a train from Omaha. And she will want some
other clothes. Perhaps you will help her, Sonia.'

'Would you?' asked Barbara, wistfully. 'Tomorrow?'

'Of course. We have time to do a little shopping this
afternoon. You will want to look nice at the hotel.'

'She will want to look nice here, this evening, at dinner,'
observed the Dean. 'You two run along now. Sonia, tell
Talbot to take care of the callers.'

Barbara responded with girlish excitement, twinkling
her fingers.

'Oh, I can't bear it!' she exclaimed. 'I'm going shopping!' Her eyes danced. 'I'm going to have some pretty
clothes again!'

'And when you go back to Nebraska,' counseled the
Dean, 'I think you should wear what you had on when
you left. You can express your new clothes to Omaha, and
pick them up there when you take your train.'

'Oh, dear,' sighed Barbara, 'do I have to wear this awful
gingham dress again?'

'Of course you do,' drawled the Dean.

'I'll go and tell Mr. Talbot,' said Sonia, slipping away.

'Sonia's nice; isn't she?' Barbara glanced toward the
door that had just closed.

'Very.'

'Does she know about Larry?'

Dean Harcourt nodded — and chuckled a little. Barbara
looked puzzled.

'What's funny?' she asked, soberly.

'Well,' said the Dean slowly, 'I've a notion that you are
plotting to get some useful knowledge out of Sonia. But
if you are, I suggest that you get some dynamite.'

'It must be awful,' remarked Barbara, moving toward
the door, 'to be so secretive.' She paused, with her hand
on the knob, to give him a reproachful, wrinkle-nosed smile.

'You should be an authority on that subject, by now,'
said the Dean, dryly.

Dinner was going to be at least an hour late, reported
Mr. Talbot, because Dean Harcourt was tied up with what
must have turned out to be an important interview.

Sonia and Barbara had returned from their shopping
tour, long since, and were waiting in the reception room for
the Dean to be at liberty. They were reading the evening
papers. Barbara was wearing a blue silk polka dot with
white collar and cuffs and the quite becoming Nebraska
tan.

'Anybody we know?' mumbled Sonia, deep in the fashion page.

'A newcomer,' replied Talbot, in his high key. 'A person named Drake. Miss Katharine Drake. Arrived a little after five. Works in a store. Couldn't get off earlier. Much agitated when she came.'

'Will she be here for dinner?' Sonia wanted to know.

'I haven't heard yet,' shrilled Talbot.

Mr. Simpson had drifted in, and remarked that perhaps dinner had been postponed to some other day. Sonia presented Barbara, who gave him a little smile. He came to the davenport and sat between them.

'Is-ums hungry?' crooned Sonia, in her deep contralto, without looking at him.

'Yes-ums,' admitted Simpson, soberly.

A young woman in her middle twenties appeared from the hallway leading to the Dean's library. She was almost pretty, her unrelieved black gown accenting a pallor that spoke of too little sunshine rather than imperfect health. Her auburn hair, primly set, but significantly stringy at the temples, suggested that she had been crying, if you hadn't already guessed as much at the sight of her slightly swollen eyes. She came into the room diffidently and made a gallant effort to seem composed. Because she wore no hat, Sonia instantly suspected that she had been invited to stay. She put down her paper, and smiled a welcome that was at least fifty per cent curiosity.

Talbot, with a proprietary air, presented Miss Drake who, by the brevity of her little nods to each of them, seemed to have something else on her mind. She walked over to Sonia, instinctively selecting her as the one to approach, and said, nervously, 'I'm staying for dinner.'

'That's good,' said Sonia, warmly. 'We'll all enjoy hav‌ing you. Won't you sit down? It will not be long.'

Miss Drake looked troubled. She was fretting about something. She stooped over to ask Sonia a question, her manner indicating that she preferred it to be private. Simpson had started down the hallway with the Dean's wheel-chair. Talbot went to answer the telephone. Bar‌bara rose and sauntered over to the big Gothic window.

'What is it?' asked Sonia, kindly.

'Well——' The girl laughed a little. 'He told me to find a Mrs. Crandall and tell her I'd be here.'

'Oh — you mustn't let that worry you,' said Sonia. 'You know the Dean doesn't get about by himself, and he probably didn't know the rest of us would be here yet; so he told you to find Mrs. Crandall yourself.'

'Then' — the embarrassed visitor raised her brows, al‌most beseechingly — 'would you tell her I'm to stay?'

'Oh — by no means,' said Sonia. 'If the Dean told you to find Mrs. Crandall, you should go and find her. We always try to do exactly what he says. There's generally some reason for it.'

'Where will she be?'

'Out in the kitchen, I should think. Go through that door, and keep going. Don't let this rattle you, Miss — what is your first name? Mine's Sonia. And you're to call me Sonia. That girl's name is Barbara.' She raised her voice a little; and Barbara remarked, over her shoulder, 'You can tell that this is a Christian institution, Miss Drake, because we all use our Christian names; though I can't recall ever hearing anyone call Dean Harcourt George.'

'My name is Katharine.'

'Kitty, I expect — at home,' prattled Sonia, ingratiatingly.

'No — just Katharine.'

'If I called you Kitty,' said Sonia, 'would you care?'

Katharine smiled mechanically and shook her head. Then she started on her errand; continued through the dining-room, pushed open a swinging door that led to the butler's pantry, and wound up in the kitchen.

'Are you Mrs. Crandall, please?' she inquired of the middle-aged woman who appeared to be in charge.

'Yes. How many are there now?'

'All I know about,' said Katharine, 'are Sonia and Barbara and the two younger clergymen and Dean Harcourt — and me. I'm invited, too.'

Mrs. Crandall chuckled good-naturedly. 'And who are you?' she asked, stirring something in a big bowl. 'I can't remember ever seeing you before.'

'No — I never was here before.' Katharine's lips twitched with nervous laughter. 'My name is Kitty. And that was never my name before.' She paused; and then added, in a puzzled tone, 'I've never been in a place like this.'

'There aren't any other places like this, Kitty,' muttered Mrs. Crandall. 'But don't let it upset you. He sends strangers prowling all over the house; especially if he thinks they are lonesome. He wants to make them feel at home. You go on back now, and don't be shy; because, if he thinks you're still scared, he'll probably send you upstairs to hunt for his glasses — or something.'

Retracing her steps through the dining-room, Katharine found the household mobilizing for dinner. Sonia slipped an arm about her, almost carelessly, as if they had been long-time friends. It flattered Katharine, for she had found herself overawed by this beautifully gowned woman who seemed so smartly sophisticated. And the comradely gesture gave her a warm little sensation of being included in this tight-meshed company of intimates.

'Dean Harcourt will probably want you to sit by him,' said Sonia, 'with Barbara on the other side, I think. He hasn't seen her for a long time. She just came today. That accounts for what's going on over there.'

On the other side of the room, Barbara was leaning over the back of the Dean's chair, listening intently, and nodding her head, as he confided something to her.

'I think I heard someone say you are employed in a store,' said Sonia, to make talk while they waited.

'Yes. Ladies' Ready-to-wear,' replied Katharine.

'It's interesting work; don't you think? I'm a toiler, too, Kitty. I have a little gown shop. Not so very far from here.'

Katharine's eyes widened.

'Are you *the* Sonia?'

'That's a sweet way to say it, Kitty. I'm going to like you.'

Katharine had dreaded this dinner, from the moment Dean Harcourt had suggested it. But Sonia had put her at ease. She wasn't frightened now. The Dean was in a playful mood. Barbara was quizzed and teased about her farm. Katharine was invited to tell how little she knew about the country, to which she had added her wish that she might know something about it.

'Barbara is driving back to Nebraska,' said the Dean, addressing Katharine. 'She starts early Friday morning, and would enjoy a traveling companion.'

'Dean Harcourt says you need a little vacation,' interposed Barbara, 'and we've thought up one for you. I have an errand that will take me away from the farm, for a couple of weeks; perhaps longer.'

'And you can take Barbara's place, you see,' explained the Dean.

'Is it something I would know how to do?' inquired Katharine, interested but not very hopeful.

'Big farm,' said Barbara. 'Lots of men to feed. You could help do that, I'm sure.'

'I'd like to,' said Katharine, 'if you think I could.'

'All right,' declared Barbara. 'It's a date. Can you go on Friday?'

'Sooner the better,' answered the Dean. 'Isn't that right, Katharine?'

She nodded, with her eyes on her plate.

IV. Brick

WHEN Mr. Drake died, Katharine became the head of their family. It was not an easy job, for she was only twenty-three and her father's place was hard to fill.

Mr. Drake was branch manager of a national concern dealing in office equipment. His intimate acquaintance with such devices had made him exceptionally methodical, for you can't spend every day demonstrating elaborate filing systems and other implements of business efficiency without developing an orderly mind.

On Sundays, it was Father's custom to collect the current household invoices and check them against supplies on hand. The family made a little joke of this weekly inventory. It was Father's hobby. He was not a niggardly fellow, nor was his income so small as to make such vigilance necessary; but he liked to know, he said, exactly where they stood. It was sound business practice.

He knew how much soap they used per annum, how many rice flakes should be found in the cupboard, how many meals an eight-pound rib roast was good for, how many times a two-dollar shirt should go to the laundry, and whether the refrigerator was consuming too much power.

Every item of expense was budgeted. Mother didn't actually have to fill out a requisition when she wanted a new hat, but she was expected to inform Father how much it cost, so he could enter the figures against the appropriation for clothing. Father was not mean; nor was he reckless. And seeing how much pleasure it gave him to keep strict account of the family's expenses, none of the rest of them offered any suggestions. He wisely arranged everything for their comfort, appointed the time and place for their annual holidays, and so painstakingly ordered their lives that it was quite unnecessary for them to do any thinking or planning for themselves.

It was Father's custom, on the night of the first day of the month, to have a family party and issue the allowances. Even Emma, who didn't actually need the money — for Bill was making good wages — was still on this payroll. Katharine, since taking a position in the department store down town, had requested the discontinuance of hers. Freddie, who was still in high school, received the smallest amount. In emergencies, he privately negotiated small unsecured loans from Katharine, for Father did not believe in spending more than your income. Indeed, a mere mention of the word 'emergency' annoyed him. Mother, too, was on an allowance; for, while she and Father were companionable enough in all other matters, she was economically related to him as a dependent. In the handling of money, business was business; and it was none of her business.

Millicent received more than the others because she really needed it. No questions were ever raised about this. It was simply taken for granted that Millicent's expenses were larger. In high school she had been interested in dramatics and an assortment of sports demanding a considerable outlay for appropriate costumes. As a college student, her requirements had not been diminished. Nobody in the family was envious. Perhaps that was because the Drakes were singularly free of jealousy, though their complete dependence on Father's will and wisdom may have accounted for their silent acceptance of whatever he felt was right.

Milly may not have been Father's pet, but she was always of much interest to him; and no wonder. She sang, she whistled, she composed funny limericks. She sneaked up behind Father, as he sat smoking his cigar after dinner, and twisted his thinning gray forelock into an absurd kewpie curl. On occasion she called him Jim, and he would mutter that she ought to be spanked; but she never was.

And Milly was lovely: corn-yellow curls, turquoise eyes shaded by long lashes; enchanting dimples, of whose purposes she was not unaware. Freddie had begun calling her 'Booful' when he was a baby. Father often called her that, too. She had never protested; it was a fact. Milly was quite pretty. And she was about as thoughtful and useful as a canary.

In the summer after Katharine's graduation from high school, Emma was married. Bill had a good job as an automobile salesman. People were still buying automobiles. But Bill hadn't saved anything. Father thought it better for them to have their own home, and provided the money to set them up in housekeeping, even in the face of his ten per cent salary cut. Nobody in the family seemed to know about the cut but Katharine, who had read it in the financial news. Father hadn't reported it at home; nor had he fretted about it, for it was no reflection on his efficiency, which was all that mattered to him. When Katharine privately ventured to sympathize, he made light of his little misfortune. Now that all business was going to hell, he said, nobody needed any new office equipment to help handle it.

It had been planned that Katharine should enter college that fall, but she figured it would be too much of a burden; so she said she preferred to get a job. Father gallantly went through the motions of dissuading her, but you could see he was immensely relieved by her stubborn refusal to spend his money and her time going to college when she would so much rather work.

If it hadn't been for Millicent's uncommonly good looks, Katharine would have been almost pretty. She had inherited her mother's burnt-sienna hair and brown eyes, and had fortunately missed having her mother's stocky physique. She was slim, lithe, shapely. Her smile came slowly and when it arrived it had an enigmatic quality that often made you wonder whether Katharine hadn't found something more amusing in the situation than had occurred to you. She didn't talk much, and never about the store, feeling that it should be left down in the Loop where it belonged. Occasionally she was invited to the homes of her fellow saleswomen for dinner and found that the whole family knew every scrap of gossip pertaining to the ladies' ready-to-wear department. It was all they talked about — and it was enough to bore you to death.

Katharine would no more have thought of packing such tittle-tattle back to her family than of entertaining the sales force with reports of table-talk at home. Sometimes she had business friends as guests for dinner, and the Drakes would be amazed to learn full details of her exciting life, down town. It was almost as if there were two Katharines, one of whom they didn't know.

Frequently, Mother would say, when the family was alone and there was a little lull in the conversation, 'Anything interesting happen today, dear?' And Katharine would say, 'No — not very.'

One noon — Katharine had been in the store for about two years — Mr. Boyle, the assistant buyer in their department, had taken some western buyers out to lunch. It wasn't his job, customarily, to entertain out-of-town clients. He was a sedate temperate fellow, not given to the kind of hospitality expected on such occasions, and when he returned at two-thirty he didn't know who he was, much less how indiscreet he was for coming back to the store at all so shockingly plastered. A few of them had quickly gone into a huddle and Katharine had volunteered to boost poor Mr. Boyle into a taxi and see him home. At no little outlay of tact and patience, she had accomplished this. Mrs. Boyle, an excitable, neurotic, easily derailed creature, had put on such an impressive scene that Katharine had had to stay with her for two hours, literally sitting on her to keep the frightened thing from phoning the Big Boss that Clarence had never been drunk before and would never, never do it again; and all this while Mr. Boyle — habitually reticent — was splashing in the bathroom to the accompaniment of roaring, ribald song. Neighboring apartments telephoned inquiries, and Katharine calmly soothed them, while holding Mrs. Boyle at arm's length to keep her from completing their social disaster.

That evening at dinner, when there was a momentary pause in the talk, Katharine's mother said, 'Anything interesting happen today, dear?' And Katharine said, 'No — not very.' In some respects Katharine took after her father, keeping her own counsel and not worrying other people with her little problems. In fact, she didn't confide anything to anybody: and, in consequence, lived a rather lonely life. She hadn't intended it to be that way; it had just turned out that way. While still in high school, she had had many friends, and enjoyed them. Sometimes she would bring boys home, or they would call for her and go to a movie; but Millicent, by merely tipping back her head and surveying them from under half-closed, adoring eyes, would take them into camp. It wasn't that she wanted Katharine's boys; it was just that she needed the practice. Milly had a lot of glamor, and it seemed ungrateful to possess such a gift and deprive it of healthful exercise.

After Katharine began working in the store, there weren't many opportunities for meeting congenial men whose acquaintance might have become cherishable. The ones she met in business, who were worth a second look or a passing thought, were either married or had their social interests established. Besides, it was no picnic to work all day; and when five-thirty came you were ready to quit, and fight your way into a streetcar. And after you had dangled from a loathsome strap for thirty-five minutes, and had walked six more blocks to Laurel Street, you didn't care whether anybody took you out that night, or not. All you wanted was to rest your feet, wash out a couple of pairs of stockings, and go to bed. Father often remarked of her that Katharine was a thoroughgoing business woman; dependable, steady as a clock. You always knew where to find Katharine, he declared. Sometimes she grinned a little when he said that. You always knew where to find Katharine. And if you wanted to find her, any evening about ten, you would find her in bed. But she didn't care much. She was too tired to care.

The only diversion in which Katharine had an active interest was her Sunday morning attendance at Trinity Cathedral. The Drakes were not church people, and Katharine was playfully teased for having gone in for religion — their way of putting it which wasn't quite true; for she hadn't embraced a creed, nor was she much concerned over the solemn enigmas that had provided an occupation for ancient saints and many a war between pious kings. Her reason for attending Trinity Cathedral was to hear Dean Harcourt.

Katharine had never met the Dean. It had not occurred to her to inquire whether she might have a personal interview with him. It was enough to sit there quietly on Sunday morning, and listen. The atmosphere of the place held certain mysterious elements of healing and repose. You sat enveloped by the symbols of a faith that had comforted so many people, for so many ages, that you accepted them without examination. Katharine never made any attempt to participate in the ritual. She knelt and stood and sat, along with the others, but she didn't read the responses or sing, or so much as hold one of the little books in her hand. She was there to look and listen; a mere spectator, if you wanted to think of it that way; but at least that was a consistent attitude, she felt, seeing how little real participation she had in the things that made life worth the bother.

Sometimes Katharine was almost startled by Dean Harcourt's uncanny understanding of her monotonous existence, her little cares, her tensions, her vague wistfulness. He was quite unlike anyone she had ever seen or heard. He was crippled, and the crisscross lines of pain endured had mapped his face with innumerable excursions into fortitude. His voice had the resonant timbre of an instrument that didn't need to be tuned; that didn't flat when it rained.

In the Cathedral tower there was a famous carillon. When it played, it made little shivers run down your back; little shudders and seizures and surges of emotion. Sometimes they made you feel like flying and sometimes they made you feel like crying; but, no matter what the bells were saying, what they said was correct — and we'll not be having any debate about it. They weren't impudent or cocky; they were just sure — and said so. The Dean's voice was like that, probably from living so long as a close neighbor to the bells. When the Dean said something, he didn't ask you whether you believed it, and you didn't ask yourself whether you believed it. You just knew it was true. Everything he said sounded sensible, perhaps because it was so simple. One day he said, 'If you were able to find your way into this mess, you should be able to find your way out; for you didn't have quite as good a reason for getting into it as you have for wanting out of it.' That, thought Katharine, made sense.

When James Drake died, in June, after a heart attack and a fortnight's illness, the family was utterly bewildered. Father had single-handedly managed everything for them but their temperature and respiration, and when he withdrew his benevolent oversight they were as helpless as so many kittens.

Mr. Abernathy came up from the office, next day after the funeral, and was amazed to discover the extent of their ignorance about their financial affairs. Mrs. Drake was embarrassed when obliged to reply to Mr. Abernathy's inquiry about the life insurance, that she really didn't know how much Father had carried, or whether he carried any. 'He never talked to us much about such things,' she murmured. It was the truth. She didn't even know how much salary Father was getting, or whether it had been paid to date. She just shook her head and twisted the end of her nose with a soggy handkerchief and told Mr. Abernathy that he had better talk it over with Katharine.

That day Katharine became the head of the family. She didn't know much about finance, but was infinitely more capable than the rest of them; so they insisted that she was to 'manage things,' which meant that they intended to lean their full weight on her exactly as Father had wanted them to lean on him. Without protest, Katharine accepted this responsibility, and they all climbed on.

There wasn't much of an estate; certainly not much if you expected to live on the income accruing from it: ten thousand in life insurance, five thousand in government bonds, a small assortment of badly battered stocks, and enough cash to defray the funeral expenses.

Freddie, who had just graduated from high school, courageously declared he would give up going to college and find a job. He had been spending most of his idle time hanging around the airport; hadn't decided whether he wanted to fly or work on the ground; but his job, when he found one, would be something in aviation, he said.

Millicent had already made arrangements to spend the summer in Provincetown, studying dramatics with a group of amateur players; would have been there by this time had it not been for Father's illness and death. She felt that if it were at all possible for the family to finance her, perhaps she had better proceed with her undertaking and prepare herself to earn some money on the stage.

Katharine had suggested that it might be a little safer, from a business standpoint, if Millicent found a job down town, and volunteered to help her make such connections. Millicent drew a sickish smile that was half a sneer.

'Now — *wouldn't* that be a career?' she sniffed.

Her sister made no immediate reply to that; simply pondered it with cloudy eyes. If Millicent had intended her remark as a forthright insult, that would be hard to take, of course, but one could bear it. But Millicent hadn't fired this shot willfully. She hadn't meant to hurt Katharine's feelings with this derisive comment on her employment in the store. She was just too damn dumb, thought Katharine, and too selfish, and too thoroughly occupied with her own pursuits, to realize what a mean thing she had said.

'It might take a long time,' observed Katharine. 'Sometimes people spend years and years, don't they, trying to get on the stage?'

'Some people; yes,' replied Millicent, her tone implying that better things could be expected of the unusually bright.

'You'd think,' interposed their mother, eager to defend Millicent's cause — 'you'd think it ought to be easy enough for young people who have had training — and have looks — and everything.'

'Naturally!' broke in Millicent. 'And if a little ignoramus like this silly Sally Singley, who had been nothing but a clerk in a department store, could learn enough at Provincetown in three days to get herself snatched out to Hollywood for a screen test, there ought to be a chance for people with some refinement.'

Katharine's lips puckered into one of her slow smiles.

'Maybe it was Sally's lack of refinement that put her over,' she drawled.

Millicent angrily struggled up out of the davenport, shook her curls, and stamped toward the stairway.

'Easy to see,' she paused to say, bitterly, 'that you don't want me to have a chance.... Oh, well ——' She capitulated with a hopeless gesture. 'If we haven't the money for an investment like that, we simply haven't the money; and I'll give it all up. All of it! All of it!' It made a fairly neat exit, and Katharine couldn't help feeling that maybe Millicent — thick-skinned as she was — really had some capacity for drama that might take a polish.

Her mother cried softly, after Milly had delivered the swan-song in which she renounced the stage and accepted whatever low tasks might be assigned to her.

'Katharine, dear,' she pleaded, when she could control her voice, 'can't we plan somehow to let Millicent do as she wants? It's breaking her heart — and mine, too.'

So — they sold some bonds at a sacrifice and rigged Millicent out for the summer's adventure. It was pretty expensive, too; for it would be no good sending Milly to Cape Cod looking like a hick.

Freddie hadn't found a job yet, but he was still in search of one. At least he was away from home all day and sometimes until late in the night. Once in a while Katharine would hear him talking on the telephone in a sort of rumble, as if the conversation dealt with a conspiracy. Freddie was growing up — and he was growing away — and he was growing rather furtive. She hardly knew him in his new rôle.

For a long time, Trinity Cathedral had been serving Katharine as a pleasant retreat on Sunday mornings. As her responsibilities increased and her problems became more

complicated, Trinity's peace and Dean Harcourt's counsel
— previously considered as luxuries — were now thought
of as necessities. Trinity had been a delightful bay in
which to sail on her weekly holiday; now it had become an
anchorage in a storm. The Dean's words had offered repose; now they were offering rescue. Katharine lived from
Sunday to Sunday.

She always took the same streetcar to the same bus-line,
which brought her to the Cathedral at ten-fifty-five; always entered by the same door, and was seated — almost
always — by the same usher, a rather dignified, bald,
fiftyish man in conventional morning clothes. He had long
since begun to recognize Katharine as a regular attendant,
greeted her with a cordial smile, and showed her to the
same seat. It was quite obvious that he held this place for
her, second to the end of a center aisle pew, about halfway
down. The end seat, he always held open for a stranger,
and Katharine couldn't help being at least mildly curious
to see what manner of woman would join her there; for it
was invariably a woman. Doubtless stray men were shown
into pews occupied by other men.

One Sunday in mid-July, as she sat there dreamily
yielding herself to the Bach Prelude that she loved best of
all — 'Out of the Depths' — her usher brought her a man.
He was probably thirty, blondish, modishly dressed in a
slate-colored gabardine. They exchanged a casual glance,
and Katharine retired into her soliloquy. The organist was
going into that sublime Coda now: it always affected
Katharine deeply; burned her eyes, suffocated her, hurt
her throat. Now it was done; and she ventured, from the
corner of a wet eye, a little look at the stranger. He was
clearly out of his element; and, now that the service was

beginning, he seemed uncertain what to do, coming slowly to his feet when they stood for the processional, and having a bad time folding up his rangy legs when they knelt. There had been mighty little kneeling, reflected Katharine, in this fellow's experience. His shoulder was closer to her face when they knelt. His sleeve smelled sort of druggy. The people all around them — all but Katharine and her unknown companion — were murmuring that they were lost sheep who had followed too much the devices and desires of their own hearts. Katharine inhaled very slowly and inquisitively through the constricted tip of her nose, and decided it was iodoform — or something like that. Maybe he was just out of a hospital, though he didn't look as if he had ever been sick. Maybe he was a doctor.

Now they were standing again, and something in the stranger's manner advised Katharine's intuition that he had observed her non-participation in the responses. It was almost as if he were saying, 'Here we are — we two — surrounded by all these people who know what to do — and we're not co-operating at all. We must do something.'

The choir had gone into the *Te Deum* now, and the congregation was joining in, too, much as it could, for it was not an easy piece to sing. Katharine's new friend stooped over, drew one of the little black books out of the pew-rack, leafed through it unhopefully, and handed it to her. She acknowledged his courtesy with a nod, promptly located the *Te Deum*, and handed the book back to him. He whispered a word of thanks; and, for a moment, his eyes searched the page. Then he returned the book to Katharine, with a deferential bow, and she closed it slowly and put it back in the rack. Then she looked up into his face, and they both grinned. Katharine felt it was one of the silliest incidents to which she had ever contributed, and it was with the utmost difficulty that she strangled a chuckle.

Now the ritual was ended and it was time for the sermon. Although she had experienced a pleasant thrill from the droll little episode with her good-looking neighbor, Katharine found herself wishing that their chance encounter had occurred somewhere else. Her mind had been distracted. It would be a misfortune, she felt, if this precious cathedral mood — which had become the most enchanting event of her drab existence — were in any way jeopardized; and it could be so easily damaged, for it was a fragile gossamer that wouldn't stand the strain of weaving into any other thought-pattern, no matter how desirable.

But presently it was as if she had given the Dean her hand, to be led along, as usual. He was talking quietly about the pursuit of happiness. He feared that this venerated phrase had been misunderstood by many people; for some seemed to think they should pursue happiness as if it were a winged thing that they must by any means overtake, even if they had to set out after it on unfamiliar one-way roads. It was probably a mistake to pursue happiness; much better to create happiness; still better to create happiness for others. The more happiness you created for others, the more would be yours — a solid satisfaction that no one could ever take away from you.... It warmed Katharine's heart when she reflected that she had been doing this. Surely, if anyone had ever devoted herself to her family, it was she. Maybe, by this process, she would realize happiness for herself, sometime. She was willing to wait. She drew a long, slow sigh; and her eyes were misty.

After a while, Dean Harcourt raised his hand and the people knelt. Again Katharine became conscious of her unknown companion. They stood, and he towered beside her. It pleased her to imagine herself dependent on him for protection. The recessional hymn flooded the great nave, and ebbed at length as the choir departed. Then they knelt for the benediction and their arms touched. Katharine did not draw hers away. That might have seemed unfriendly.

After a moment's silence, everybody rose and there was a general stir. The stranger paused, after stepping out into the aisle, and waited for Katharine to precede him. Then he fell into step beside her and they drifted with the crowd toward the high-arched doors. Now they were out in the blinding sunshine.

They had not spoken, on the way; nor had they exchanged a glance. Side by side, as a part of the dissolving multitude, they walked down the broad steps to the street level where Katharine paused, looked up into his eyes, and smiled tentatively.

'I take a bus here,' she said; and then she surprised herself a little by offering him her hand. 'Good-bye. I hope you will visit our Cathedral again, sometime.' It seemed all right to say this much to him; proper way for Christians to treat a stranger in their midst. Surely Dean Harcourt would approve of that.

'The bus stops again, a couple of blocks farther down; doesn't it?' said the stranger. 'Would you mind?' Releasing her hand, he took Katharine's arm and propelled her through the crowd. When they were a little more in the clear, their steps slowed and he said, 'Now may I introduce myself? I am Doctor Harrison. I live in Cleveland and am in Chicago for a few days on a professional errand. The chief of staff at our hospital insisted that I should hear Dean Harcourt. . . . And you?' He smiled into her eyes.

'I am Katharine Drake,' she replied, matching his mood. 'I have always lived in Chicago, at home, with my family. I work down town in a department store. I always hear Dean Harcourt on Sundays.'

'I thought you were a stranger.'

'Because I didn't sing or read verses.' She nodded, understandingly. 'I go just to listen — and I don't like to do anything myself.'

'I don't have a chance to go to church very often,' said Doctor Harrison. 'If I did, I might feel the same way.'

'The trouble is,' explained Katharine, 'the words they want you to read aloud are really very beautiful and impressive; but if you should read them as they deserve, your neighbors might think you were trying to be elocutionary — or something. And if you just mumble them ——' She hesitated, and finished lamely, 'That's not so good, either.'

They were nearing the second corner now and Katharine paused at the curb. 'I can take my bus here,' she said.

'Must you?'

'No — not exactly must. But we have dinner at home on Sundays at one-thirty, and they'll be expecting me.'

'Couldn't you telephone and say you were having dinner down town with a friend?'

'Have we been acquainted long enough,' asked Katharine, soberly, 'for me to say we are friends?'

'I think so,' declared Doctor Harrison. The big double-decker was careening down the street, but she made no effort to signal it. 'Was that yours?' asked the doctor.

Katharine nodded.

'We'll take a taxi,' he said. 'I don't like busses.'

It was a funny thing, Katharine thought, what being in

love would do to you. You were in love not only with him:
it made you feel warm and tender toward everyone else.
Maybe that was the way you could tell. Anyhow — she
had never felt like this before.

Only a week had passed, but it seemed a long time.
Perhaps that was because she had done so much thinking;
staying awake to all hours, and not wanting to go to sleep;
waking early in the morning, and starting another twenty-
hour day. It was a wonder she didn't go to work heavy-
eyed and absent-minded, but it hadn't had that effect on
her, at all. Indeed, she must have been looking unusually bright, for several of the girls had spoken about it and
were eaten with curiosity to know what had happened to
her.

She had risen at daylight, this morning. There was no
reason, for it was Sunday. She tried not to make any noise,
tiptoeing out to the wicker swing on the little verandah.
About six her mother came down, wondering sleepily if
anything was the matter. Nothing was the matter, Katharine assured her, and she should go back to bed.

'And I'll get your breakfast,' she said.

'You mustn't,' protested her mother. 'The idea — you
working all week — and then having to get breakfast on
Sunday.'

However, she did consent to go back to bed, and Katharine went to the kitchen; for Mother liked to have her
coffee soon as possible after she woke up. It was heart-
warming to be doing this for Mother. She knew plenty of
girls in the store who resented having to do anything at
home, but she didn't feel that way, at all. Some people
shirked their duties to their families, and some who per-
formed their duties did so with sour complaints. But

Katharine didn't mind. She rather liked doing things for others, even at a considerable sacrifice. Last week she had sent Millicent twenty dollars out of her pay. Millicent really shouldn't have asked for more money when she couldn't help knowing how they were economizing at home; but Katharine hadn't felt indignant over Milly's request. Indeed, she had realized a peculiar pleasure in sending the bank draft — a curious sensation of an inner glow.

When her mother's breakfast tray was ready, Katharine carried it upstairs and put it on a chair by the bed. It made her feel good to be doing this for Mother. She would have been glad to get Freddie's breakfast, too, but knew that Freddie would resent being wakened so early. Poor Freddie wasn't making much progress in finding a job. Katharine hoped he wouldn't be discouraged. She was glad to note that he hadn't begun to fret about it yet. It would be nice, she thought, if Freddie could earn something, pretty soon; for it was costing quite a little for his meals and fares. Of course, as Mother had said, you couldn't expect the boy to go about with empty pockets. And Freddie was such a high-spirited youngster, anyway, Mother had added, that it simply wouldn't do to let him lose his self-respect.

After Katharine had seen to it that her mother had everything, she took her own cup of coffee out to the swing where she re-read the letter she had had on Thursday. It would be more than three hours before she would leave for the Cathedral. It was going to mean more to be there today than it had ever meant before. For the thousandth time she reviewed last Sunday's events, item by item, beginning with that funny little pantomime over the prayer-book, and their walk down the aisle, and her missing the bus, and their ride in the taxi.

They had lunched in the Renaissance Room at the swankiest of the big hotels on the Boulevard, having a little corner to themselves. Phil had wanted to go there because of the string quartet. He hated a loud racket, he said, when he wanted to talk with someone.

Katharine remembered everything they had said to each other. She had accused Phil of being lonesome, but he had pondered that remark with an uplifted eyebrow. Maybe — today — he had been lonesome; but not ordinarily: didn't have time to be lonesome. Didn't have a home; didn't want a home; wouldn't know what to do with a home if he had one. He was all wrapped up in his work: you could see that. And it was wonderful the way he talked about his chief, Doctor Paige. Doctor Paige, he said, had a wonderful story. Phil would tell her about it, some time. Katharine remembered how her heart had jumped a little when he said that, for it meant that Phil wanted to see her again, another day.

Then they had taken a long drive in a taxi until it was time for the organ recital at the University. She had told him — Phil was crazy about organ music — how fond she was of Bach's 'In Thee Is Joy' — and how it kept on piling up joy until you were all but smothered by it. Strangely enough, that was the closing number of the recital. When it came on, Phil had reached for her hand and gripped it; not with a sneaking little squeeze, but an honest handclasp that he had made no effort to conceal. Then their fingers had interlaced and stayed that way until the music ended with a triumphant chord that vibrated the air for all of two seconds before it vanished. Katharine had been so happy that she couldn't keep the tears back, and when they rose he had looked down into her swimming eyes and whispered 'Sweet' — the way you do when you look at somebody's little baby asleep.

Then they had driven about some more in the University grounds and back to the Loop where they had dinner at a place Phil knew of where lobsters were a specialty. Katharine had never eaten any but the canned kind, and it was fun to have Phil teach her how to get it out of the shell. After that, he had taken her home. She had wondered, as the taxi turned into Laurel Street, whether Phil might want to kiss her good-bye. She had made up her mind to do that without protest if he insisted; but he didn't, and she was glad. It seemed to bless the whole day's experiences — that he didn't try to kiss her — this time. Her mother had been reading when she came in.

'Well — you *have* had a full day, haven't you?' she had said, inviting a report.

'With a doctor.' Katharine had paused at the foot of the stairs, momentarily. 'I want to get into something cooler, Mother.' She took a couple of steps up. 'He lives in Cleveland. I met him at the Cathedral.' She took a few more steps. 'We had a nice day.' She was at the top of the stairs now, and called down, 'Is Freddie home?'

'Not yet,' her mother had replied.

Upon her return, Katharine was relieved to find that Mother was apparently contented with her account of the day's doings, and eager to talk about Freddie.

'He thinks he might get a job in Dayton, but I'm sure I don't know how we are to find the money; not unless you can lend it to him, dear.'

'I can't until next pay-day,' Katharine had replied. 'Think he can wait that long?'

'He'll have to, won't he?' said Mother. 'If we haven't

got it, Freddie will just have to wait. He says he needs some new shirts, too, Katharine, whenever we get around to it — and some shoes, too.'

It always amused Katharine a little — Mother's use of 'we.' 'Whenever we get around to it.' 'We' were Katharine. However, it was all right. Katharine was carrying a heavy load, but she liked it. They were all leaning hard on her, but she could stand it. It was a funny thing — but the sensation was far from unpleasant; a sort of almost painful little ecstasy. Funny thing. Maybe the martyrs had it. Of course they would have had it in great abundance, because they really suffered.

Katharine sipped her coffee slowly, now looking with meditative eyes at the heavenly blue morning-glories that trailed over the trellis, now glancing again at the open letter. There really wasn't anything personal in Phil's note. He was back at work again. He had enjoyed their day together — immensely! Perhaps he could wangle a week end off. In October — maybe. If so, he might drive to Chicago. He would hope to see her. And he was Very Sincerely hers. It wasn't much — but Katharine had been carrying it — folded into a small square — very close to her. Sometimes it wasn't very comfortable.

After a while, Mother came down and joined her in the swing. Then Mrs. Andrews, next door, came out on her verandah. She and Mother were close friends. They all said good morning, and Mother said, 'Won't you come over and join us?' And Katharine rose to give Mrs. Andrews her seat beside Mother, and went to the kitchen to get a cup of coffee for Mrs. Andrews. When she came back and was nearing the open front door Katharine heard her name spoken in the low-voiced conversation. Mother was telling

Mrs. Andrews how much Katharine was sacrificing and how hard she was working and how she had got up this morning early to get breakfast for her mother when it was the only day in the week that she could sleep as long as she liked, and ——

'I know,' Mrs. Andrews murmured, feelingly. 'Katharine certainly is a little brick — if ever there was one!'

'That's what she is,' Mother declared. 'I never saw anything like it. If I do have to say it — about my own child — Katharine's a brick.'

Again Katharine felt this peculiar warming sensation in her heart. She came out onto the verandah with two cups of coffee, gave them to her mother and Mrs. Andrews, and went back into the house. She drew a pensive smile. It was nice to have people feel that way about you. Brick. Little Brick.

When Katharine arrived home, hot and weary, on the afternoon of the last Friday in August, her mother met her with a telegram. She had opened it, thinking it might be from Millicent or Freddie, and was appropriately regretful over having done so when she discovered it was from Katharine's new friend, Doctor Harrison.

'He is going to be here Sunday,' she announced.

Katharine took the telegram without comment and started up the stairs, her mother calling after her jocularly, 'He must be getting quite fond of you.' Without replying, she went to her room, closed the door, tossed her hat aside, sat down on the edge of the bed, and luxuriated in the unexpected message. He was driving and would arrive in Chicago late Saturday night. Could they have lunch together, down town, Sunday, and then take an all-afternoon drive? Would she have a reply waiting for him at the hotel? Katharine, with shining eyes, drew a deep breath and hugged herself delightedly. Oh! This was wonderful! Marvelous!

After she had read the telegram until she knew it by heart, Katharine took a shower, got into some comfortable clothes, and went down to help with the evening meal. Of course she couldn't blame Mother for having opened the message, but it would have been ever so much nicer, she felt, if she had been permitted to break the news in her own way.

'If he likes you that well,' Mother began, as Katharine sauntered into the kitchen, 'I should think he'd like to see your home. Why don't you ask him to come out here for dinner on Sunday?'

Katharine murmured that that would be nice, and began setting the table.

'Of course,' she added, after a couple of trips to the dining-room, 'Doctor Harrison and I don't know each other very well yet. Perhaps it isn't time to show him the family.'

'He knows you well enough to sign himself "Phil,"' said Mother, significantly. 'And there's only me. I'd like to meet him. Surely he can't raise any reasonable objections to calling on you in your own home; not if his intentions are ——'

'That's just it,' Katharine broke in, impatiently. 'If I ask him here, he'll think the family wants to look him over — and see if he'll do. And — as for his intentions — I think I'm old enough to be the judge of that, without any help.'

It was the first time that Katharine had let herself go

so bluntly, and when she went back to the kitchen she was dismayed to see what she had done. Mother was leaning against the kitchen table, crying into her apron.

'I never thought' — she gulped — 'that you'd talk to me like that.' It was dreadful, the way Mother was trying to speak through her racking sobs. 'I — I get so lonesome — sitting here — all day — everybody gone. I just wanted to see your — your friend. Can't you understand? I didn't want to spoil your good time. But I won't say any more. You go down and see him. It's — all right. It's all right.'

Naturally there was only one thing for Katharine to say, and she said it. It would have been callous cruelty to have stood there unmoved by her mother's pitiable breakdown. She put her arms around the slumped figure, and with murmured repentance and endearments succeeded in gradually calming the emotional storm. Of course they would ask Phil to come out for dinner, and she was very selfish not to have suggested it herself. After a while, Mother's grief had ebbed to the stage of amazingly bountiful nose-blowing, and Katharine — sobered and depressed — continued setting the table. The hilarious joy over the promise of a visit with Phil had been throttled down. However, she had done her duty by her mother; and the consciousness of having made this sacrifice gave her a pleasurable heart-warming sensation. She knew what Mrs. Andrews would say, if she heard about it — as she probably would. And she felt that if Dean Harcourt had been here, he would have commended her prompt compliance with her mother's wishes.

'You aren't eating a thing, dear,' said Mother, a little reproachfully, as if to imply that it was high time we forgot all about our little misunderstanding now, and resumed our normal appetite.

'It's so sultry,' explained Katharine. 'I'm not hungry.'

'Maybe it's getting ready to rain,' remarked Mother, leaning toward the window to inspect the sky. 'Well — we certainly need it. I'd be willing to see it pour for a couple of days.'

Katharine pretended to sip her tea. All we needed now, to make everything just perfect, was a couple of days of pouring rain. Her mother observed the slow smile that was bending her lips; and, brightening, inquired what was so funny. But Katharine didn't explain. She shook her head a little, to signify it was nothing of consequence, and pushed back her chair.

'You sit still,' she said, dutifully, 'and I'll bring in the berries.'

Now that we had decided to have Doctor Harrison with us for dinner on Sunday, Mother immediately gave alarming signs of planning a stunningly abundant hospitality. She was a good cook and believed in hearty food. Mr. Drake had been an earnest eater, in his time. It would be a pleasure to have a full-grown man at her table again. Katharine had been appalled upon learning, Saturday night, what all they were having besides the stewed chicken, noodles, sweet potatoes, avocado salad, pickled peaches, and deep apple pie.

'He has his dinner in the evening, Mother,' cautioned Katharine. 'Please don't have too much.'

'Pooh!' scoffed Mother. 'You can't give a man too much to eat; no matter when you serve it.'

There hadn't been much use in arguing the point. Katharine felt that the whole affair was likely to be embarrassing, in any event; and if Phil couldn't overlook

Mother's childishness in preparing this rustic feast, he wouldn't be able to understand her at all; so she had said no more about it.

They had risen early, this Sunday morning, Mother eager to have breakfast over so she could set to work on the vast enterprise of the day. The dinner was going to require a great deal of time and hard labor — and when it was ready, thought Katharine, it was going to look as if it had been produced at ruinous cost and infinite bother. But Katharine didn't often bring anyone home for a meal, said Mother, and it was no more than right that the dinner should be a credit to her home. When Phil called up, at nine, to say — not very enthusiastically — that he had had the note and would be out at one o'clock, Katharine was sorely tempted — her mother being out of earshot, engaged in a high-keyed conversation with Mrs. Andrews — to say:

'Maybe you'd rather go with me to the Cathedral, and then have a bite somewhere on the Boulevard'; but she didn't have the courage. My Goodness! — why couldn't Mother let her alone — to see her friend in peace — without all this fuss and muss!

At eleven, Katharine gave up trying to simplify the table, and went to her room. She stretched out on her bed and closed her eyes. Doubtless she had been exaggerating her anxieties. Phil would understand. Mother was as transparent as glass, and naïve as a six-year-old child. Anyhow — the ordeal would not last very long. They would get into Phil's car and leave it all behind them. How glad she should be that it was such a fine day. She tried to recover a mental portrait of Phil, in various moods. It was pleasant — day-dreaming.

Presently she was startled out of her enchanted languor

by the sound of her mother's voice in a series of shrill exclamations.

'Why — of all things! My precious baby! I can't believe it! How did you get here? . . . Katharine! Come down — and see who's here! You can't guess!'

She could, though. She guessed it was Milly. And that was right. She rose up on one elbow and stared at herself in the mirror, meeting a pair of troubled eyes. First we had to have this terrible dinner to go through with. And now we had Milly. She smiled wanly. She had borne a good deal: this was just one thing more. She would try to be a brick.

Milly greeted her with a dutiful, sisterly peck, but was in a dour mood, and anxious to explain it. She had left Provincetown before the season closed because she was simply all fed up. It was just an impenetrable little clique. They hadn't given her a chance. Wainwright was nothing but a bluff, anyway; didn't really know the first thing about directing, much less acting; was an insufferable snob; gave all of his attention to people with money. She was glad to be home — and out of the whole mess of them. Then she cried a little, admitted she hadn't eaten any breakfast, and consented to have a cup of coffee.

'What's all the big doings?' she asked, glancing over the table; and when Mother had explained, brightly, 'Katharine's having a guest — her beau — if you'll believe it,' Milly turned toward her sister with pleased interest.

'You don't tell me,' she said, caressing her yellow curls with both hands. 'And he has never been here before,' said Mother, 'so we'll have to be nice to him.'

When the mantel clock downstairs had struck three,

Katharine reached an important decision. It had been a sultry night, but she was shivering, for she wasn't used to crying and the past two hours of incessant and uncontrollable sobbing had nearly destroyed her. What a dreadful-looking object she was going to be tomorrow at the store. However, she felt a measure of relief. She had resolved to talk with Dean Harcourt.

It wasn't that she had any expectation of his clearing up her troubles. The Dean believed in one's doing things for others, and he would probably repeat what she had so often heard him say; that the highest joy in life was to be found in loving service. She would tell him about her problems, and he would commend her. He would counsel her to carry on bravely. And it would be easier, after that.

It had been the most unhappy day of her life. Millicent had taken full charge of Phil from the moment he arrived. And Mother had seemed bent on hurling them at each other. Of course, it wasn't intentional. Katharine knew that allowance must be made for the fact that Milly had just now come home, humiliated and discouraged; and Mother was fairly bursting to make her happy. And Milly, who — on her own lugubrious testimony — had been negligently if not infamously treated for many weeks, was sorely in need of admiration, and was bidding for it with every light turned on and the band playing. Milly knew how to do it, too. She was a gifted flirt; and, as a flatterer, she handled a brand of molasses that would sweeten everything for a thousand yards in all directions.

Phil — poor, bewildered Phil — had done his utmost to emphasize his special interest in Katharine, but they wouldn't consent to it. As if saying, 'Katharine can talk to him any time,' Milly and Mother — maybe without realizing what they were doing — had crowded her out of the picture. And because she had no talent for out-talking and out-dimpling other people, she was putting up a pretty poor show — and knew it. Milly had the floor. Mother hadn't yet heard all the details of her eventful summer on Cape Cod, and encouraged her to go on and on with her fascinating story.

Katharine had tried to appear pleasantly interested in this interminable narrative, but she felt it must be a rather sickly smile. Milly was making full use of all the implements of allurement. One quite effective device — Katharine had seen her do it on innumerable occasions — was to tip her head forward a little, prop her elbows on the table, lace her fingers under her chin, and gaze straight into the eyes of her victim, as if she had just made an amazing discovery; the eyelids would lift slightly, and there would come a radiant smile, instantly followed by a sobered, startled expression, as to say, 'Merciful Heavens! Have I let him see how much I care!'

Once in a while Mother and Milly would pause to toss a crumb of sympathy in Katharine's direction. Katharine was the man of the house; steady as an old plow-horse. No, sir — they certainly wouldn't know how to get along without Katharine. Poor Katharine worked like a dog — down there in that stuffy store. Poor Katharine. That sort of talk. Poor Katharine. Dear Katharine. Mother patted her hand once, and told Phil she was a brick.

After about ten years of this insufferable dinner, they rose from the table; and Phil, glancing at his watch, said, 'Katharine and I are taking a drive — up along the north shore.' And Mother said it was a wonderful day for a drive;

and, turning to Millicent, inquired, 'What are you doing, dear?' Then Phil said, 'Perhaps you would like to go with us?' Of course he was saying it for sheer courtesy's sake, expecting Milly to decline. But Mother promptly exclaimed, 'How nice of Doctor Harrison! Why don't you go?'

So, Milly had come along — after making a feeble protest that she didn't want to be a crowd — and sat between them, doing most of the talking. Sometimes she would turn to beam on Katharine briefly. The yacht races: how you would love to see them, Katharine! You will simply have to see the ocean, some day, Katharine. Well — as I was saying — so then we drove down to Woods Hole and took a boat across to Nantucket. You'd love it, Katharine.

On the way back from Lake Forest they had stopped for tea at a nice little place. Phil was attentive, but quiet. Katharine had hoped for a chance to slip him a private word, but there was no opportunity. When they turned into Laurel Street, about nine, Phil said he supposed they were tired, and he would go directly down town. Katharine thought Milly might go into the house and leave them alone together for a moment, but Mother had heard them arrive and came out to the car. Phil shook hands, all round, and pushed off toward town. Milly called after him that he must come back soon, but he didn't turn his head. Perhaps he hadn't heard her. Perhaps he was bored stiff with the whole lot of them feeling that Katharine was a stick, and her mother a magpie, and her sister an agonizing pain in the neck. How glad he must have been to drive off alone, probably saying he was right thankful to have found out — in time — what he would have been letting himself in for, if he had pursued this friendship any farther.

Well — we couldn't go on this way, without some sort of moral reinforcement. Katharine was going to see the Dean and hear him say that she must be strong. Maybe she could be strong — if Dean Harcourt commended her. She crept out of bed, turned on the light, and wrote him a note. She was in trouble, she said, and wanted to talk with him. She further deposed, in a brief postscript, that she had been a regular attendant at the Cathedral for a long time. It helped; just to write. Then she went back to bed — and slept.

All day Wednesday, Katharine was nervous. A Mr. Talbot had replied to her note, telling her to come on Wednesday afternoon. She had telephoned him that she was working, and would it be all right if she came late. Mr. Talbot had said that the Dean would see her whenever she arrived.

As the day advanced, Katharine's courage dwindled. Habitually she was quite conscientious about her work and applied herself to it with undivided attention. But, this afternoon, she knew her smile was stiff and her manner detached.

'Yes, madame, I think this little model would be very good for you,' she would be parroting, while her mind was busy with such self-defensive measures as, 'I don't bear them any ill-will. They haven't meant to make me unhappy. I didn't come to complain. I just thought it would be a relief to tell someone, and I knew you would understand — and sympathize.' . . . 'Wouldn't you like to slip it on, madame? Yes — it's your size, I think.' . . . 'I don't expect you to try to do anything about it, Dean Harcourt. There's nothing to be done. It's my cross; and I'll try to bear it.' ... 'Yes, madame; sixteen ninety-five Yes, madame; the alterations would be at your expense. Lottie, tell Mrs. Squick to come and take a measure.' ... 'I hope I'm not just taking up your time with my little troubles. Perhaps I shouldn't have come. I'll try not to make the story too long.'

When the gongs rang at five, and everyone set to work spreading the covers over the stock, Katharine's hands trembled and her knees were unsteady. This was supposed to be the best moment of the day. 'What's eating you?' demanded the Renschler girl, as their elbows touched. 'Feel all right?' Katharine said she guessed it was a little touch of indigestion. 'If it's heartburn,' said Renschler, 'I've some soda tablets.' Katharine obligingly took one, though she didn't suppose it would do much for that sinking sensation. There was a lot of difference, she reflected, between heartburn and heart-burning.

Because she was going late in the afternoon, Katharine decided to take a taxi to the Dean's House. She did not have long to wait for one to come along. It picked her up at Wabash and Washington, and they were soon making good time on the Boulevard. Katharine's depression had lifted considerably. After all, it was a silly thing to do, this interview with Dean Harcourt. He would probably wonder why she had bothered him with such a small matter, and wonder why the Drakes couldn't smooth out their family difficulties without dragging him through their troubles. Indeed, she had a notion to ask the taxi-driver to let her out, but she couldn't do that, for the appointment had been made. It was like going to the dentist. The pain would ease up, while you were on the way to the office; but you knew that it would be just as bad as ever if you got cold feet and failed to show up.

The Dean's House was almost a part of the Cathedral; same sort of windows, though smaller, of course. The door was opened by Mr. Talbot. He seemed to be expecting her; inquired if she was Miss Drake, led her down a long hall, opened a door, announced her name.

Dean Harcourt was sitting in the far corner of the room, at a large desk. His chair had a tall back, very much like the one in the Cathedral; so, it was almost like seeing him as he looked on Sundays. He asked her to come in, and pointed to the biggest chair she had ever been offered.

'Mr. Talbot tells me you are one of my flock,' said the Dean, gently. 'It's high time you came to see me.'

'I'm sorry I had to come so late.' Katharine's mouth was dry and her voice sounded very thin in this large room. 'I work in a store.'

'You're to have all the time you need, Miss Drake. Don't feel hurried. Won't you take off your hat? Put it in that little dressing-room over there.'

She thought it an odd request, but obeyed mechanically. Returning, she tried to fit into the chair so she wouldn't look or feel uncomfortable, but the arms were far apart and the seat was so deep that she couldn't lean back; so she drew her feet up under her and snuggled into one corner. The Dean watched her with a twinkle of amusement.

'Like that chair?' he asked.

'I do — now,' said Katharine, responding to his smile.

'It is a known fact,' he drawled, 'that it's difficult to confide in anyone if you have your feet flat on the floor.'

'So — that's why you have this big chair.' Katharine grinned, and risked a query. 'Do your men callers sit on their feet, too?'

'It's a good question,' approved the Dean. 'They draw the chair closer and hook their heels on that lower rung. And they're never ready to talk — about the thing they came to talk about — until they do that. . . . Now — if you're quite comfortable, Katharine, begin at the beginning and tell me all about it. I can see that somebody has been hurting you.'

It seemed easy to talk to this man. Katharine even went back to the death of her father for a starting place. Occasionally the Dean put in a brief question; but, for the most part, he let her tell her story in her own way. She didn't want Dean Harcourt to think that she had come to complain. She knew, she said, that making sacrifices for others was the way to acquire nobility. Bearing burdens was not only a duty — but should be a source of happiness. And she was willing to admit that it had made her happy to do so — until just lately. It was getting very hard — lately, she said.

'What has been happening — lately?' inquired the Dean.

So — she stammered through the humiliating experiences of last Sunday, trying to make short work of it, but being pressed for more details; and before she had finished with it she was crying.

'He'll never want to see me again,' she said, dismally, 'but that's all right. I've made a lot of sacrifices. I suppose I can bear this one, too.' She broke down completely at this point, and shook her head disconsolately when the Dean asked gently if she wanted to tell him anything more.

'Your trouble, Katharine,' began Dean Harcourt, deliberately, 'is largely due to an error of judgment. You think that sacrifice gives people a certain nobility of spirit, and that is true; but if sacrifice is such a good thing, it ought to be passed around, a little, so that other members of one's family may benefit by it, too. Your household has never had this advantage. I'm afraid you have been a bit selfish. There is always more joy in giving than getting. You have unwittingly deprived your family of that joy.'

Katharine lifted her bowed head and listened with a baffled look in her wet eyes. She could hardly believe her ears. She had thought Dean Harcourt would sympathize — and commend her.

'This is a pretty serious mistake that you have made, my dear,' the Dean went on. 'It may be a long, hard job repairing the damage you have done. When you became the head of your family — manager, treasurer, wage-earner — you were in a position to bring out the best they had and make them useful and happy through co-operation with you. Instead of developing them, you have all but ruined them. And you have had a sort of grim pleasure in doing it — as if you were accomplishing a very fine service. You thought you were being good to your mother by permitting her to outrage your natural rights. Was that a kind way to treat her — your own mother — letting her become a person of that sort? You abetted your young brother into becoming a parasite. Do you think that was good for him? And you have ruined your sister to the point where she may never amount to anything!'

'You mean' — asked Katharine, thickly — 'I should have fought it out with them?'

'It wouldn't have been necessary to have a fight,' said the Dean, 'if you had handled it the right way at the beginning. It's never a kindness, Katharine, to provide other people with the weapons for their own destruction. See what you've made of your sister!'

'What do you want me to do?' murmured Katharine.

'Well — you will have to right this wrong, and it will not be easy. A couple of months ago, when you were all mellowed by your father's death, you might have welded them together in a common cause. Now you'll have to attend to it by surgery! It will hurt them — and it will hurt you. But it must be done — and without any further delay.'

'You mean — I must tell them not to impose on me, any more?'

'Of course! And here is another problem that should be solved; just as serious as that one. You have done a great injury to yourself. You have been enjoying what you are doing; getting a nice little emotional tug out of feeling abused; feeling like a martyr. Of all the degrading psychoses, this is the worst one! You can still scramble out of it, I think; but you must not waste a minute. Had you gone on, this way, a little while longer, you might have been utterly ruined.'

'I thought I was doing the right thing,' cried Katharine.

'That's the pity of it.' There was a long silence. 'Come here,' said the Dean, gently. Katharine groped her way around the big desk and put both of her hands in his. 'You have made a serious mistake, my dear,' he continued, 'but we will think of a way out — for all of you. You must go away. Your mother and sister and brother will have to be given a chance to reorganize themselves. My sympathy is with them, almost as much as it is with you. We must plan to save all of you.'

'You want me to leave home?'

'Immediately.'

'I'm sure I don't know where I'd go. I've never been away from my people. I'd have to find a job.'

'We can talk about that, later.' The Dean glanced at his watch. 'Now it's away past the dinner hour. I want you to stay; so we can go into this matter further.... There's a mirror over there, in case you want to make some repairs.'

'I know I look a sight,' muttered Katharine. 'But — please! — I don't want to stay for dinner; not if there's to be anyone else.'

'You won't care, once you're in there,' promised the Dean. 'It's quite fashionable at our table to have red eyes and leaky noses.'

When Katharine emerged from the dressing-room, some minutes later, she had rehabilitated herself considerably, and wore what might — if encouraged — resemble a smile. Dean Harcourt rewarded her gallantry with an approving nod.

'Now, to save time, Katharine,' he said, 'I wish you would go and find Mrs. Crandall, my housekeeper, and tell her you're to be here for dinner.'

'Oh — must I do that?' Katharine's tone pleaded to be excused from this errand. 'What would she think, my coming to tell her I'm a guest?'

'Mrs. Crandall, you'll find, is not easily upset by such announcements. You go down the hall, the way you came in, and someone will tell you where to find her.'

In the reception parlor, there were four people waiting for dinner. She thought she wouldn't have the courage to face them, for it was easy enough for them to see that she had been crying. But the Mr. Talbot introduced her. The beautifully gowned woman, who seemed somehow to belong to the household, turned out to be Sonia who had the most expensive and exclusive gown shop in the city. Katharine had admired her from the first moment. And there

was a very pretty girl named Barbara, who had been working on a farm in Nebraska; though you wondered why, for
she didn't look as if she needed to. It was very funny,
finding Mrs. Crandall.

At dinner, they got to talking about Barbara's driving
back to Nebraska on Friday, and before they were through
with it, Katharine had been asked to go along as a traveling companion; and maybe she would find a job out there
for a while. It was all arranged in about two minutes.
Katharine didn't have much to do with it; just listened
while the others planned it.

After dinner, Dean Harcourt asked her into the library
for another private talk. She was quite at ease with him
now.

'In many a home,' the Dean was saying, 'some one member of the family carries the whole load; serves as the official
clock-watcher, tells them when it is time to get up, when it
is time to start if we are to catch the 8.19 car; serves as the
official calendar, telling them that next Tuesday is Emma's
birthday, and we mustn't forget that the Chester wedding
is on the nineteenth; serves as the official errand-boy,
whose duty it is to turn the night-latch on the door, put out
the porch-light, check the furnace, call the cat, and drape
a towel over the bird-cage. Nobody knows or cares how
you happened to be appointed to these thankless positions;
but, once you're recognized as the incumbent, there'll be
no other nominations as long as you live.'

The Dean had been so sober about all these trifles that
Katharine couldn't help laughing; for she thought he was
having a bit of fun.

'I'm surprised, Dean Harcourt,' she said, 'that you know
so much about little household duties.'

'I hear about them, Katharine. Sometimes people come to talk with me about the flatness and staleness of their lives, and how difficult it is for them to achieve happiness; and mostly it turns out that they have been harried by just such trifling cares. It wasn't the costly renunciations that wore them down. It wasn't the big sacrifices that made them unhappy. It was the aggregate of all the small things they were expected to do. It may not be much of a care to cover the canary every night; but you'll find that the same person who covers the canary rebaits the mouse-trap, tightens the tap that someone left running in the kitchen, puts the half-filled milk bottle back into the re-frigerator, and closes the window in the pantry. The official bird-cover-up-er is the same person who tells Grandma it is time for her pill, and Father that he has a loose button on his overcoat. I maintain that whenever one member of the household discovers that he has been appointed — for life — as the family drudge, he should resign without delay; for the sake of the whole tribe.'

'And run off?' asked Katharine.

'That depends on circumstances. In your case, I seri-ously doubt whether you could restore justice and amity in your home, with yourself present. You are fortunate in having a chance to go away. Sometimes people take on so many obligations that their only escape is in death.'

The Dean paused, thoughtfully, and then went on.

'A few days ago, a woman came to tell me that her three half-grown children had got completely out of hand. They were impudent, disobedient, selfish, quarrelsome. She said, tearfully, "I don't know why they treat me this way. I've done everything I could for them." She told me of her sacrifices; hadn't bought a new dress for two years, because she wanted the girls to have pretty things; had neglected her teeth until several of them had fallen out; hadn't felt it was fair to the children to spend money on herself; so she had done nothing for her face or her hair or her hands. And now — after all these givings-up — they despised her, disobeyed her, and seemed ashamed to have their friends see her. Should I have advised her to go home and make the best of it?'

'Please tell me,' said Katharine.

'I told her to go home and publish a declaration of independence, partly for her own sake, and mostly for the salvation of the family.'

'Will she do it?'

'No,' said the Dean, bluntly. 'She will not do it. She has rejoiced in her martyrdom too long. Her self-pity now means more to her than her self-respect. She is a very unattractive person to look at, and she knows it; but eventually, she thinks, she will be paid off for her sacrifices.'

'Will she?' asked Katharine, soberly.

'I don't know,' said the Dean. 'All I know is that she has not been rewarded very nicely here. Any love that costs your self-esteem isn't worth having.'

'I believe that,' said Katharine. 'I'm glad you are helping me to get away. You are right. It was time.'

She rose and put on her hat.

'It isn't going to be easy to tell them,' she said. 'I'm afraid there will be quite a scene.'

'Very likely,' agreed Dean Harcourt. 'But — keep it in mind that if you do not succeed in protecting yourself now, you are probably saddled with this dilemma for life!'

When she arrived home at eleven, Katharine found them

waiting up for her. She explained briefly that she had gone to dinner with some friends, and was very tired, and wanted to go to bed; but they sensed that something important had occurred, and tried — without success — to detain her with amiable queries.

After a while, Millicent followed her up to her room and sat down at Katharine's vanity table where she toyed absently with her sister's toilet things. She seemed to have something on her mind.

Sometimes, when Millicent was appropriately ashamed of a request she was about to make, she would try to give the situation an air of comedy by pretending she was a little lisper of six.

'Kath-ar-ine,' she wheedled, 'Ickle sister's hair is the baddest ever. She's ist got to have a permanent.'

Katharine was standing in the open doorway of her clothes closet, pulling her dress off over her head. She paused midway, with only her eyes in view, and grinned.

'Ickle sister' — she rasped, dryly — 'ickle one-hundred-and-forty-pound, college-graduate sister can crimp her own hair.'

'Why — Katharine!' Millicent's eyes were wide. 'What's come over you?'

'A little touch of common sense, Milly,' she muttered. 'By the way — I forgot to tell you. I'm leaving on Friday for a month's vacation.'

'What? But how can you? Won't you lose your job?' Millicent's voice was full of genuine alarm.

'Sure — but I don't care. I need a vacation. And so do you, Milly. We've been depending entirely too much on each other.'

'Yes — but what is going to become of Mother and me, while you're gone?'

'Don't know,' said Katharine, grinning light-heartedly. 'That's *your* problem.'

Millicent stood up, majestically, and tipped back her head.

'Listen, Katharine! You wouldn't dare to walk out — on Mother — like this!'

'Wouldn't I?' Katharine laughed. 'You wait — and see!'

V. Beam

IT WAS not until they had escaped the tangled traffic of down-town Chicago and were making better time on the commodious suburban boulevards that Barbara and Katharine exchanged more than a glance and a smile. And they were miles west of Oak Park before there was anything like a sustained conversation.

The Drakes had never owned a car, and Katharine had not learned to drive. Relying upon the public utilities for her transportation, she knew — for were not surly warnings posted in busses and streetcars? — that you mustn't talk to the motorman, a superfluous injunction, so far as she was concerned; but there must be some good reason why a driver didn't care to talk; so she had kept still as a mouse in her far corner of the well-worn leather seat; had kept so quiet that Barbara wondered if she were not repenting her decision to make this trip. Perhaps, reflected Barbara, they might travel all the way to Nebraska in silence.

Not that she cared very much, for she had plenty to think about and she had no special interest in this Katharine Drake. All she knew about her was that she had been heartlessly imposed upon by her selfish family whom she had been single-handedly supporting; and, on the somewhat surprising advice of Dean Harcourt, was leaving home in sheer self-defense. The demure creature had never been at large before. Judging by her half-frightened expression when, at eight, she had turned up in front of the hotel with a man's-sized suitcase, Barbara suspected that she was already doubtful about her bolt to freedom, and might prove to be a morose companion.

But that wouldn't matter much, for Barbara's mind was busy. What she should be thinking about, of course, was the distressing predicament of poor Sally Singley, repudiated and marooned in Hollywood. It brought no relief to say to oneself that Sally was responsible for her own débâcle. Dean Harcourt had effectually disposed of that alibi. After the manner of Pygmalion's miracle that had brought Galatea from a block of ivory into the realm of the living, Barbara had given Sally a similar newness of life. Pygmalion was responsible for his creature. Barbara was responsible for hers.

In a few days she would be out there in Hollywood, trying to help the hapless girl, who wouldn't be in this humiliating plight at all, had it not been for the encouragement and the subsidy that Barbara had given her. Just what she was going to do for Sally, beyond settling her bills and buying her a ticket home, was still to be planned. She had hurried to Chicago for a consultation with Dean Harcourt, and he had been sympathetic enough, but unwilling to suggest a course of action.

'This is your problem, Barbara,' he had said, 'and I think you may have a better chance to solve it if you follow your own judgment. You'll know what repairs are necessary when you find out how badly she has been damaged.'

Well — she would do her best; but, for the moment

Barbara wasn't caring two little whoops about Sally. She was going back to clear things up with Larry. And that, she felt, would require a great deal of careful thought.

It was a beautiful morning and the roadster, freshly lubricated, was putting its heart into its work. Barbara turned to smile amiably at Katharine, who seemed to have cheered up, to the point of going on record that it was a lovely day for a drive, to which Barbara assented cordially. Then, with eyes on the road ahead, she resumed her deliberations. She decided to organize everything she could remember about Larry; what a doctor would call a case history. She would even go back of that and recapture her own mood and the Wendell Farm atmosphere before Larry arrived.

She had joined the Wendell organization with the fixed purpose of discovering whether she could make her way successfully with strangers, meeting them on their own level. Within a day or two she had almost forgotten what she was there for. Mr. Wendell's cordiality had been so effortless that Barbara had promptly begun calling him 'Uncle Andy,' as did the other girls. 'Midge' had shown her the little dresses of the baby that had died.

'Yes,' Midge had said, with an audible sigh, 'he would have been ten this November. Here is the little silk cap that Aunt Clara — that's Andy's oldest sister — crocheted for him. Sweet; isn't it? I had such a hard time when Donald came that the doctor said we couldn't have any more.'

Barbara had been there just three days — it was the first Sunday afternoon — when Midge had offered this tender confidence. She remembered now that she hadn't said to herself, at the time, 'I should be satisfied now. Midge wouldn't have bared her heart to me if I weren't capable of making friends — on my own account.'

It was pleasant to recall the easy attitude of the girls as they accepted her into their company. Her room, at the end of the row in the single-story barracks, soon became a rendezvous. After the supper work was done, they would come in and sit on her bed and chatter. And they had come singly, too, in the afternoon, as freely confiding as if she were a life-time friend. Hattie Prentiss had had a bad quarrel with her 'steady,' back home in Onlyville — or some place — and they had broken their engagement; and Hattie had cried until she couldn't see, and Barbara had held her in her arms and joined in the crying; and had held a handkerchief to the freckled little red nose, and said 'Blow' — as if Hattie were five instead of nineteen, after which they had both laughed through their tears. And Maud Bemis wanted to go to college so badly that it made her throat ache when she thought about it; and Barbara had said that maybe some way could be figured out. She had resolved, instantly, to see that Maud's wish came true; only she couldn't tell her yet.

It had been a truly sweet experience, well worth all the little inconveniences and drudgeries it had cost. And then she had begun to ask herself, occasionally, how much longer she should stay on the farm; until the threshing was completed, of course; but — how long after that?

And then — one day — Larry had drifted in off the dusty road, with his messy paint-box and his lazy smile. And the Wendell Farm had become enchanted ground.

Barbara smiled, with narrowed, reminiscent eyes, as she re-experienced that first conversation. She had always thought apple trees quite pretty, but she had not realized how ineffably lovely they were until Larry had set up his easel in the orchard, and she had looked at them through his observant eyes. It was funny what love would do to you. After Larry had come, so many things became lovable, just because he loved them. Barbara remembered how she had negligently admired the supple strength of the huge, heavy-maned Clydesdales, but had never known how companionable they were until she saw them nuzzling at the pockets of Larry's threadbare jacket.

'They like you,' she had said.

'And sugar,' he had replied, lazily.

The remark was typical of his gentle cynicism. In most matters he was a skeptic, probably because he had been disillusioned; but he wore no chip on his shoulder. It was evident that he had experienced some hard knocks that weren't to be talked about, but nothing had happened to numb his appreciation of simple beauty. Sometimes, when Larry had dodged a question bearing upon his past, Barbara had been momentarily alarmed, fearing he might have run away from something he had done; and then she knew that it couldn't have been anything shameful. No fugitive from justice would be spending whole afternoons painting pictures of apple trees.

That first time they were together, they had talked — mostly in play — about the Pygmalion-Galatea legend. They had trifled with the old story, outdoing one another in the invention of absurd contretemps suggested by the miracle; but the fact remained that each knew the other had done some serious thinking about the privileges and penalties of inviting people and things to step forth into a larger life.

Somehow that chance reference to the legend had established the mood and pitch of their friendship. After supper, they had chatted briefly with Andy and Midge,

on the verandah; and when Midge had been called to the
phone and Andy had followed her, they had sauntered
down the lane. Again Pygmalion and Galatea had appeared — not as puppets, this time, providing grotesque
entertainment; rather as symbolic figures in a significant
drama.

'I was talking with a friend, not long ago,' Larry was
saying, 'who had thought deeply about the joys and sorrows
of genius. One man calls out the latent activities of another and gives him a new life. If this man becomes a
menace to his generation, the blame must be traced back
to the person who inspired and empowered him. And then,
my friend added, "There are certain penalties, also, at-
tached to the fashioning of *things — inanimate things*. How
much better off our civilization would be," he said, "if the
aeroplane had not been invented. Add up our gains and
losses which have accrued from the automobile." And then
he went on to say that the inventor should hold himself
responsible for the thing he sets in motion.'

That kind of talk.

It was a wonder she hadn't guessed who Larry's thoughtful friend was; for it all sounded like Dean Harcourt.

They had seemed to have an understanding, from the
first, that they were to be excused from talking about
themselves. Barbara couldn't help feeling that each knew
the other knew they were both out of their natural element.
They didn't belong here on Wendell Farm: they were mere
spectators. And this implied that each had sought escape
from something neither wanted to discuss.

Sometimes — when Barbara was a senior in college —
a few of them would collect, late in the evening, for an
hour of more or less futile windbagging about the old

riddles; Design, Destiny, Duty, Desire — and What's-it-all-about-anyhow. And she had never felt very much improved or entertained by their owlish concentration on the old jigsaw puzzles of metaphysics which (she had once remarked to Larry) had been played with until lots of the pieces were missing. And Larry had drawled, 'Lots of the pieces were never made.'

But it was a different thing entirely when you talked over these intangibles with Larry. They weren't mere antiques, smelly of mothballs, in the museum of Philosophy Hall. They were vital issues — as clamorous as your appetite; practical as a tankful of gasoline; demanding as much attention as a locomotive siren.

Larry had remarked — Barbara knew now where he had heard it — 'This man I spoke of said to me, "It does make a difference what you believe about Destiny. If you think the world is going to smash, that may seem to be a mere academic theory; but it isn't! If you believe the world is on a decline, it will show up in your face, in your talk. It will handicap you in making friends. People will be afraid that you may accent their forebodings at a time when they're not in the market for apprehension — but assurance. It will hurt you in business. You can't sell a man an annuity, if he detects, by your tone and manner, that you think we are on the edge of a catastrophe. If you have a private suspicion that civilization's fingernails are turning blue, you'd better not try to interest anybody in a century plant." '

This had sounded so much like Dean Harcourt that Barbara had been almost on the point of asking Larry if — by any chance — he had ever attended Trinity Cathedral in Chicago; but she had decided against it for fear it might involve her in some talk about her own acquaintance with the Dean. She heartily wished now that she had asked that question. It might have led to an exchange of confidences.

What in the world was she going to say to him tomorrow?

The pointer on the speedometer dial had been creeping up until the aged roadster was jingling at every rivet. Barbara slowed to forty-five, shook herself loose from the wool she had gathered, and took note of her passenger as if she had just now come on board. Katharine gave her a wistful, lonesome little smile.

'One has to keep one's eyes on the road, when driving fast,' she remarked, obviously helping Barbara to an explanation of her detachment.

'No; one doesn't,' said Barbara, self-reproachfully. 'One can drive and talk at the same time. One has been very impolite. Forgive me, please. I've had lots to think about.'

'I haven't felt neglected,' lied Katharine, pleasantly. 'I've been thinking, too; about the farm, mostly; wondering what it is like. I know so little about the country.'

There was nothing that Barbara could talk about with more enthusiasm. She began at the beginning of her experience, and told Katharine how she had resolved to spend some time among strangers; had thought it would be good for her to make her own way in a new environment.

'I never heard of anyone doing that before — on purpose, I mean,' said Katharine, 'when they didn't have to. I've always stayed so close home; too close, I suppose. Dean Harcourt thinks so.'

'It will be good for you to get away,' remarked Barbara,

wondering if Katharine wanted to pursue the subject. 'I think people can see entirely too much of their families.'

'Did your parents object to your going out on your own?' asked Katharine, blandly.

Barbara's reply was somewhat delayed while she debated whether to dodge the question. Then it occurred to her that inasmuch as she was about to plunge into a grand debauch of truth-telling when she encountered Larry, it might be well to take a preliminary work-out.

'They don't know about it,' she said, trying to make it sound casual. 'My mother and my stepfather are in Europe.'

'And they wouldn't take *you?*' sympathized Katharine. She understood the whole situation now. Barbara's mother had married a well-to-do and selfish man, and they had turned Barbara adrift. 'I thought I had a pretty rough time at home,' she went on, companionably, 'but — not like that.'

Barbara did not comment immediately; was about to let it pass, and return to her description of life on the Wendell Farm; then, in a spirit of family loyalty, she amazed Katharine by drawing a different picture of her affairs.

'No — I've given you the wrong impression of my people,' she confessed. 'They would have taken me with them, gladly, if I had wanted to go. My mother is very good to me; and my stepfather, too.'

Katharine shook her head, incredulously.

'Dear me!' she murmured. 'If I had a chance to go to Europe, I'd certainly snap it up. Why didn't you go?'

'Because I've spent the last half-dozen summers over

there, and I wanted to stay in the States this season. Europe's no treat to me. I was two years in school in Switzerland when I was in pigtails.' Barbara didn't know she was bragging; didn't know it was anything to brag about. Katharine listened with wide eyes. It was the first time she had ever heard anyone refer to 'the States.' It sounded almost as if Barbara didn't belong to our country. She had begun to have a comradely feeling toward Barbara. Now she felt suddenly lonesome.

'I thought you were poor,' she said.

'Not much wonder,' agreed Barbara. 'These clothes — and this dreadful old car.'

There was an uncomfortably long silence, Barbara wishing she had not confided, Katharine trying to think of something to say. Now you could see, reflected Barbara, how a story of this sort would be received by anyone of small resources; by Larry, for example.

'Do they — do these people on the farm — have you told them?' inquired Katharine.

Barbara shook her head and stared straight down the road.

'No,' she said, grimly, 'and it's worrying me. I have to tell a man about it tomorrow, and I don't know what to say to him. He hasn't a nickel — and we like each other very much — and I've pretended I didn't have anything. And now I've got to tell him.' She paused — and went on — as if to herself: 'He couldn't provide for me, and I know he's too proud to let me provide for myself; much less for him.'

'Why do you have to tell him?' asked Katharine.

'Because he is going to find it out, presently. I'd rather tell him myself.'

'Maybe he'll take it all right.'

'If he does,' said Barbara, 'I'm afraid I won't care for him any more.' They both laughed a little at this paradoxical speech. 'You know what I mean,' explained Barbara. 'I'll tell him all about it, because I must. Then — he will say that we can never be anything more than friends. And that will be the end of it. I know he wouldn't consent to let me support him, and I couldn't respect him if he did. So — there you are.'

'How about giving your money away?' suggested Katharine. 'Then you'd be on an equality.'

Barbara turned and stared briefly into Katharine's eyes.

'There's an idea,' she said, soberly. 'I hadn't thought of that.'

'You'd have to like him — very much,' observed Katharine. 'Wouldn't that be giving up a good deal — for a man?'

'Have you ever been in love?' challenged Barbara, as if her query answered the other.

Katharine nodded her head slowly, her eyes averted.

'And I'd give up everything,' she admitted. 'But — I haven't anything; so — it's no matter,' she finished, clumsily.

'You mean, you can't marry him? What's the trouble? Is he married?'

No; Phil wasn't married. She had just lost him through too much family interference. And, finding Barbara ready to listen, Katharine told her all about it.

'Oh, he'll come back,' said Barbara, negligently optimistic.

'No,' muttered Katharine. 'He won't come back.'

'It's a wonder you don't despise your sister,' commented Barbara.

'What makes you think I don't?' Katharine's tone was so unexpectedly bitter that Barbara couldn't think of a suitable rejoinder.

'Because,' she remarked, after an interval, 'you seem to have such a sweet disposition.'

'That isn't sweetness, what you see.' Katharine's voice was hard. 'It's just deadness. The light is out, that's the trouble.' She was glumly silent for a while. 'I'll bet there are plenty of people,' she went on, 'who get credit for being sweet and uncomplaining when the fact is that they're numb.'

'Why don't you write to Doctor Harrison,' suggested Barbara, bright with this new idea, 'and tell him you're sorry about the way everything turned out on that horrid Sunday. He is fond of you, or he wouldn't have come. It would take more than that to destroy his interest in you.'

'If he came back because I asked him to, I wouldn't want him. I couldn't care for a man who would love a girl with so little self-respect.' Katharine laughed a little. 'It seems to me,' she continued, 'that you and I are facing the same sort of problem. If our men are reconciled to us, we won't be able to love them any more.'

That kind of talk went on, intermittently, all day. They became so freely confidential that Katharine pitilessly diagnosed herself. She had not only permitted her family to impose on her; she had encouraged them in it; she was getting a curious, morbid, sweetish pleasure out of it; privately nursing the thought that she was 'a little brick.' And then, Dean Harcourt had talked her out of that delusion.

'And now,' she had confided, 'I find that I'm going in the opposite direction. A week ago, I was anxious to give up everything to make my people happy, and I was entirely

contented with doing so. Now that I see what a fool I've
been, and what a simpering little nobody I had come to
be — well — now I don't care to do anything for anyone.
I'm still a brick; but not because I'm willing to be run over.
I'm a hard, cold brick now.'

'You'll get over that,' promised Barbara, brightly.

'I hope so,' murmured Katharine. 'I don't want to feel
this way toward Mother and Millicent. Do you know,
Barbara, I left the house this morning without saying
good-bye to them; just sneaked out; got my breakfast at
a little hole in the wall on Canal Street; and feeling pretty
good, too, that I'd given them a bad day. It's funny; this
feeling is almost exactly like the other one. It's around
your heart, somewhere, and in your throat. Same sensation
— pity, I suppose it is. I had been pitying them until I
gave up everything for them; and now I want to hurt them,
so I can pity them. Do you think I'm going crazy?'

Barbara remembered something they had studied in
Psychology that tried to explain this, but she decided not
to venture upon it.

'I think what you need,' she said, 'is sunshine, new
friends, not too much time to brood over your troubles,
plenty of milk — and a long talk with Larry.'

At eight, they were both weary enough to put up for the
night at a little hotel in Wonderly. After a lengthy debate
with herself, Barbara decided to give all of her money away.
She felt comforted by this resolution — and slept.

Unless they were very hard-pressed with seasonal work,
on the Wendell Farm, there was a half-holiday on Saturday.
Barbara was regretting that their arrival, probably about
two, would find so many of the girls either gone or anxious

to get away. She had forgotten about that. But Larry would be there. She would spend Sunday on the farm, and perhaps Larry would want to drive her to Omaha. They would have a long talk, this afternoon. She would tell him everything. Whatever he might think of the way she had deceived him, they would still be friends.

They were nearing Axton now, and Barbara's agitation was increasing. In about twenty minutes she would meet Larry. She dreaded the interview, but was anxious to have it over. He would be out in the grove, or the orchard, or under a tree in one of the pastures. And would he be surprised to see her coming? He would be so surprised that he might want to take her in his arms and kiss her. And if he wanted to, she would let him. Perhaps it would be better to encourage him to kiss her before she told him. Perhaps he wouldn't care to, afterward. And it would be something nice to remember.

They turned into the lane, Katharine sitting alert and bright-eyed.

'And those big barns — away over there,' she pointed. 'That's the next-door neighbor, I suppose.'

'No, sir — that's all Andy Wendell — God bless him!' boasted Barbara. 'There isn't a neighbor in sight! We don't believe in neighbors!' It was plain, from her prattle, that Barbara was trying to out-talk her excitement.

Midge and Andy were sitting on the verandah. They both rose and sauntered across the lawn as the roadster rolled to a stop.

'We had your telegram, but we weren't looking for you quite yet,' said Midge. 'Get out — and come in. You're tired from that long trip. Andy'll put the bus away.'

They got out of the car and Barbara presented Katharine, hugged Midge, shook hands warmly with Uncle Andy, told him not to bother about her dusty little wagon, and briefly explained why Katharine had come along — Midge accompanying all this talk with solicitous purrings and cluckings, almost as if she were sympathizing with Barbara about some misfortune. Of course, she said, they would be more than glad to have Katharine, and would try to help her have a good time.

Andy stood by, quietly interested, a bit perplexed.

'So — you went to Chicago,' he said, when there was a chink in the talk. 'We all thought at first that you'd started for California, on account of your being interested in that movie girl.'

'And I do have to go to California, Uncle Andy,' said Barbara, grateful for this cue. 'I'd like to take the Streamliner from Omaha on Monday. I am not sure that I can do anything very useful for my friend Sally; but I can at least let her know that I tried.'

'That's what Larry thought you'd be doing when you left here so sudden like,' said Midge. 'He was afraid you might get into some kind of trouble.'

'Where is Larry?' inquired Barbara. 'I want to see him.'

'Oh — he left,' said Midge, 'that same day, soon as he found out you were gone.'

'He left!' echoed Barbara. 'Where did he go?'

Midge glanced at Andy, rather helplessly. Katharine, instinctively sensing that they might be able to talk more freely if she retired, strolled across to the clump of asters and cupped one of the larger flowers in her hands.

'Well,' drawled Andy, deep in his throat, 'it's all sort of mixed up like. Larry said he'd have to push off at once for California. We knew he hadn't any money, and would have to hitch-hike; so Midge and I drove him over to the highway.'

Barbara shook her head, self-reproachfully, and made a little murmur of regret.

'Yes,' said Midge, 'we left him standing there beside the road, with his old suitcase. He looked kind of pitiful — and lonesome; as if he didn't know whether to go, or not; as if he didn't know whether there was any use going.'

'That's too bad,' murmured Barbara, disconsolately. 'And, of course, you haven't heard anything from him since?'

'Well — yes,' replied Andy. 'Not directly, we haven't; but here's where the funny business begins, that we don't understand. Soon as we were out of sight, Larry went to the garage and hired Maxie Pepper to drive him to Omaha.'

'How could he?' asked Barbara. 'Larry didn't have any money.'

Andy grinned, and rubbed his jaw.

'I know,' said Midge. 'That's what we all thought; but there's something about Larry that we can't explain.'

'Yes — Maxie called up here,' said Andy, 'a few minutes after we'd got home, that night, and said this seedy-looking young fellow that had been painting pictures over here was in his garage, wanting to be drove to Omaha. And I said, "Well — that'll be all right; far as I know." And Maxie said, "I told him he'd have to pay me in advance, for he doesn't look very darned prosperous, and he pulled out a wallet thick enough to choke a horse, and handed me a fifty-dollar bill, and when I asked him if he hadn't something smaller he said No."'

'Why! — of all things!' exclaimed Barbara.

'Yes — we just couldn't understand it.' said Midge.

'He seemed so quiet — and kind — and sort of pitiful like — if you know what I mean.'

'Well — I told Maxie,' Andy went on, in a business tone, 'that we had no reason, over here, for thinking that there might be something crooked. He hadn't stolen anything from us. And he hadn't behaved as if he was scared of anyone turning up to catch him. Of course' — Andy's tone became confidential as he faced Barbara's troubled eyes — 'for a young fellow to come into your family, as you might say, and stay for weeks, passing himself off for a poor guy that can't even afford to get his pants pressed — and then turn out to have maybe a thousand dollars cash in his pocket; and wanting to be driven in a big hurry to the Omaha airport ——'

'Airport!' repeated Barbara, mechanically.

'Yes — to take a plane for Chicago — after we'd just left him on the road — a-hitch-hiking to California — well — all that calls for a hell of a lot of explaining. And that's a fact!' Andy nodded, firmly, a couple of times. It was — indeed — as Andy had indicated, a chapter that needed a few footnotes.

'So — he went to Chicago,' muttered Barbara, half to herself.

'That's what Maxie thinks,' said Midge. 'He didn't wait at the airport and Larry didn't tell him where he was going. But this old chatterbox Meggs, at the station, had told Maxie about your sending a telegram to some fellow in Chicago that you were coming; and he said Larry was quite upset about that.'

Barbara felt weak and sick. She couldn't bear anything more. She motioned Katharine to get into the car and they drove back to the single-story dormitory. No — Larry hadn't gone to Chicago to find her. He wouldn't do that. There was something wrong about Larry. Where did he get all this money? And if he had come by it honestly, why was he making such a big secret of it?

Leaving Katharine to unpack her clumsy luggage, Barbara started toward the house. Hattie came bounding out of her room, next door, noisy with her greeting; but dampened a little when she noted Barbara's preoccupied air.

'I'll be back, in a few minutes, Hattie,' said Barbara, absently, 'and we'll have a little visit.'

Midge and Andy were still on the verandah, talking in subdued tones. They invited Barbara to join them, and waited to hear what she might say.

'Uncle Andy,' she said, weakly, 'you don't suppose Larry sto—— got that money wrongfully.'

'Of course he didn't!' declared Midge, loyally. 'You could see he wasn't that kind of a boy.'

'Yeah — I wouldn't worry,' rumbled Andy. 'Larry wasn't what he seemed to be, but that doesn't mean he's a criminal.' He stared into Barbara's bewildered eyes, drew an awkward grin, gave her a labored wink, and added, audaciously, 'Same thing goes for *you*, young lady! We always felt that you were something else than you made out, but we didn't think you had run off from some crime; especially when you told us you knew Dean Harcourt. But there's an awful lot that we don't know about you; and, of course, it's none of our business. Everything you've got on didn't cost ten dollars, all told; and you're poor as a church mouse; but you're planning to take the Streamliner for Los Angeles.' Andy laughed, noisily. 'Maybe you've got a pass to ride the Streamliner — though I don't think anybody else has; but you'll have to pay for your Pullman and meals. That's hard to understand, Barbara: but we don't think you're a thief.'

She sat there for a moment with downcast eyes; then reached out a hand to Midge, and faced Andy, repentantly.

'I'll tell you everything — now,' she said. 'I know I've treated you badly. Many times I have wanted to tell you, but I knew that when I did so it would change everything. And I was so happy.'

'We didn't hold it against you, dear,' murmured Midge. 'Naturally we were curious about you; especially after Larry came; and that made two of you with secrets. Dean Harcourt hadn't told us anything about Larry, except that he wanted a place to put up, in the country, while he painted some pictures. But as soon as he came we could see that he'd had a good education, and had been around, and we wondered why he was out here, doing nothing, as you might say. And when we saw that you were falling in love with him, we began to feel a little responsible for you. And so — one day — Andy ——'

'Thought you weren't going to tell that,' growled Andy, grinning.

'She may as well know it, Andy, so long as she's going to tell us all about herself. . . . Andy up and wrote to the Dean and wanted to know whether you had any folks, and told him we would like to know a little more about you, if he could tell us.'

'He didn't tell us very much,' interrupted Andy. 'He just said that you were all right and we needn't worry.' He chuckled and turned to Midge for advice. 'Shall we tell her?' he asked.

'Sure! Why not? Let's not have any more secrets.'

'Well ——' drawled Andy, with exasperating deliberateness. 'The Dean said you were a very good girl who was trying to get away from half a million dollars long enough to get acquainted with yourself.'

'So you *knew!*' whispered Barbara, flushing a little.

'It was awfully funny sometimes,' said Midge, folding her chubby bare arms and rocking gently. 'Remember the afternoon, Barbara — we were sitting right here on the verandah — and I was trying to head off a runner in my stocking? And I told you that you could have 'em if you liked.'

Barbara nodded and grinned.

'And you knew — about me — *then*,' she said.

'Yes — I knew. And I had a hard time keeping my face straight.'

'I wore them,' said Barbara, jauntily.

'I know you did, dear,' said Midge. 'Andy and I laughed about that. But no one else knew.'

'That's good. Thank you, Midge. Thank you, Uncle Andy, for keeping my secret.' Barbara was thoughtful for a minute. 'I may help at supper, this evening, same as ever?'

'Not quite,' replied Midge. 'You see, we had no notion when you were coming back — or whether you would come, at all; so I told Letty Swanson to take your place. Of course, you can help wait table — along with the other girls — if you'd like to.'

'I'd like to,' said Barbara, softly.

Andy rummaged in the breast pocket of his overalls and brought out a broken cigar, licked its wounds, and struck a match on the seat of his trousers.

'Well — all I got to say is,' he remarked pontifically,

'you're a darned good sport, and I wish you were my daughter.'

Tuesday morning the porter put up a table in Barbara's compartment and brought her a dozen sheets of stationery. She had some letters to write, she told him; which was true, though she wanted the paper mostly for the recording of memoranda.

Now that she was no longer an employee at the Wendell Farm, Barbara was going to do a few little favors for the people with whom she had lived and worked. And she wanted to occupy her mind with this pleasant task, for she was dreadfully lonesome. It was almost as if Larry had died.

Her thoughts, as she stared out at the window, skipped about dizzily. She must write to Dean Harcourt, but what had she to say? Perhaps he'd tell her now what ailed Larry — now that she was so worried — and really needed to know. . . . She must write to Maud Bemis and tell her to arrange for college. Maud would find it hard to believe that the way was clear for her to go now. . . . Just fancy! — Larry's pretending to be so low in funds that he couldn't have his hair trimmed if he bought her a dish of ice cream; with his pocket full of money! . . . She would have to think up a nice Christmas gift for Midge and Uncle Andy. . . . Larry must have been very much ashamed of the way he got that money, to be so careful that no one found out he had it. . . . Hattie had patched things up with her boy and was going to be married this fall. Chest of silver. It would probably be better sense to send her the money and let her spread it out over a few other things. . . . That's why Larry didn't want to kiss her when he couldn't help knowing that she loved him: he was ashamed. Well — you'd have to give him credit for that much. Whatever it was that shamed him, he at least liked her well enough to want to keep her out of it. . . . Letty Swanson was too unattractive to make a good match, poor dear. And she had been so keen on saving up enough to buy a second-hand car. Very well — Letty really needed a car; a nice one; a nice bright blue coupé with silver stripes. A car would be the making of her. . . . That was funny about Larry being so upset when he thought she had started alone for California; must have changed his mind suddenly after Midge and Andy had left him standing there beside the road. Probably didn't want them to know he had funds for nicer travel. Oh, dear! Why hadn't he told her the truth? . . . Old Mr. MacLeod wanted a lot more type for his little printing-shop. And that Jewel Stiles might really go places if she had a good dentist make her a pretty mouth so she could smile without putting her hand over it. It wouldn't be an easy letter to write, but Jewel would forgive her. . . . Imagine! — his knowing Dean Harcourt — and then having this secret that he couldn't tell; not even to her. . . . She must think of some appropriate little gifts for these other girls. Angie Lawton was dying to visit her married twin in Oregon. That would be easy enough to do. There would have to be a little extra for clothes. . . . Maybe Larry would have called on the Dean by now. Perhaps it would have been better to have told the Dean he might let Larry know every-thing about her. Silly thought; for she hadn't known Larry was going to Chicago when she left there. Maybe he didn't go to Chicago. This Maxie person didn't know certainly.

As soon as Larry had made himself presentable — and

it was with considerable satisfaction that he outfitted himself in modish clothes — he set forth to find Sally. The Gigantic Studios had no notion where she was and frankly didn't care; but her agent, Dick Veddar, might know something about her. Larry looked up the address of the agency and called there shortly before noon.

'Friend of yours?' inquired Dick, when Larry had stated his errand.

'Not exactly,' Larry had replied, with some hesitation.

Dick Veddar nodded his head approvingly, and went through the pantomime of patting his caller on the shoulder.

'If Sally Singley isn't exactly a friend of yours,' he said, solemnly, 'don't involve yourself in her complicated affairs. If you're looking for trouble, better find yourself a nice big nest of yellowjackets to play with.'

Larry laughed a little at Veddar's droll speech; couldn't help feeling that he might find this chap congenial.

'Perhaps I should explain,' he said. 'This summer I have been seeing something of a young woman in Nebraska who knows Sally very well and is much distressed over her little ——'

'No — brother! Not little!' interrupted Dick, drawing a doleful face. 'You were perhaps about to speak of Miss Singley's little mishap, or little misadventure, or little unpleasantness; but if you had seen as much of Sally as I have — during these recent days — you would know that nothing connected with Sally Singley would be little. When Sally is succeeding, she is immense: but when she fails, she is simply super-colossal! Now we have straightened out her tangles, at least enough of them to get her cleared away, and off our hands. She has gone back to Chicago, her point of origin, and all is well. I advise you to leave it at that. As for me; if I ever sight her again, I'm going to break the Olympic record for the quarter-mile.'

'Well, thanks for telling me,' laughed Larry. 'I hope she doesn't have too rough a time getting herself re-established.'

'Oh, Sally'll be all right,' promised Dick, confidently. 'She has friends back there and a family — of sorts. She used to talk quite freely about a priest who had taken an interest in her, and given her a lot of good advice which I wish she'd made use of. By the way Mr. Runyan, how much do you know about Sally?'

'Almost nothing,' Larry admitted. 'Just what I've told you. I never met her.'

'It's a queer story. And so long as you've concerned yourself about her, perhaps you ought to know it.' Dick glanced at his watch. 'How about a bite of lunch together — if you have no other plans?'

They sauntered down the street to a restaurant, and were given a booth, Dick proceeding meanwhile with his story.

'Yes — but' — Larry broke in to inquire — 'what induced this Breckenridge girl to cancel her summer plans, and send Sally out to Provincetown in her place? And what has become of *her?*'

'Well — there you've got me stuck. Sally never wanted to explain that. Tim Wainwright, who directed the Summer Theater, knew Miss Breckenridge very well. Immensely wealthy family. The girl had a large fortune of her own. She expected to show up on the Cape, soon after Commencement; had made a sizable contribution to the Players' School. Then, one day, Wainwright gets this telegram from Chicago telling him she can't come, but is sending a friend, Sally Singley, in her place, and would Tim take her in.

Of course he was willing to do that, sight unseen, for he was under obligation to Barbara.'

'Barbara?' echoed Larry.

'Yes. Did you think you'd heard something?'

'A mere coincidence,' mumbled Larry, relaxing his sudden tension. 'Plenty of girls named Barbara. The girl I met in Nebraska was named Barbara, but she can't be this Barbara Breckenridge. Except that she is interested in Sally — there's nothing to it. Go ahead, please, with your story.'

'W-a-i-t a minute!' Dick signaled a 'hold everything' with both hands outspread.

Larry shook his head doggedly and regarded Dick with a tight-lipped, incredulous grin.

'This Nebraska girl' — he lowered his voice confidentially — 'hasn't a nickel. She was working on a farm — in the kitchen and dining-room — feeding the threshers.'

'Did she act as if she belonged there?' Dick wanted to know.

'N-no; she didn't,' stammered Larry. 'I felt that she had a story; but she never wanted to talk about herself, and I didn't care to seem too inquisitive.'

'What were you doing there, if I may ask?'

'Sketching. Painting farm scenes.'

'Is that your profession — painting?'

'Well,' drawled Larry, 'if I had a profession, I suppose it would be painting.' For a few moments, they gave themselves with interest to their luncheon. Then Dick glanced up and tilted a finger at Larry.

'Did you ever,' he inquired, 'hear your Nebraska woman speak of the Chicago priest that Sally was always quoting, out here? It seems that the Breckenridge girl saw a lot of him and was much influenced by him. That's how Sally came to know him, I think.'

'No,' replied Larry, without pausing to consult his memory, 'she never spoke of him.' After a little hesitation, he added, 'You probably wouldn't recall his name?'

'Got it here, some place, I think.' Dick dug up his memorandum book and leafed untidily. 'Yes — here we are. Harcourt . . . Sally gave me the address when we took her on: person to notify in case anything happened to her.' He chuckled dryly. 'Plenty happened to her, all right; but we didn't bother the holy man with her misfortunes. . . . Dean George Harcourt, Trinity Cathedral, Chicago.' He glanced at Larry, inspected his face briefly, and ventured, 'Ever hear of him?'

'Yes,' admitted Larry. 'In fact, I have seen something of him, rather recently. He seems to have quite a large following. People go to him for advice on all manner of questions.'

'Including you, perhaps?'

'Yes — I found myself at loose ends, and decided to have a talk with Dean Harcourt.'

'Instead of a fortune-teller,' commented Dick.

'He's not a quack,' countered Larry, crisply, 'if that's what you're trying to say. This man has a sort of peculiar talent for dealing with personal difficulties. He impressed me so deeply that I took his advice, even when he counseled me to go to that big farm in Nebraska, and paint country scenes.'

'Picked out that particular farm for you, did he?' It was evident that Dick Veddar's curiosity was mounting. 'Now — see here, Mr. Runyan,' he went on, earnestly, 'I don't mean to be prying into your affairs, and you stop me if

I'm talking out of turn; but this whole thing interests me. We have some hook-ups here that are a little too neat to be merely coincidental. Let's imagine a case. We know — to begin with — that Miss Barbara Breckenridge was in close and frequent consultation with this Dean Harcourt, known as a reliable trouble-shooter. So, we may as well surmise that she feels the need of advice. She has been in some sort of mess; disappointed in love, maybe; just bored, perhaps, as many a rich girl is. Let us say that Dean Harcourt suggests her going away into another atmosphere for a while. He knows about this big farm in Nebraska, and sends her there.... By the way — what was your Barbara's name?'

'Brown.'

'Mmm — Brown,' muttered Dick. 'Breckenridge. Kept the initial.'

'Nonsense!' scoffed Larry. 'This girl that I knew was stony broke. She hadn't run away from anything, and she wasn't fretting about anything — not even about her poverty.'

'Oh — that's easy enough.' Dick carelessly dismissed Larry's deduction with a flick of his fingers. 'She saw that you were a person of means. Naturally she would be sensitive about calling attention to her empty purse — if she had any self-respect, at all.'

'But — she didn't know I had anything,' argued Larry. Instantly, upon observing Veddar's ironical grin, he regretted his comment.

'Oh, oh! So you were poor, too?'

'Dean Harcourt,' explained Larry, coolly, 'thought I might have better luck, getting these farm scenes, if I just strolled in as an itinerant.'

Dick laughed.

'I think that you and the girl were kidding each other, and apparently doing a swell job. Your friend Dean Harcourt must have had a good time. First, he sends the girl out to the country. Then he sends you to see that she isn't too lonesome. That's my guess — and I think it's a safe bet.' Then he frowned a little, and added, slowly, 'The only thing about my theory that needs a bit of nourishment is the fact that she didn't come out here and do something for Sally, if she was so immensely upset about her.'

'I was going to tell you,' muttered Larry, reluctantly. 'Soon as she heard the news about Sally, she left.'

'Ah! — for where?'

'I don't know. Nobody knew.'

'Perhaps she discovered that Sally was returning to Chicago — and has joined her there.'

Larry did not reply; sat absently sipping his coffee, his eyes preoccupied. A tall young fellow, trying to avoid a congestion in the aisle, accidentally bumped the table, and paused to beg pardon. Larry glanced up, gave a start, flushed, and hastily bent over his plate. The other man stared at him intently for a moment, shook his head as a swimmer dashes water out of his eyes, and reluctantly passed on. Larry's heart pounded hard. Dick, keenly observant, noted his agitation, and wondered what this pantomime was about. Now the newcomer retraced his steps; and, leaning over the table, looked hard into Larry's face.

'Sorry — but — you couldn't possibly be *Lee Richardson*. He — he's dead, you know. Got drowned. So — you can't be Lee — but — listen! — Lee — what's it all about?' His voice was husky and trembling.

'Sit down, Freddie,' muttered Larry, sliding along on the semicircular seat to make way for him. 'I'll tell you everything. First; I'd like you to meet Mr. Veddar. Veddar, this is an old college friend, Freddie Burlingame.'

'Yeah — but look!' Freddie had given Dick a perfunctory nod, and had thrust his face close to Larry's. 'Don't you know you're supposed to be dead?'

'Sh!' cautioned Larry. 'Pipe down, please — and be calm.'

'Calm?' growled Dick. 'He's talking to a dead man, and you want him to be calm!' He grabbed a passing waiter by the coat-pocket. 'Hey, you. Bring me a Scotch and soda — pronto. Perhaps you'd like one too, Burlingame.' He turned sourly on Larry. 'Think a drink would do you any good?' Larry shook his head.

'So — you did get out of that car when it went down stream,' said Freddie.

'I remember!' The light was breaking for Dick. 'Richardson! Swept off the bridge at Cuyahoga Canyon; night of the big flood, mourned for dead; the old folks crazy with grief. Well — you certainly have a nice little job of explaining, ahead of you.'

'Maybe it isn't quite as bad as it sounds,' said Larry, defensively. 'I was pretty badly banged up, that night. It was a long time before I could think straight.'

'Aphasia — or something like that?' suggested Freddie, helpfully.

'Call it whatever you like,' said Larry. 'It was a tough experience — and I didn't get over it straightway. I have communicated with my family and I have been intending to resume my right name, tell my story, and take a chance on what my friends might think.' He searched their eyes for a sympathetic reaction, without assurance. 'It's no small thing,' he went on, 'to have yourself kicked through the newspapers. I wasn't quite up to it. After all — it's my affair. I've explained to the people who had a right to know. I'm under no obligation to entertain the public.'

'I'm not so sure about that,' drawled Dick. 'There must have been at least fifty coast guards and policemen and things like that trying to find you.'

'They were paid for it; weren't they?' Larry retorted.

'I suppose so,' admitted Dick.

'They won't be any better off, when they read in the papers that I'm alive?'

'Probably not.'

'Then they can wait, a few more days, until I am ready to tell it. . . . How about some lunch, Freddie?'

Dick looked at his watch and said he would have to go back to his office.

'Where will you be, Mr. — er — Richardson — in case I want to reach you?'

'Beverly Wilshire — through tomorrow, at least — and then at my Uncle's place, likely. Thanks for your kindness, Veddar.'

Dick took a few steps and came back to say, confidentially, 'I see Skippy Drew — over there at the bar. Why don't you let me bring him over, and give him a break? There's a big scoop in this — for somebody: why not let good old Skippy have it.'

Larry laid a hand on Dick's sleeve and pulled him closer.

'Now — get this straight, Veddar!' he growled. 'I'm going to tell this story — in my own way — when I get around to it. I am under no obligation to Skippy Drew or his gossip column. Maybe you are: and, if so, that's your business. But — I'm telling you! If you give this out to Skippy — or anyone else — there'll be *two* scoops. One of 'em will be about your going to the hospital with a pair of black eyes and a busted beak.'

Dick grinned, and patted Larry soothingly on the shoulder, with a wink in Freddie's direction.

'If you think I'm joking,' added Larry hotly, 'you go ahead and try it. . . . And see what comes of it.'

After he had parted from Freddie, Larry went up to his room and sat for an hour beside an open window. The fact that he had been recognized, and must now resume his rightful identity without delay, did not disturb him very much. There would be a little flurry of talk. People disposed to give a man the benefit of a doubt would be sympathetic. Those who habitually attributed bad motives to persons who had done something irregular would revile him. But the racket wouldn't last long. The public had a short memory. Some fresh scandal would come along and sweep his story out of print in a few hours.

Presently he would call up the house and talk to Uncle Earnest or Aunt Patty. And they would ask him to come down immediately. And he would go. There might be some constraint, at first; but he felt assured of an affectionate welcome.

For the moment, all this did not weigh very heavily; for he had something much more important to think about. Barbara! Freddie Burlingame's unexpected arrival had postponed until now any serious thought concerning her identity.

Larry put his feet up on the windowsill, lighted a cigarette, and tried to remember every little scrap of Barbara's conversation that might have some bearing on this matter. She couldn't have run off from anything or anybody. Nothing of that sort was apparent in her talk or behavior. He believed he could have sensed it, if Barbara had been in trouble serious enough to warrant flight. To be sure, she wasn't a typical country lass; but neither was Andy Wendell a typical yahoo, according to the accepted tradition. It was an exceptional farm. His employees were above the average.

Barbara wealthy? Nonsense! Larry chuckled as he recalled that Saturday night in little Axton when she suggested an ice-cream cone because it cost only a nickel. That was because she was accustomed to small frugalities; had been pinching pennies to make ends meet; knew how to do it without any discomfort; could make a little joke of it.

Well — we wouldn't have long to wait. Dean Harcourt would probably know what had become of Barbara Breckenridge. After a few days with Uncle Earnest and Aunt Patty, Larry was going back to Chicago; get a good description of the Breckenridge girl; and then — well — if this wasn't his Barbara (and he still strongly doubted that she was) he would return to the Wendells' and pursue a thorough search.

This much having been determined, he went to the telephone and put in a call for Uncle Earnest. His hand trembled a little as he waited. Presently he heard old Bunner's discreetly dry voice saying, 'Mr. Richardson's residence.'

'Bunner, this is Lee.'

'Indeed, sir. May I ask where you are, sir?'

'In Beverly Hills. Is my uncle at home — or my aunt?'

'No, sir. They are up in Alaska. We expect them home about the end of next week. Will you be coming down, sir?'

'I'll see, Bunner. May have to go back east at once on an errand. But I shall return before long. Tell my uncle and aunt that, please.'

At seven, next day, after an aimless stroll, during which time he had tried to make up his mind whether to return first to the Wendell Farm or go directly to Chicago, Larry went up to his room to change for dinner. He could hear his telephone ringing before he unlocked the door. It was Veddar.

'Well — she has been here to see me.'

'Who has been here?'

'Your Miss Breckenridge.'

'Mine?'

'Yes, sir. Came in at three to inquire about Sally. I told her that Sally had returned to Chicago. I asked her if she had come directly from Chicago; and she hesitated. Then she said she had driven from Chicago to Axton, Nebraska, taking the train at Omaha. Does that clear up your — your little dilemma?'

There was quite a pause before Larry said, 'Obviously.' Then he asked, 'I suppose you told her I had inquired about Sally.'

'No. It was a temptation, I'll admit. But I didn't mention your name; either of your names. This called for a good deal of self-discipline, and I hope you'll give me credit for my restraint.'

'Thanks. I do. Where's she stopping?'

'She's not stopping. She was at the Ambassador, but she is going back to Chicago on the Superchief tonight.'

'Thank you very much, Mr. Veddar.' Larry tried to keep his excitement out of his voice. 'It was mighty good of you to call me.'

There was an unmistakable tone of amusement in Veddar's reply. 'O.K.,' he drawled. 'I'll not detain you. You'll have to hurry! That train leaves at eight.'

Reflecting that he must have been as transparent as glass when he talked to Veddar about Barbara, Larry made a short job of packing; insisted, at the cashier's window, that he must be served without delay; had everybody scampering to facilitate his quick departure. The last thing he did was to grab up a pad of telegraph blanks; and, in the taxi, he composed a wire to Dean Harcourt, 'Sally's friends are leaving tonight for Chicago. Warm regards.' The Dean had done him an amazingly good turn, and he felt it no more than right that he should express appreciation.

Now it occurred to him that he might be unable to secure space on the train. But he wasn't going to fret about that. They'd have to take him. He'd never heard of a train that hadn't room for at least one more. The red-cap asked him where he was going; and when Larry told him he wanted the Superchief, he picked up the bags and shouted, 'We suah gotta shake a leg, boss. What's yuah space?' Larry said he hadn't any; he'd stop at the ticket window. 'No-*suh!* We-all get that on the train.' That's how close it was. The gateman didn't stop him; just grinned and waved his hand and shook his head doubtfully. They pushed him into the first open vestibule and the porter picked up the little step. The red-cap took the telegram and the five-dollar bill, and mopped his forehead. The Superchief slipped quietly out.

There was, thought Larry, no need for haste in consulting the Pullman conductor. If he had no space left, it wouldn't be likely that the matter could be remedied by a frantic pursuit of him. So he decided to go to dinner. As he entered the dining-car he saw Barbara. The steward had met her at the other door and was showing her to a small table. She was wearing a blue polka dot with white collar and cuffs. He liked polka dots; especially on a blue dress, and white collar and cuffs. She was seated with her back toward him. Larry's voice was a bit husky as he asked the welcoming steward if he would seat him with 'that young lady — a friend of mine.' The steward was happy to oblige; led the way; drew out the chair.

It was quite clear that the young lady was annoyed. The steward's professional smile gave way to a look of anxiety. Conscious of receiving a male dinner companion, in face of the fact that there were unoccupied seats to be had, she had evidently decided to ignore the intruder. With her face turned toward the window, and a little frown between her eyes, Barbara was intently interested in the railroad yards. The steward moved away, troubled. Presently a waiter came, bowed deferentially, and laid menu cards on their plates. Then he placed an order blank and a pencil at the unwelcomed gentleman's elbow.

Larry's pulse was hammering inside his warm collar. He felt himself in a very awkward position. The waiter, who would instantly have sensed the young lady's coolness even if he had been blind — for the very air was charged with it — decided to take himself off, for the present, and wait until things got better — or worse. At length, Larry found his voice.

'Do you prefer your consommé hot or cold, Miss Breckenridge?'

She gave a little start, turned toward him, winked rapidly a few times, and then frankly stared at him with wide, unbelieving eyes.

'Larry!' she whispered. 'How did you get out here?'

He extended both hands, and she slowly gave him hers, too dazed to smile a welcome.

'I hitch-hiked,' he replied, soberly, 'same as you. Aren't you glad to see me?'

Her eyes wandered over him, taking him in, item by item, trying to accommodate herself to the much improved state of his clothing. Then she gave him a slow, tight-lipped, reluctant smile.

'You have been deceiving me,' she said, reprovingly. '*Haven't* you? Do you think that was a nice way to act?'

'What do *you* think?' countered Larry, amused. 'You ought to know.'

The waiter had returned now, apparently much gratified to find his customers holding hands. It was evident that a reconciliation had been effected, and the young man would probably be good for a substantial tip. They paid no attention to him. He moved the salt and pepper, cleared his throat, and said 'Yassuh.'

'Who told you my name, Larry?' asked Barbara.

'Dick Veddar.'

'Oh — the man who was Sally's agent. Do you know him?'

'A little. Couple of days. I came out to see if there was anything I might do for Sally.'

'So — you were acquainted with Sally — and never told me; just sat there and let me talk about her.'

'That's all I knew about Sally; what you told me. I never met her. But — you had at least implied that you were somehow related to her — and it seemed clear that you weren't in a position to do anything for her; so I thought I'd better act — in your behalf.'

Barbara's eyes softened into a smile.

'That was good of you, Larry,' she murmured.

'You would have done as much for me, I think.'

'I could get you-all's steak started,' interposed the waiter.

'Want a steak, Barbara?' asked Larry.

She retrieved her hands, and nodded absently.

'Medium or rare, Miss?' inquired the waiter.

'Yes, please,' said Barbara.

Larry competently assumed charge at this juncture; and, without consulting Barbara's wishes any further, scribbled their order on the card, warmed by his sensation of proprietorship. Barbara's eyes followed his hand as he wrote.

'Think you'll have enough money left — after that — to get your hair trimmed?' she asked, dryly. She lowered her voice. 'You *were* a fraud; weren't you?'

'A harmless one, Miss Brown,' chaffed Larry. 'And what I did was in compliance with advice from the head of a highly respected institution. It had been suggested that I should try to make country life glamorous by painting some pictures. The man who proposed it told me I should go to the Wendell Farm, where I would be cordially welcomed. He thought my work there would be more spontaneous and enjoyable if I simply turned up, one day, as a shabby-genteel wayfarer. And, once in that rôle, it wasn't easy to discard. Many times I wanted to tell you, Barbara.'

'Yes — I know how you must have felt.' Her eyes were

downcast. She sighed and glanced up with a brooding
smile. 'I wasted a lot of sympathy on you, Larry. You
seemed so detached from life as if it didn't mean anything.
I thought that perhaps — if you had a little money, to
give you a start — you might find a fresh interest in
living.'

Larry made no rejoinder when she paused, and she
went on, dreamily.

'It seemed to me you were one of those cases that needed
to be brought out. I often wondered whether I might do
something, without being misunderstood.'

'That's funny,' said Larry. 'I wanted to do a Pygmalion
miracle for *you;* but didn't know how to go about it. You
seemed so self-sufficient; which was, of course, exactly the
right way for you to be. But I wanted you to have a few
more of the good things of life.'

'Such as — what, Larry? What are the good things of
life?'

'Oh — freedom from drudgery; a chance to play a little;
the means to ride the Superchief; a beautiful blue silk
polka-dot dress; lots of things like that.'

'But — that's no Pygmalion miracle, Larry,' objected
Barbara. 'He couldn't have made Galatea come alive by
putting a blue silk polka-dot dress on her.' After a moment's thought, she added, 'I think men often try to make
something of a woman that way.'

The waiter had removed the soup. Larry's hand slipped
across the table until it touched Barbara's fingertips. His
eyes were meditative as they met hers.

'It has often occurred to me as a peculiar thing,' he said,
'how often we were reminded of that Pygmalion legend.'

'I know,' nodded Barbara. 'It was almost the first thing

we ever talked about. Remember — that day in the orchard — when you had just arrived?'

'Of course. The story was quite fresh in my mind. Only a few days before, it had come up in a conversation I was having with the man who suggested my going out to Nebraska.'

'You needn't try to make a riddle of that, Larry.' Barbara smiled archly. 'I know who the man was — Dean Harcourt.'

'Did you know that — from the first?' asked Larry.

'No — the Wendells told me, when I was back there, this time.' She studied his eyes. 'You can't help knowing, Larry, that the Wendells are fretting about you. They can't understand you, at all. They are just as loyal as they can be — but — oh, Larry, you did leave such a lot of things unexplained. Why — if they hadn't been so fond of you, they might almost have thought you weren't straight. About being so poor, you know — and then suddenly having money.'

The waiter had brought their dinner now. Conversation was briefly interrupted.

'I know,' said Larry, contritely. 'I left in a great hurry. I was worried about you. It would have been better if I had told them.'

Barbara's face brightened.

'It was something — then — that you could have told them?' she asked, anxiously.

'Of course, dear.'

'And me?' pursued Barbara. 'Can't you tell *me?*' Her eyes were beseeching. 'Oh, Larry — I've worried myself almost sick. We had been such close friends, and I couldn't understand why you didn't confide whatever it was that had happened to you.'

'Well — how about *me?* How do you suppose I felt when I learned from that Axton garage man that you had wired some fellow in Chicago — that's the way he put it — "some fellow in Chicago" — that you were anxious to see him, and would be with him "tomorrow."' Larry searched her face, bewildered by her ingenuous smile.

'That "fellow" was Dean Harcourt,' she said; and then she laughed at Larry's explosive sigh of relief.

'Tell me,' he inquired. 'Did Dean Harcourt send you to the Wendell Farm?'

'No — I went there on my own hook. The Dean learned about the farm through me.'

'It's an odd thing,' said Larry, thoughtfully, 'how completely you and I have been under Dean Harcourt's influence. Every day, some comment of his seems to prescribe for a current problem. I find myself quoting him. It's a strange grip he has on one's mind, even at a distance. The other night, on the plane, when I was thinking about the ship's course through the darkness, guided by the radio beam, it occurred to me that Dean Harcourt — no matter how far one gets away from him — serves in the same capacity.'

'What a lovely way to put it!' agreed Barbara, softly. 'I shall always think of Dean Harcourt, in the future, as *the beam* on which I must depend for safe flying.'

'Apparently he wanted us to get acquainted,' said Larry.

'And we didn't.' Barbara's face was sober. 'We've never been acquainted. Just good friends, who didn't know each other, at all. Perhaps we'd better begin all over again, Larry.'

'And be entirely honest,' he assented. 'Shall we begin now?'

'Why not? It's high time.'

There was a little pause. Obviously it was Larry's turn to speak. It was a serious moment.

'Very well,' he said, unsteadily. 'I hope this isn't going to make matters more complicated than they are now. I shall have to begin by introducing myself; for my name is not Larry Runyan.'

Barbara's eyes widened in surprise.

'But you are not to leap to the conclusion,' he went on, 'that Lee Richardson adopted an alias because he had fled from a crime.'

'I'm sure of that,' murmured Barbara, weakly; and then she added, 'May I still call you Larry?'

'Yes, my dear. I don't believe you would have liked that other fellow very well, anyhow.'

'But you will tell me about him; won't you?'

Larry decided it would be easier to do in the third person.

'He was a very restless chap, Barbara; unappreciative of everything that had been done for him by his uncle and aunt, with whom he lived in California. One night there was a flood. A bridge collapsed while he was driving across it. He managed to escape from the car as it careened toward the sea. Pretty badly shaken and bruised, he made his way to the road and began to walk. The farther he walked, the more he dreaded the thought of going home to resume his velvet-covered chains. So he continued to walk, knowing he should return and aware of the sorrow he was causing. But — after a couple of days, he knew he was not going back to spend his life in a bank, when he had no appetite for it, and marry Caroline whom Aunt Patty had picked out for him.'

'Was she pretty?' Barbara couldn't help asking.

'Well — perhaps not pretty, any more, but making the most of what was left; and certainly the soul of generosity; gave Lee expensive presents; insisted on ordering his clothes; took him with her on long trips ——'

'She *was* generous!' exclaimed Barbara.

'That was the trouble,' Larry went on, straight-faced, and much occupied with his dinner. 'Aunt Patty was much too generous.'

'Oh,' said Barbara, 'Aunt Patty. Well — go on, please. And let's try not to frighten each other.' Then she added, 'Do you think that was funny?'

'Yes.' Larry grinned mischievously. 'I think you would say that Caroline was pretty. She was sweet and gracious. I supppose Aunt Patty selected her mostly for her passive disposition. It was arranged that when they were married they would live at his home.'

'With Aunt Patty?' asked Barbara, in a husky whisper.

'Absolutely! And Aunt Patty — in all love and kindness — would have planned their lives so that neither of them would ever have had to make a decision — about anything.'

'I'm glad you ran away!' declared Barbara, relieved.

They glanced up simultaneously as the conductors paused at their table. Barbara offered her tickets. The Pullman conductor took his share and announced, 'To Chicago. Car 64: Drawing-room C.' Then turned to Larry.

'I have neither transportation nor Pullman space,' he confessed. 'Didn't have time to get it.'

The Pullman conductor glanced through his charts — and frowned. The train conductor said he'd take the money for the transportation.

'I'll see you later, sir,' said the Pullman conductor. 'After we leave San Bernardino. You will find a seat in the club car, perhaps?' The train officials moved along.

'But — aren't you ever going to clear that up?' asked Barbara.

'I have — partly. Uncle Earnest and Aunt Patty know. Dean Harcourt attended to it. That was what I went to see him about, when he advised me to go out to Nebraska.'

'But — but aren't you ever going to tell — and be Lee Richardson again?'

'That depends,' he said, moodily.

The waiter was inquiring about their dessert.

'I'd like a ten-cent dish of ice cream, Larry,' said Barbara, 'now that I know it won't break you.'

'By the way,' said Larry, 'are you going back to the Wendell Farm again?'

Barbara shook her head.

'I think I've done everything I went there to do,' she said.

'You haven't told me what that was,' said Larry. 'It's your turn now.'

So — she told him, with simple sincerity and a rigid economy of words, prefacing her story with the comment that he might find it hard to believe. As she proceeded, his face grew more and more strained.

She had wanted to find out whether she was the sort of person who might be liked for herself alone. All her life she had been surrounded by people who knew her to be well-to-do. Sometimes they said affectionate things to her; but how could one tell what they really thought? . . . The servants obeyed your wishes, consulted your whims, laughed at your little jests. Almost all the boys you knew told you that you were pretty, and their mothers told you that you were clever. But you didn't know. So you thought you would find out about yourself.

And that, confided Barbara, was why she had put on the

cheapest clothes she could find, and had gone out where nobody knew her, just to see what attitude people would take toward her.

Larry's eyes had grown rather hard, as Barbara's strange story was confessed.

'So — it was just an experiment,' he remarked, dryly. 'Well — you should be gratified over the success of it.' He bowed, looking at her from under level brows.

'Why' — said Barbara, a little breathlessly — 'I'm afraid I don't understand, Larry. Have I said something that has offended you?'

'Oh, no,' he rejoined, ironically, 'I have no right to take offense. As I say, I think the project was enormously successful. Everybody liked you. Even I liked you. You certainly scored there!'

'Shall we go now?' asked Barbara, in a strangely husky voice. They rose, and Larry stood aside for her to pass.

'Would you like to sit in the club car with me?' he asked.

'No, I've some letters to write. Thank you very much for my dinner, Larry. We will meet in the morning, no doubt.'

She slipped away quickly, leaving Larry half-stunned by her impulsive departure. He sauntered forward to the club car, slumped into a chair, scowled at the attendant who handed him an evening paper. At least, he felt, they might have talked the thing over amicably. It had been a pretty cold-blooded bit of laboratory work that she had done, but he could be a good sport about it if she'd give him a chance.

The whole business was utterly beyond comprehension. Larry closed his eyes and let a long panorama of events unroll, picturing Barbara sketching by his side, so reckless with her friendship that she didn't know how much self-restraint her nearness cost him. Surely she couldn't have been playing with his feelings. Why, she couldn't have put on such a deceitful show of honest affection if she had been crafty as Satan!

Well — he could call it all a closed incident now. She had blandly told him why she was on Wendell Farm. He had often wondered about that. Now he knew.

After a while the Pullman conductor found him and roused him from his sullen torpor. The conductor was dismayed. He had hoped there might be a cancellation wired to them from some place along the line. But there hadn't been. And the train was booked solidly. He was immensely apologetic, but breathed more easily when — to his amazement — he observed that the discommoded passenger didn't seem to care very much.

'Very well,' said Larry. 'I'll get off. Let me settle with you for my seat to Barstow. I'll wait there for the next good train.'

He settled back into his chair and resumed his gloomy meditation. The train screamed across the dark desert. After a while the porter touched him on the shoulder.

'Bags in de vestibule, boss,' he said. 'We'll be in dere now, right smart soon. And she doesn't wait long.'

Larry rose, dully, strolled forward to the passageway, and leaned against the steel wall. The train was rapidly losing speed. Ahead of him were four or five passengers, waiting to step off for a brief glimpse of the hot little city. His heart thumped when he saw Barbara, pushing past them; coming toward him.

'The conductor just told me you were getting off,' she

said, unsteadily. It was easy to see that she had been crying. 'I can't let you go; not this way,' she whispered. 'I'm so sorry. You don't understand, dear. I — I wasn't experimenting on *you!*'

The train had stopped now, and you could hear the vestibule doors opening with a metallic slam. Two big men were in the passageway behind them, saying 'Excuse us, please.' And were trying to push their way through.

Larry put both arms around Barbara, and they were propelled steadily toward the door. It was almost as if they were on a crowded dance-floor.

'Barstow!' shouted the porter. 'All out for Barstow!'

They were out in the vestibule, now, still holding tightly to each other.

'No, sir, gem'n,' the porter was saying. 'We's no time here, *at* all. Here's a gem'n wants off. Gangway, please, sir.'

'Sorry, darling,' whispered Larry, in her ear. 'I'll have to get off. Meet you in Chicago.'

'At the Drake,' she said, brightening.

'B-o-a-r-d!' sang the conductor.

'B-o-a-r-d!' urged the porter. 'No foolin', boss,' he shouted. 'Iffen you wants off at Barstow!'

Larry detached himself and ran down the steps. The train was in motion. The porter closed the lower half of the vestibule door. Barbara crowded in beside him. The two biggest men moved in close behind her. Larry was trotting alongside.

'Barbara!' he called. 'You know what I want to say; don't you?'

The train was rapidly gathering speed. Larry was losing ground.

'Is it all right, darling?' he shouted, breathlessly. 'Will you?'

Barbara leaned far out and waved a hand.

'Yes!' she cried. 'Forever — and — ever!'

The train was slipping smoothly, swiftly into the darkness. Barbara backed away from the door. The tears were streaming down her cheeks, but her face was radiant. She elbowed her way through the wide-eyed group of spectators.

The porter swung the top door shut with a decisive bang, and remarked to nobody in particular, 'Ah reckon dat young man done feel pretty good now.'

VI. Curtain

THE largest bell in the taller of the Cathedral towers having tolled five, the carillon played Trinity's stirring theme-song. The last of Dean Harcourt's afternoon visitors had left.

Sonia, who since two o'clock had been meeting callers in the reception parlor and directing them, one by one, to the spacious library for their appointed interviews, came in and curled up wearily in the big Gothic chair facing the mahogany desk.

Mr. Talbot had just brought in a special-delivery letter that had come by air, and the Dean was reading it with deep interest and keen amusement. Sonia, tired as she was, fidgeted with impatient curiosity.

'Aren't you ever going to tell me?' she complained.

'In a minute,' mumbled the Dean, absorbed.

'From Larry, maybe?' nagged Sonia.

'It's from Mr. Andrew Wendell.' The Dean handed the letter across the desk. 'And it deserves to be read aloud. Kindly proceed. You will observe that our interests in Nebraska are becoming somewhat complicated. Barbara, returning to the farm with her mind made up to explain herself to Larry, finds that he had left, probably in pursuit of her.'

The letter was long and involved. Much of it incorrectly assumed that Dean Harcourt had been in full possession of certain details which he did not have.

Larry, learning that Barbara had rushed away in her roadster, on some mysterious errand to aid 'a friend,' had set out after her. It was his belief — and the Wendells', too — that she had started for California to see what she might do for the unfortunate Sally Singley. Andy and Midge had driven him to the highway where Larry hoped to beg a ride.

'Half an hour afterward,' continued Andy's letter, 'the garage in Axton called up to say that Larry wanted to be driven to the Omaha airport. He had a lot of money on him. They wanted to know whether everything was hunky-dory, for Larry was poorly dressed and the people around here thought he was just a good-mannered tramp. I told them he was straight, far as we knew; but naturally it worried us.'

'Perhaps,' Sonia interrupted her letter-reading, 'you should have told Andy something about Larry's circumstances, in the first place.'

'I wish I had, now,' agreed the Dean. 'Well — read on. The thing keeps going steadily from bad to worse.'

Sonia resumed her reading. On the drive to Omaha, the garage man had informed Larry that Barbara had sent a telegram 'to some fellow in Chicago ——'

'That was *you*,' laughed Sonia.

In the telegram, Barbara had said she would be seeing him, next day. This had upset Larry so badly that he had had nothing more to say. The driver did not tarry at the airport, but it was his guess that Larry had taken a plane for Chicago.

'Why — maybe he's in town now!' exclaimed Sonia.

'No, no — Andy has cleared that up. You read on.'

'"So ——"' continued the letter. '"After we had put Barbara on the Streamliner, yesterday, Midge hectored me into driving out to the airport, because I know a fellow in the express department. And he looked it up, sort of on the quiet like. Larry had gone to Hollywood, all right. Wish I had found that out before Barbara left. It might have eased her mind. For, of course you know that she and Larry are mighty fond of each other."'

'Isn't that a shame?' commented Sonia. 'Just imagine! Those poor things; chasing each other about; half crazy with worry!'

'It won't injure them permanently,' drawled the Dean. 'And it isn't as if they couldn't afford to pay for their tickets. This anxiety gives them a chance to find out whether they really care; whether it's close friendship based on loneliness and propinquity — or the real thing.' He folded his arms on the desk and regarded Sonia with a twinkle which she recognized as a warning that he was about to reminisce. 'When we were little tads, at home,' the Dean went on, 'and there'd be an epidemic of chicken-pox, if we were a bit under the weather Mother would inundate us with prodigious quantities of saffron tea. The idea was that if you had the makings of chicken-pox in your system, the saffron tea would bring out the rash; and then they would all know what you had — and could do something about it.'

'I see,' observed Sonia, dryly. 'The anxiety of Barbara and Larry is a sort of saffron tea that brings out the love-rash. That's certainly a glamorous way to put it.'

'I shall write to Andy in the morning,' said the Dean,

'and reassure him about Larry's honesty. . . . You're staying for dinner, aren't you?'

'Am I? Very well. I'll call Simpson. You look tired. Maybe you can rest a little before dinner.'

While the salad was being served, Talbot was called to the telephone. They could hear his high-pitched voice as he attended to it. Apparently the message was of interest. Returning, he paused in the doorway.

'I say, sir,' he called to the Dean, 'it's a young lady who seems quite upset; insists on speaking to you.'

'Didn't she give her name?' asked the Dean.

'No, sir. She is very much agitated; says she thinks you would be willing to talk to her if we give her a chance.'

'Oh, very well,' consented the Dean. 'Bring it here.'

It wasn't often that Dean Harcourt took telephone calls directly at his dinner table. It had to be something urgent. Talbot brought an extension phone, and connected it.

'Yes?' said the Dean.

It was a tired, whipped little wisp of a voice that seeped out of the instrument, indistinct but audible to the group about the table.

'Know who?' queried the disconsolate voice.

'Yes. Where are you?'

'At home. When may I come?'

'Whenever you wish.'

'Tonight?'

'Yes.'

There was a momentary pause.

'Are you — are you just terribly disgusted?'

'No; just sorry.'

Another lengthier pause.

'Oh — I'm so — so dreadfully unhappy.' The over-wrought voice trailed off into a childish little whimper.

'That's good,' consoled the Dean. 'It will make a fine place to start from. Come — and tell me all about it, my child. I shall be looking for you.'

'You won't scold me?'

'I won't need to. I see that you have attended to that, yourself.' He closed the telephone and Talbot came to put it away. Nobody said anything for a long minute. Then the Dean turned to Sonia. The big tears were standing in her eyes.

'Know who that was?' he asked, quietly.

Sonia nodded, and murmured, 'She has hit bottom, all right.'

The Dean's voice was resonant when he replied. He glanced about the table to include them all.

'That was Sally Singley,' he said. 'She is rather fortunate tonight. As Sonia says, she has hit bottom. The only way Sally can go now — is *up!*'

After dinner, the Dean and Sonia repaired to the library for a private conversation about Sally's predicament, pending her arrival.

'If she has anything to her, at all, and she surely must have,' Sonia was saying, 'perhaps I might find a place for her in my shop.'

'No — not yet, my dear,' cautioned the Dean. 'It's good of you and very like you to suggest this, but let's not confuse Sally with sudden prosperity. That has been her trouble, you see.'

They were both surprised when Talbot came to announce that Sally had arrived. She had wasted no time. Dean

Harcourt told Talbot to show her in. She appeared presently in the doorway, sober-faced and diffident, but when she realized that the Dean was not alone, she brightened instantly and marched across the room with all the self-assurance of a majorette, to the astonishment and delight of Sonia, who wasn't a bad actress herself. Sally's magical change of front was as easily interpreted as if she had announced, 'I'm willing to take a well-earned licking from Dean Harcourt — but nobody else is going to *see* me take it!'

She approached the Dean with clipped, confident steps and greeted him with the voice and manner of a philanthropic dowager who had dropped in to make a large subscription to Trinity's endowment fund. It was nicely done. Sonia's eyes sparkled.

Dean Harcourt extended his hand warmly; and, still holding it, said, 'Sally, I thought it might be pleasant for you to meet a good friend of mine, Sonia Duquesne. I asked her to wait until you came.'

Sonia had unfolded herself from the big chair; and, rising, offered her hand. Sally took it, tentatively at first, and for a moment they studied each other's eyes. Then the almost defiant look of self-containment left the girl's face, to be replaced by an expression of wistfulness. Gradually her lips responded to Sonia's understanding smile.

'Sonia knows all about it, Sally,' said the Dean, gently.

'Yes — I see,' murmured Sally. 'Well — I'm glad.'

Sonia pointed to the big chair.

'Sit down, Sally,' she said. 'I'm going now. Come and see me, if you like. Dean Harcourt will tell you where I live. Good night.' She gave her hand to the Dean, and was moving away, Sally's eyes accompanying her. And then, as if magnetized, Sally followed along to the door.

'Did you mean that' — she asked, unsteadily — 'about coming to see you?'

'Of course,' said Sonia. 'And now — I quite insist!'

When the door had closed, Sally returned and sat down opposite the Dean. There was a little silence. Sally's eyes drifted again to the door and she gave her head an inquiring little toss in that direction.

'Is she in trouble too?' asked Sally.

'Not any more.'

Quite a pause followed before Sally said, 'I like her.'

'I thought you might,' said the Dean.

'Does Sonia belong to the Cathedral?'

'About the same way you do.'

Sally shook her head, pensively.

'I'm afraid I wouldn't be very good at it,' she confessed. 'I'm not even sure that I believe in God, at all.'

'That's not very important, just now,' said the Dean, casually. And when Sally's eyes registered surprise, he added, thoughtfully, 'I mean, it isn't quite so urgent — at present — whether you believe in God as whether He believes in you. If you will conduct yourself in a manner that might encourage Him to believe in you, the time may come when you will feel that you should return the compliment. But there's no hurry about that. He is very patient.'

'What a funny thing to say,' murmured Sally.

'Want to take off your hat now?' asked the Dean, smiling.

Sally nodded knowingly, drew a deep sigh, and laid her very becoming and expensive hat on the desk. Then, without further delay, she began at the beginning and gave a full recital of her adventures. She did not spare herself when giving an account of her spectacular failure, and before she was through with it she was crying.

'What shall I do?' she sobbed. 'Everybody will be laughing. I'm ashamed to be seen. I thought I had brass enough to face it out, but ——'

'Sally,' said the Dean, feeling it was now his turn to talk, 'one of the curious traits of human nature is that the people are always more cordially drawn toward someone who has failed than toward someone who has succeeded. The successful excite their envy, but they feel a bond of kinship with those who have met defeat. Sometimes the successful are scornful of persons who have tried to climb up where they are — and have failed. But you can count on the friendship of most of the people who either failed, or never tried; provided — you don't sulk.' The Dean folded his arms on the desk, and searched Sally's wet eyes.

'Do you know what I should do, if I were in your place?' he went on, earnestly. 'I should go back to the store, tomorrow, and ask for my old position.'

'Oh — I simply couldn't!' exclaimed Sally. 'I know what the girls would say — and do. They're awfully catty, down there. They would get together in little clumps — and whisper — and giggle.'

'Would you do that, Sally,' asked the Dean, soberly, 'if one of the girls came back to the store after having an unhappy experience like yours?'

Sally debated this question with herself for a moment, and slowly nodded her head.

'If you want me to be honest — yes,' she confessed.

'But, after you had giggled, behind her back, wouldn't you feel mean — especially if she made no effort to retaliate?'

'I certainly ought to,' Sally admitted.

'And then you would probably try to do something for

the girl, to make up for your cruelty and bad manners. Perhaps you would show her more friendly attention than ever before. Don't you think that might happen?'

'Maybe. Yes — I suppose that's what would happen.'

'Are you willing to go back there, tomorrow, and ask for your old place in the basement?'

'Do you really want me to?' asked Sally, thinking fast.

'You can do it, my dear. You are, temperamentally, quite elastic and resilient, but you're not likely to bounce unless you strike something hard. You'll not rebound if you sink into a swamp of self-pity and remorse.'

'All right,' she agreed, impulsively. 'I'll do it!'

'You are a brave girl, Sally,' declared the Dean, 'and I am proud of you.'

And Sally, to show how brave she was, buried her face in her hands and cried like a little child. Then she slowly straightened, shook the tears out of her eyes, smiled pensively, and reached for her hat.

'You will find a little dressing-room over there,' said the Dean, gently.

She accepted the suggestion. Leaving the door open, Sally surveyed her tear-smeared face in the glass.

'I expect that's what this place is for,' she mumbled, half to herself, as she began to apply the powder and rouge. 'Sort of a service station for people who cry.' She turned toward the Dean, still busying herself with her make-up. 'It must be pretty tough for you — seeing so much of this, every day. I should think it would make you sad.'

'My vocation, Sally,' replied the Dean, 'has always been acquainted with grief. But ——' he added, encouragingly, 'I do not think you will cry, the next time you come.'

Having attended to her repairs, Sally was ready to go. She looked quite another person now. She came to the Dean's side and took his hand.

'I forgot to tell you,' she said, 'about the girl I found, that night, in the Cathedral. Do you remember — the one I fed and sent home? Well — she mailed me the money I had spent on her dinner and railroad fare, and I sent her one of my studio portraits.' Sally drew an ironical smile. 'She seemed glad to get it — but I don't suppose she is bragging much about it now.'

'You should have a new picture taken, Sally,' said the Dean. 'She will like it better than the other one, I think. This will be a picture of the friend who came to her rescue. The girl in the other picture was only an actress.'

Sally was rummaging in her handbag. Presently she came up with a small parcel wrapped in tissue paper which she laid on Dean Harcourt's desk.

'These are Barbara's pearls,' she said. 'Will you put them in your safe? I don't want to be responsible for them, any longer.'

The Dean opened the little package and spread out the beautiful necklace on his desk.

'I suspect that this is very valuable,' he said, 'probably worth many thousands. Did you know that?'

Sally nodded.

'You could have pledged this jewelry for enough money to keep you going in Hollywood for a long time; perhaps until you reinstated yourself.'

'Yes — I know. But the pearls weren't mine.'

'You weren't a bit tempted?' The Dean looked up into Sally's eyes, studying them soberly.

'No,' said Sally, firmly, 'not a bit.'

'Well — I'm not surprised, but I am gratified. You are made of excellent stuff, Sally. It's going to be a pleasure to work with material like that. Something important can be made of you, I think.'

Sally smiled appreciatively.

'Like the ivory girl — that Barbara talked about?'

'Exactly!' said the Dean. 'Like the ivory girl! I don't think Pygmalion would have spent much time or skill on the release of Galatea if she'd been made of putty. It had to be something precious to justify all that labor.'

'I must write to Barbara tonight,' said Sally. 'She'll be awfully disappointed in me, but I'm going to tell her everything.'

'That's right, Sally. The Nebraska people will forward your letter to her.'

'You mean — Barbara has gone somewhere else?' Sally's eyes were wide with interest.

'Barbara,' said the Dean, 'is on her way to Hollywood — to see what she can do for you, Sally.'

'But she mustn't!' exclaimed Sally. 'How can we reach her?'

The Dean shook his head, and said he didn't know.

Through her locked teeth, Sally drew a quick little breath that sounded like an instinctive response to pain.

'I've made so many people unhappy,' she cried.

The Dean was thoughtful for a moment.

'Sally,' he said, gently, 'when one makes a bad mistake, the penalty is almost always shared by one's friends. But — don't fret. We will be hearing from Barbara, presently, I think.'

'May I come back, tomorrow evening, and see if you've had any word from her?'

'Yes — and I shall be interested to learn how your friends greet you — at the store.'

'I'm afraid I'll be snubbed,' murmured Sally, ruefully.

'I'm afraid so, too,' agreed the Dean.

Sally's eyes were perplexed.

'But you advised me to do it,' she reminded him.

'I didn't advise you to go there expecting to be snubbed,' said the Dean. 'That's the surest way to get it. Run along, now, my dear. Come back tomorrow about eight-thirty.'

It was a custom of the curates to spend some time with Dean Harcourt before he retired for the night. Sometimes they discussed their parish problems. More often it was an informal, comradely chat that had very little to do with their professional cares.

After Sally Singley had gone, they appeared in the library, Simpson bringing the Dean's wheel-chair, Talbot carrying a special-delivery letter.

'Talbot,' said their chief when they had helped him make the transfer from his tall Gothic chair, and the little procession was moving toward the door, 'have you ever thought much about handwriting as an interpreter of character?'

'A little,' admitted Talbot. 'I've never won any prizes for proficiency in it.'

'What do you make of this one?' The Dean handed back the letter, and the procession halted while the senior curate squinted intently at the large square envelope.

'Well, sir,' shrilled Talbot, 'it seems to be from a lady of substance, judging by the quality of the paper; a lady of lofty social position, I should say, if these tall, perpen dicular letters are indicative of her own altitude; and, from the unusual size of the period at the end of it, I surmise that when she is through talking she expects the meeting to adjourn.'

'Very penetrating, Doctor Watson,' approved the Dean. 'Now, Mr. Holmes, let's have your deduction.'

Simpson took the envelope and inspected it gravely.

'It's from a very self-conscious young woman,' he decided. 'She is ambitious, conceited, and eager for distinction. But she is not a person of means, as Talbot thinks, or she would have a supply of two-cent stamps on hand for mailing local checks. This is a three-cent stamp. And she is not a customer of ours or she wouldn't have addressed it "Trinity Cathedral, 9721 Marlborough Street."' Simpson put the letter in the Dean's hand and they continued their journey down the hall, emerging in the reception parlor.

'And what do you think, sir?' inquired Talbot, as they paused at the door of the little elevator. He gave Simpson a slow wink.

'I'll open it,' replied the Dean, 'and tell you later.'

'Very shady practice; eh, Simpson?' squeaked Talbot.

'By such humbuggery Columbus made an egg stand on end,' said Simpson.

They pushed the chair into the elevator; and, mounting the stairs, met the Dean on the second floor. He had read the note en route.

'This is from a young lady who wants to see me tomorrow,' he reported. 'She intends to scold me, I suspect, for advising her sister to leave home for a while — where she has been shockingly imposed upon — and give her family a chance to reorganize itself.'

'Are you,' ventured Talbot, 'going to let her scold you?'

'Just a very little,' said the Dean, dryly. 'It's a rather difficult case to handle. And she must have her innings.'

It was evident that what Millicent Drake had come to say wasn't going to take very long, for she sat on the extreme edge of the big chair, her elbows on its broad arms, leaning forward as if poised for a track event.

As one with unlimited time at the disposal of his visitor, Dean Harcourt had relaxed comfortably. He had greeted her with a warmth of cordiality that might easily have been mistaken for a gesture of apologetic weakness; and it was apparent, by the low temperature of Millicent's dignity, that she was about to make this mistake.

'I have come to inquire about my sister,' she began, crisply. 'I think you know where she is.'

'She didn't tell you where she was going?' asked the Dean, artlessly.

'She did not.'

'Perhaps she didn't want you to know,' suggested the Dean. 'In that case, you will not invite me to violate your sister's confidence, will you?'

Millicent took a little time to digest this.

'We sim-ply can-not understand Katharine,' she resumed, pointing up her syllables with emphatic nods that shook her blond curls. 'It wasn't a bit like her. It would never have occurred to her to do such a thing if someone hadn't put her up to it.'

'You're worried about her?'

'Of course! Naturally! Mother is almost frantic!'

'Well — we can't have that,' sympathized the Dean. After a moment's reflection, he went on, 'Your mother is a widow, I believe.'

Millicent bowed with appropriate gravity.

'Katharine told me something of your home life,' the Dean continued, 'but so many people come here, on various errands, that it's not always easy to remember the details of their stories. Katharine told me something about herself, and a little about you. Now — help me refresh my memory. You're the sister who supports the family: is that correct?'

Millicent wasn't going to reply but the Dean waited.

'Katharine has a position down town,' she muttered, reluctantly, 'if that's what you mean.'

The Dean nodded, absently, and said that was what he meant.

'And you don't have a position?' he went on, quietly. And when — after some delay — she had shaken her head, he remarked, 'Perhaps that is because you are younger. Sometimes it happens that way. The older children get all of the attention and the advantages. And by the time the later ones come along, there's no money left for college.' He paused to give Millicent a chance to comment on that, if she wanted to; and when she remained silent, he asked, 'What year did Katharine graduate?'

'She did not graduate,' replied Millicent, sullenly.

'Fail — maybe?' asked the Dean.

'My sister' — a slow flush was creeping up Millicent's throat — 'my sister did not go to college — at all.'

'Oh? I thought one of you was a college graduate.'

Millicent rose, indignantly.

'I fear I am just taking your time, Dean Harcourt.' Her voice was trembling with anger. 'I thought you might tell me where Katharine is. If you do not want to do so, there is nothing further I care to say.'

'I'm sorry to see you leave in this mood, Miss Millicent,' said the Dean, gently. 'Won't you sit down again, and let me talk to you, for a little while? I'm not sure that I can be of any assistance to you — but — it's worth trying.'

Millicent shrugged a pretty shoulder; and, after a brief period of indecision, sat down.

'Well?' she snapped, impatiently.

'You appear to be a very unhappy young woman,' said the Dean, in the tone of a diagnostician. 'It is your mirror, I think, that has done it. You are an extraordinarily beautiful girl. I daresay you have been told that, many, many times. They probably began telling you when you were a little child. And it was true.'

Millicent's face softened perceptibly, and a dimple deepened.

'And that,' continued Dean Harcourt, 'became your distinguishing quality. You couldn't be much blamed for consulting your mirror. People who complimented you upon your beauty might be telling the truth, or they might be merely flattering you insincerely; but the mirror was honest. And it became your friend, your confidant, and your comfort. Whenever anything went wrong, the mirror reassured you.'

Millicent broke in to murmur that she hoped she wasn't quite that vain.

'Then — at an early age,' pursued the Dean, indifferent to her comment, 'you began to develop another quality. I surmise that your family must share the blame for your selfishness. Your parents and your sister should have helped you deal with this menace to your happiness. You were the one who got the pretty clothes, and went to the parties, and played tennis, and attended college. Those were busy days. And when you looked in the mirror, you didn't have time to peer deeply. Now that you are a little older, and not so hard-pressed with engagements, you have been finding something in the mirror that isn't very satisfactory. And that is most distressing, because the mirror was your closest friend. Now it has become your most severe critic, and you can't bear to consult it.'

Millicent was angry, but she did not speak.

'Now — if you want to say that all this is none of my business, you will be within your rights. I am making it my business because I know you are wretchedly unhappy and I want to do something about it. I am talking candidly to you, but I think you will agree that I haven't given you any such drubbing as you have been getting from the mirror! You have imposed upon your sister for years; leaned your full weight on her, dazzled the boys who came to see her, borrowed her wages, and so completely drove her into eclipse that she was losing confidence in herself as an attractive personality. You would like to be an actress; but how are you ever going to succeed in a convincing interpretation of somebody else's character when you are so woefully perplexed about your own? You couldn't get along with the young actors at Provincetown, and left before the season was over. That was because you couldn't get along with yourself. People who can't co-operate harmoniously with others discover — if they're brave enough to look — that they have been unable to consolidate the warring elements in their own minds.'

The Dean came to a full stop, with this, and there was a long silence. Millicent did not look up.

'Well,' he said, gently, 'that's all I wanted to say, my

friend. If you wish to present your side of the case, I am ready to listen — respectfully and sympathetically. Or — if you like — you are quite at liberty to go.'

Millicent did not reply; nor did she make any move to leave.

'I have often wished,' continued the Dean, meditatively, 'that there might be a little more emphasis placed upon family courtesy. We have talked a great deal about the importance of being a good neighbor, and we like the thought expressed in the poem about living in a house by the side of the road, with a friendly attitude toward passersby. And that's very fine.' He hesitated, smiling enigmatically. 'Occasionally someone remembers the old adage, "Charity begins at home," though I think this maxim is quoted mostly by persons seeking an alibi for their stinginess. In any event, what we need most, at home, is not charity, but courtesy. If the members of a family have a proper consideration for one another's rights and wishes, there'll not be much need for charity.'

Millicent sighed, and glanced up with clouded eyes.

'I haven't meant to be selfish,' she said, glumly.

'That's what makes it so bad,' murmured the Dean. 'It has become automatic. You had practiced it so long that you could do it without exercising your volition, at all. Sometimes people think it is a reasonable excuse to say, "I didn't mean to do it" — but that is the very worst explanation there is for bad conduct. Why, it even became so natural and effortless for you to defraud your sister that you made off with her friends when you didn't need them or want them. Be quite honest, now, Millicent. You don't care anything about Doctor Harrison; do you?'

'No,' she admitted.

'Well — Katharine does; or did. It was the only serious attachment she had ever made. And he liked her — until you came.'

'I'm sorry,' said Millicent. 'I didn't realize that she was so fond of him. They really didn't know each other very well. If you'll tell me where she is, I'll write to Katharine and apologize.'

'You mean — you'll write to her and say you are sorry that you took her man away from her? Is it possible that you have arrived at the point where you don't know the difference between an apology and an indignity?'

'Then — what do you want me to do?' She was almost in tears.

The Dean sighed and shook his head.

'I don't know,' he confessed. 'But I am sure that there is nothing you can do with a letter or telegram saying you are sorry. There is no insult that can possibly salt a wound more painfully than, "I'm sorry." The total damage you have done to Katharine cannot be quickly repaired. You see, she gave up and gave up and gave in, and sacrificed, and played second fiddle until she began to find pleasure in it! You thought she loved you so much that she wanted to surrender everything to make you happy. That wasn't it, at all! She had become a martyr; loved her bruises; nursed her wounds in secret. And that's where she made her great mistake. She was so bent on sacrificing herself that she permitted you to mistreat her. And so — it's partly Katharine's fault that you have become' — the Dean hesitated, and finished lamely — 'what you are.'

Millicent slowly rose. Her face was distorted.

'I'll go now,' she muttered, huskily, 'if you've nothing more to say.'

The Dean's face brightened a little.

'It is possible that we may be able to repair all of this damage,' he said, more hopefully. 'We have sent Katharine out to Nebraska where she is waiting table and working in the kitchen on a very large farm. Perhaps the different environment, new friends, fresh air, sunshine, and relief from the extortions and impositions of her home — perhaps these changes may restore her emotional balance. It's by no means certain. This mental trouble of hers has been at work for a long time.'

'*Mental* trouble!' Millicent's eyes were frightened.

'What else?' demanded the Dean. 'Your sister is headed toward a definite persecution complex, and there isn't a more serious mental condition than that.'

'Why — this is terrible!' exclaimed Millicent, her voice breaking.

'I suggest that you take a long walk, Millicent,' advised the Dean. 'Think it all over. Perhaps you will want to come back, sometime, and have another talk.'

'What shall I say to Mother?' asked Millicent, half to herself.

'About you — or about Katharine?'

'Well — naturally — I was thinking about Katharine's trouble.'

'When you talk to your mother,' said the Dean, 'you had better concentrate on what ails *you*. Perhaps she will notice that she, too, is in need of a little — interior decoration. If you and your mother begin thinking straight about yourselves, you will be well on the way toward doing something for Katharine.'

Millicent turned, rather unsteadily, to go. She fumbled with the latch of her handbag.

'Does this cost anything' — she asked, weakly — 'this interview?'

'I'm afraid so,' replied the Dean, 'but you don't pay it here.'

She walked toward the door, where she turned to say good-bye.

'I want to see you again, Millicent,' said the Dean. 'Sooner the better.'

'Tomorrow?' she asked, with some earnestness.

'Yes.'

'What time?'

Dean Harcourt was studious for a moment. Then his face lighted.

'You plan to be here in the evening — about half-past eight.'

'There's a young Mr. Price,' announced Sonia. 'Says he has an appointment. Will you see him now?'

'Yes,' said the Dean. 'Did you find out anything about him?'

'No. He was pretty far upstage when I tried to make myself agreeable, and didn't seem inclined to be chatty. He is with a firm of architects, offices in the Loop; family lives in Evanston; parents and a sister Jean. He is unmarried, a graduate of Cornell a year ago, has a small apartment, likes to paint, would follow it as a profession if he could afford it.'

'Umm,' ummed the Dean, with a dry grin. 'Didn't want to talk, eh? How much talking did you want him to do?'

Sonia assumed the defensive, purse-lipped expression that she knew was so amusing to Dean Harcourt when she stood accused of having fairly gouged people's personal stories out of them, and asked, in an elaborate tone of injury, if she should bring Mr. Roger Price in.

'A friend of Larry's,' she added, 'in case you don't already know.'

'Yes, I know. He told me on the phone. Good-looking fellow?'

'Immensely! If he was about seventeen years older ——'

'Then what?' asked the Dean, as Sonia moved toward the door.

'He'd be forty,' she drawled.

Presently she returned with him and closed the door behind him. The Dean pointed to the big Gothic chair, and Roger, bowing, accepted the invitation.

'Well, Mr. Roger Price,' began the Dean, 'what's the latest movement in the field of architecture?'

'About 1930, sir, I'm told,' replied Roger, with an ironical chuckle.

It was immediately apparent that Dean Harcourt enjoyed the prompt sally; for, in spite of its cynical implication, Roger's remark had not been spoken bitterly. The Dean folded his arms on the desk and leaned forward on his elbows, an appreciative smile playing about his eyes.

'Not operating under forced draft, then, I take it,' he rejoined, adopting his visitor's mood.

'In a way, yes — if you will pardon an atrocious pun: I am forced to draw. Most of us youngsters have resorted to anything we can pick up. Hack work. We call it "commercial art," which is a pleasant way to say it. There's only one thing to be said for us, sir. We're not pretentious. No job is too small.'

'For instance,' prodded the Dean, interestedly.

'Well, sir, tonight I am going to do an illustrated menu-card for the Long Wing Chop Suey Grotto, and shall charge them ten dollars.'

'No likee?' asked the Dean, shaking his head.

'No likee,' sighed Roger. 'No likee job, no likee wages; but — allee same must eat. "I cannot dig, and I am ashamed to beg."'

'You seem to be familiar with the Scriptures,' observed the Dean.

'No, sir; not very. I just happened to recall that sentence. I heard you quote it, last Sunday. That fellow was a pretty smooth grafter; wasn't he? Why, he made our politicians look like a lot of cooing doves.'

'You attend the Cathedral regularly?' asked the Dean, amused.

'Lately, yes. Came here, one Sunday, with Larry Runyan. He told me he had talked with you, sir. And you advised him to go out into the sticks and paint haystacks. I have missed him horribly! Week ago I had a letter from him. He was upset and restless; wanted to get away from that farm; wanted me to join him in a long trek up into the Rockies. I don't know what he thought we'd use for money. He hasn't any, and he knows I haven't. I wrote, asking for more details. I'd like to go with him, if we could hit on some plan to finance the trip; for I'm doing nothing here. Yesterday my letter came back undelivered, accompanied by a note from the Mr. Wendell on whose farm he had been painting. He said that Larry had left suddenly for California. That was all; just "California." That's what I came to see you about, sir. I thought you might know.'

'I know that much,' said the Dean. 'Larry went by air to Hollywood on an emergency errand for a friend.'

'By air!' exclaimed Roger. 'Then landscape painting must have met a bull market in Nebraska; or else Larry robbed a bank.'

'Nebraska is a great cattle country,' said the Dean, slyly pleased to pay off Roger for his recent pun. 'I think,' he added, seriously, 'you will be hearing from Larry, one of these days. He has not left us permanently.'

Roger's face cleared.

'Well — it's a relief,' he said, 'to know that Larry had some object in scooting off like that. His letter worried me. He was quite depressed. Something had happened to him. Everything had gone stale and sour. Larry's a moody fellow, you know: not very good company for himself. I have wondered whether — somewhere along the line — he hadn't had a lot of trouble. He never wanted to talk about himself.' Roger studied the Dean's eyes with candid inquiry.

'It's going to turn out all right, presently,' said the Dean. 'I am not worrying about him — now.'

Roger, in much better spirits, rose and prepared to leave. Dean Harcourt motioned him back into his chair.

'Don't go yet,' he said, quietly. 'Let's talk about *you*.'

'What about me?' asked Roger, obeying.

'I gather that you are disappointed because you have not found satisfactory employment. You think it is unfortunate that you had to launch upon your career as an architect when all business is sluggish. I want to talk to you about that.'

'I wish you would, sir,' agreed Roger, attentively.

'When your father was of your age,' pursued the Dean, 'there was a good job waiting for every college graduate — and every other young fellow who wanted to work. Things were booming. Production couldn't keep up with demand.

Young men hopped off the Commencement rostrum into well-paid positions. That abnormal condition continued for a decade. Then the markets were saturated and industry slowed down. Good jobs were not so easily to be had by inexperienced youngsters. And it strikes you that this is a time of unusual stress and hardship for youth. Isn't that so?'

Roger admitted that this was a fair statement of the case, and waited for the Dean to continue.

'Now — the only fault to be found with your view, Roger, is that the actual facts do not support it. We have not met an emergency: we have been readjusting to the usual thing. The normal, traditional procedure has demanded that youth shall wait its turn, speak only when spoken to, apprentice itself, run the errands, turn the grindstone, accept small wages or none — and wait — until developing skill and sound experience, plus a few funerals at the top of the business, brought opportunities for advancement. Until this recent unexampled inflammation in all industry, that was the rule.'

The Dean paused and a slow, reminiscent smile crinkled the crow's-feet at his temples.

'Roger,' he went on, 'I don't want to weary you with an old man's memories; but, during the summer following my graduation from college, I worked in a planing-mill for seventy-five cents per day. I walked two miles to get there and we began work at seven o'clock. I carried my lunch in a tin bucket and ate it sitting on the ground in the shade of a pile of lumber. When the whistle blew at five, we quit, went home, and washed the sawdust out of our ears at the iron pump in the back yard.'

'That must have been pretty hard to take,' observed Roger.

'After supper,' the Dean went on, half in soliloquy, 'I went out to the truck-patch and hoed weeds and killed potato-bugs and fought mosquitoes until dusk. I had no feeling of revolt. It was the normal thing to do. I didn't realize that this was degrading employment for a newly fledged Bachelor of Arts. All I knew was that the profession to which I aspired wasn't ready for me yet. My father had gone through such experiences in his youth, as had his father before him. That was the way the world had been rigged up. Youth was expected to work at small tasks — and be patient.'

For a long time, Dean Harcourt sat with half-closed eyes, busy with his recollections. Then, as if suddenly rousing to the fact that he was not alone, he drew a long breath, smiled, and said, 'I hope I haven't been too tiresome. I'll let you go now. You have work to do; drawing the picture for the chop suey place. Try to enjoy it — even if you're getting only ten dollars for it.'

'Thanks for the tip,' said Roger, taking the Dean's extended hand. 'I'm a little bit ashamed — for complaining.'

'I don't want you to be ashamed,' rejoined the Dean. 'I want you to be patient. Come and see me again.'

Sonia met him as he walked through the reception parlor on the way out. He turned to smile and nod good-bye. She moved toward him and held out her hand.

'You must have had a pleasant talk with Dean Harcourt.' Sonia's tone invited a comment. Roger's brows contracted thoughtfully.

'He makes one's troubles seem unimportant,' he said.

'The Dean has that effect upon everyone who talks with him,' declared Sonia.

'Everyone but you, perhaps.' Roger surveyed her with

an almost disconcertingly frank avowal of admiration, and added, 'You don't look as if you had ever had any trouble.'

'That's good,' murmured Sonia. 'You must come back, often, and see us.'

'Does the Dean do this sort of thing all day long?' inquired Roger.

'And far into the night,' nodded Sonia. 'Lots of boats — big and little — want Dean Harcourt to take the wheel, and see them through the narrows.'

'It must be a very exacting job,' remarked Roger.

'Yes — but pilots have steady nerves,' said Sonia.

Dean Harcourt was so quiet at dinner that Sonia, who had been induced to remain, divined by his preoccupied manner that something of unusual interest was in the air. And she was perishing to find out what it was. When, having made short work of his coffee, he invited Sonia to join him presently in the library, she knew that he was ready to tell her.

'Millicent and Sally are coming here,' he said, 'at eight-thirty.'

'You're having them meet?'

'Yes. Do you think that's odd?'

'Rather. I can't see that they have anything in common, except that they're both females — and Caucasians.'

'People do not have to be of the same intellectual or social stratum, Sonia, to have similar interests. You know that. Here we have Millicent, who studied dramatics in college and probably has a sound theoretical knowledge of the stage; and Sally, who knows next to nothing about the professional patter of acting, but is, nevertheless, a gifted impersonator. Might they not have a profitable friendship?'

'From what you've told me of Millicent,' observed Sonia, 'she would consider Sally beneath her.'

'That might have been the case, a few days ago, but Milly has had a chance to do some thinking. We shall see, presently, just how much thinking she has done. Now, when Sally arrives, I want you to look after her while I have a preliminary chat with Millicent. Let her tell you all about the warm welcome she had at the store. She telephoned me about it at six; couldn't wait; bubbling with joy. Encourage her to talk about it. Later, we will have the two girls together, and I shall want Sally to give us a glowing account of her occupation.'

Mr. Talbot came in, at this point, to say there were two visitors waiting in the reception parlor, Miss Drake and Miss Singley. Sonia followed him out, after a brief interval, passed Millicent in the hall, and found Sally wandering about looking at the pictures. The quick, bright, sincere happiness on the girl's face, when they met, warmed Sonia's heart.

'You won't mind waiting a little,' she said, 'while the Dean talks to that other girl?'

'Not if I can talk to *you!*' declared Sally.

Millicent walked slowly to the guest chair and sank into it without waiting to be invited. Her face was sober but not sullen.

'How goes the battle?' asked the Dean, pleasantly.

She shook her head, without speaking.

'Wouldn't you like to take off your hat?' The Dean pointed to the door of the little dressing-room. 'Put it over there. You'll feel ever so much more like talking.'

After a moment of indecision, she rose with evident reluctance and obeyed, giving the mirror a scowl. As she was returning doggedly to her chair, the Dean said, 'I wonder if you would do a little favor for me, Millicent. At dinner, I had only one cup of coffee and I'd like another. Will you be good enough to find my housekeeper, Mrs. Crandall? And tell her to bring a pot of coffee and two cups, please.'

'Why — of course, Dean Harcourt; if you will tell me how to find her.' Millicent's face was puzzled, but her frown was clearing.

'Just go down the hall, the way you came, and ask anybody you see. Someone will tell you.'

She strode off with a confident air. In the reception parlor she asked directions of the modishly dressed woman, who seemed familiar with the house, and was told how to proceed toward the kitchen.

'Are you Mrs. Crandall, please?' asked Millicent, of a competent matron seated at the kitchen table.

'Yes — but I'm afraid you have struck me at a bad time. We had chicken patties for dinner, and there were just enough to go around. But we have everything else — and I can give you some nice cold tongue.'

'Thank you; I've had my dinner,' said Millicent, amused. 'Dean Harcourt asked me to tell you that he'd like a pot of coffee, in the library.'

'Just enough for himself?' queried Mrs. Crandall.

'Well — I think he did say ——'

'That's what I thought. Want cream in yours? He doesn't take it. You've never been here before?'

'Yesterday.' Millicent's smile faded out.

'Well' — Mrs. Crandall, busying herself with the coffee, assumed a tone of encouragement — 'you'll get along all right with him, this time. Whenever he begins sending them all over the house, on trumped-up errands, it means he likes them. You'd better hurry back, now.'

Millicent laughed. She was being treated like a six-year-old, but she didn't resent it. As she passed through the reception parlor she observed the stylish woman in intimate conversation with a pretty girl of her own age. They gave her only casual attention.

'Find Mrs. Crandall?' asked the Dean, when Millicent was seated opposite him.

'She offered to feed me. Do I look hungry?'

'Not for food — but for the satisfaction of making an investment; which prompts me to suggest a project. We have a young woman, extraordinarily talented but without any training, who needs instruction in dramatics. She works in a store, at small wages; can't afford a dramatic school. I have been wondering if you wouldn't take her in hand.'

'But — would I have time?' asked Millicent. 'I'm looking for employment.'

'I know; and you're not going to like it; not unless you can find some delightful avocation that will keep building you up faster than the drudgery of your work can tear you down. That's what ails many people who earn their living down town in shops and offices. Their lives are regimented. Their work is a more or less genteel form of slavery. It has the effect of destroying their personalities — *unless* they can find something to do, outside the working hours; something that gives them a chance to be creative, expressive, ingenious.'

'Perhaps I might give this girl a couple of hours in the evenings,' said Millicent, 'though, really, I don't believe I could do very much for her.'

'But you'd try?'

As they settled to a serious discussion of this matter, over their coffee, Millicent's attitude gradually changed from one of indifference to something like interest. At the end of twenty minutes, she was committed to the Dean's project. He was delighted with her mood, and told her so.

'Now you *are* going to be beautiful!' he declared. 'That was what ailed your beauty, Millicent, and that's where the mirror fooled you. Your beauty was all on the outside. Now it will be welling up from within.' He smiled into her eyes, and added, 'You'll see!'

'When may I meet this girl?' asked Millicent.

'Now. I was so sure of what you'd want to do that I asked her to come here.' He pushed a desk button, which amused Millicent. The Dean caught her fleeting smile and raised his brows inquiringly.

'I was just wondering,' she explained, 'why you couldn't get coffee that way — by pushing a button.'

'Oh, no,' he replied, pretending to be serious, 'I have to send for coffee. We don't have a coffee button.'

Sonia appeared, and the Dean introduced them. It was easy to see that Millicent was impressed.

'You may bring Sally in now,' said the Dean. She breezed into the room like a young tornado, danced across to Dean Harcourt's desk, took his hand, and began pouring out a torrent of highly carbonated hallelujahs extolling the store that had treated her so magnificently.

'Mercy! — what a racket!' said the Dean. 'Hold up — a minute. I want you to meet Miss Drake. Millicent, this is Sally Singley.'

Whatever may have been Millicent's faults, she was not an expert dissembler. She stared into Sally's face with such unabashed curiosity that Sally couldn't help saying, with playful impudence, 'It's me — all right. Only — now I'm working in the store again.' She turned to the Dean. 'And they've promoted me. I'm up in the nice lingerie now.' Sally tipped back her head, raised a shoulder languidly, gave her curls a caress, and remarked coolly, 'Here's something quite chic, modom, in petit point; just arrived; so very nice.' She snapped out of her part with a quick little sigh and a smile.

'Is that the way you carry on, up there — really?' asked Sonia, shaking her head, incredulously.

'Why not?' countered Sally, defensively. 'They love it. You ought to know they do.'

This amused the Dean greatly. He caught Sonia's eye, chuckled, and was promptly punished for it by her pursed expression of reproach.

'Sounds like fun,' put in Millicent, a little to her own surprise.

'Nothing like it,' declared Sally. Then, impulsively, to Millicent, 'Do you work at anything?'

'No; but I am hoping to find something.'

'In a store, maybe?'

'Anywhere. I need a job.'

Dean Harcourt, gently tapping his open palm with a paper knife, watched this conversation grow. He was keenly interested, as was Sonia.

'Ever work in a store?' asked Sally, in the business tone of the personnel department.

Millicent shook her head.

'I suppose one has to start at the bottom,' she surmised.

'Yes,' rasped Sally, indifferently. 'Them mittens would be awful nice and warm fer the little boy, lady. They's priced to sell, too. Nineteen cents.' She instantly came out of that, and said, naturally, 'I can get you in — if you think you want to.'

'Thanks,' said Millicent. 'It will be good of you.'

The Dean and Sonia exchanged glances. He nodded, several times, much pleased.

'I'll be going now,' said Sonia. 'Good night.'

'And I have some work to do,' said the Dean. 'I suggest that you girls repair to the reception parlor, and talk as long as you like.'

'Thank you — for everything,' murmured Millicent, as she and Sally moved toward the door.

Returning impulsively to the Dean's desk, Sally bent over him to say, in a stage whisper, with a toss of her head toward her new friend, 'What do you bet — if I went at it with a mallet and chisel — I could make something nice out o' that.'

'Well — you want to be careful,' muttered the Dean, from the corner of his mouth, 'or she'll try to make something nice out o' *you!*'

'Don't like me any more?' whined Sally, in the tone of a badly spoiled eight-year-old.

'I *couldn't* like you any more, Sally,' said the Dean, gently. 'You're perfect. You're refreshing. It's pleasant to have you about.'

'About to what?' she asked, impishly.

'About to leave,' chuckled the Dean. 'Skip along now. They're waiting for you. Come back soon. Good night.'

After she had opened the door, and was halfway through, she turned, and gave the Dean a stiff bow that was heavily coated with ice. It was very funny; but the Dean, with a sober face, matched her dignity with a courtly inclination of his head. Neither smiled. Sally drew the door almost shut. Then opened it a little way — and childishly blew him a kiss, which stuck to her fingers. Much chagrined, she blew it again; and, apparently failing to dislodge it, she soberly licked it off — and closed the door behind her.

Sonia returned, at that moment, colliding with Sally in the hall. Dean Harcourt was wiping his eyes.

'What's the matter?' she asked, with an inquisitive smile.

'Sally and I,' he said, 'have a new act.'

'That child!' said Sonia. 'She has no respect for anybody; not even *you!*'

'No, no, Sonia. Sally has just paid me a little compliment. She thinks I'm human. She thinks I should be able to play. Rather pleasant,' he added, half seriously, 'to find someone who thinks I should be able to play. I wonder if Sally is trying to bring *me* to life.'

Barbara had decided, en route, that she would await Larry's arrival before going to see the Dean. She wasn't sure which train he would take. There was one stopping at Barstow at four in the morning which was much too early, and another at nine. She felt he would take that one. As the afternoon wore on, and time hung more and more heavily, she impulsively resolved to run over to the Cathedral — it was only five minutes by taxi — and have a glimpse of Dean Harcourt.

But she was going to keep their secret until Larry came. That is, she was going to try to keep it; though it was possible, of course, that he might get it out of her. The Dean had such a funny way of reading your thoughts.

Leaving a note for Larry at the desk — just in case —

she proceeded to Marlborough Street, and was met by
Mr. Talbot. It was five-thirty, and the day's work was
done.

'I say!' shrilled Mr. Talbot. 'How jolly well you look!
That must be an uncommonly healthful country, out there
in — where was it — Minnebraska?'

'Nebbasota,' corrected Barbara, waving at Sonia who
was coming forward to welcome her with outstretched
hands.

'How perfectly wonderful!' purred Sonia. 'And where's
Larry?'

Barbara's eyes were puzzled.

'Larry?' she echoed. Then it suddenly occurred to her
that the Dean might have heard from him. 'Well ——' she
stammered. 'You see — Larry isn't in town. What made
you think he was coming?'

'Now, Barbara,' said Sonia, maternally, 'please don't be
difficult. Goodness knows! — we have enough to bear. . . .
Haven't we, Mr. Talbot?' This last remark was practically
shouted into the genial curate's face, in a tone that meant
'Why don't you go away — so she'll tell me what's up?'

'Oh — quite!' he agreed, drifting across to the radio.

'Sonia,' said Barbara, reproachfully, 'what a dreadful
way to use that dear, good man.'

'Would you mind,' called Talbot, 'if I turned on the
news?'

'Not at all,' said Sonia. 'That's what I'm about to do.'

She slipped an arm around Barbara's slim waist and led
her to the cushioned window-seat.

'He wired the Dean,' whispered Sonia. 'Said you were
both coming — together. Didn't you?'

'Part of the way,' confessed Barbara, turning her face
aside.

'You mean, he got off the train?' Sonia's voice was so full of apprehension that Barbara could hardly keep her face straight.

'Yes, Sonia,' she replied, dejectedly.

'Is there something' — Sonia paused, for station identification; and, not getting any report, went on, gently — 'is there something you want to tell Mamma?'

'No, Mamma. Little Barbara can't talk veddy well yet.' Then she laughed a little, and added, roguishly, 'Think you can keep yourself all in one piece, Sonia, until you find out what's gone wrong?'

'You're very ungrateful,' remarked Sonia, making an elaborate show of disappointment. 'Here we sit — and steam — and fret.'

'I know,' murmured Barbara, pensively. 'Keeps you from getting fat. Could I say hello to the Dean?'

'Not for a minute or two, darling. He has been upstairs, for a half-hour, resting. You'll see him at dinner. Shall I tell Crandall you're staying?'

'Let me tell her, Sonia. I want to see her.'

'Very well. I'll wait here, and comfort poor Talbot. He likes to have someone at hand to listen to his comments on the news commentator's comments while the commentator is commenting. It is rawther confusing, don't you know; but Talbot enjoys it.'

Mrs. Crandall was rolling out the delectable paste for a berry pie.

'You'll get all over flour,' she warned, in response to Barbara's hug. 'And I'll be smeared with lipstick. How are you, Precious? It's good to have you home.'

'What are you going to have?' Barbara stepped to the range with an inquiring sniff.

'Liver and bacon,' muttered Molly, the cook.

'And there isn't much more than enough,' added Mrs. Crandall. 'Don't know why they sent such skimpy pieces. When the Dean serves you, Barbara, tell him you want just a bite. Tell him it gives you the hives — or something. You haven't any business to come barging in here, this time o' day. Ought to call up — and make a reservation.'

'It's lots more fun — this way, Mrs. Crandall,' said Barbara, making a new bow of her apron-strings.

'For who?' interposed Molly, laughing immoderately at her own quick wit.

Barbara was lifting something from the large wooden salad-bowl, and had her back to the swinging door when it was gently pushed open.

'For Mercy's Sake!' exclaimed Mrs. Crandall. 'If here isn't another one! Oh — you'll all be the death of me!'

Larry gave her a pat on the shoulder. Barbara turned, and slowly exhaled a luxurious 'Oh!' without making a sound.

'This is Miss Breckenridge,' said Mrs. Crandall. 'Barbara, this is Mr. Runyan.'

Larry wrapped his arms around her, and Barbara reached up both hands and twisted his hair in her fingers. He kissed her hungrily, again and again. At length, a bit breathless, she drew away, and looked up into Larry's face, beaming.

'Well ——' said Mrs. Crandall, dryly, 'I'm glad I had a chance to introduce you. Maybe you've met somewhere before. I hope so. Now I've got to make another pie.'

'Forgive us, please, Mrs. Crandall,' said Larry, holding Barbara close. 'You would have been informed about our engagement, but — it has all been rather sudden, and ——'

'This is the first time we've seen each other,' said Barbara, 'since Larry asked me.'

Mrs. Crandall put down the rolling-pin, and, with arms akimbo, surveyed them with candid curiosity.

'You see,' went on Larry, 'when we became engaged, Barbara was on a train.'

'And you?' she asked.

'Larry was outside, running along.'

'Well' — Mrs. Crandall rubbed her forehead with the back of a floury hand — 'you'd better go now and tell that to the Dean. He believes everything that anybody says to him.'

Sonia stepped in. Her eyes were dancing.

'Oh! So you found each other!' she said gaily. 'That's fine! How are you, Mrs. Crandall?'

'Not so good,' she mumbled. 'I'm losing my mind.'

They met at the dinner table. Dean Harcourt offered them his hands.

'And so the pilgrims have returned,' he said warmly, 'doubtless to live happily ever afterward.'

'The message I sent you, sir,' said Larry, 'wasn't quite correct. We did start together, as I reported, but there was no place for me on the train; so I had to get off.'

'Sonia told me,' said the Dean. He turned to her with a half-teasing smile. 'I think she feels,' he went on, 'that the affair of the train was badly managed. I suggest that from now on you would do well to let Sonia arrange things.'

'It's a good idea,' agreed Barbara. 'It would take a lot off your mind, Larry.'

'I don't think I've done anything to earn the reputation of a planner,' put in Sonia, pretending pique. 'I almost never make a suggestion.'

'Huh!' said Mrs. Crandall, from the end of the table.

'How do you mean — "huh!"' countered Sonia. She turned to Larry. 'There's an unfortunate tradition taking shape here. I'm accused of being an organizer, when the fact is that everything is always arranged before I hear about it. And just because that's so, I think I have a right to offer one little thought.'

'About what?' asked Mr. Simpson.

'The wedding. Any child could see that the wedding must occur here in the Cathedral, for neither of them would consent to anyone else doing it but Dean Harcourt. Barbara's mother and stepfather would undoubtedly approve. And Uncle Earnest and Aunt Patty would love to come here for it, too. They travel a good deal; don't they, Larry?'

'May we have Andy and Midge?' asked Barbara.

'Yes,' agreed Sonia, 'and Sally, of course, and Katharine.'

'Don't forget Millicent,' said the Dean.

'And Roger,' added Sonia.

'By the way, Larry,' interjected the Dean, 'I have been seeing something of Roger. Will you be looking him up?'

'Tomorrow.'

'Some valuable work to be done there, Larry,' said the Dean. 'Roger is very good stuff. Needs a little shaping. You'd better limber up your mallet and chisel. You're the fellow who can do it. Roger will do anything you say.'

'When is the wedding to be, Sonia?' inquired Talbot.

'How ridiculous!' she retorted. 'As if it was up to me.'

'You might express your opinion, Sonia,' advised the Dean.

'Well,' she said, thoughtfully, 'it seems to me that October — about the middle of October ——'

Everyone enjoyed this and the laughter was general. Sonia did not join in the merriment.

'So you could have your honeymoon,' she said, 'before the bad weather comes on.'

'Where are we going?' asked Larry, eagerly.

'I thought Bermuda would be rather nice,' she replied.

'What shall I wear?' asked Barbara.

'That pink gingham,' said Larry. 'It's the first dress I ever really liked.'

That kind of foolish banter prevailed, all through the dinner, and when they rose Barbara and Larry, at Dean Harcourt's request, accompanied him to the library, Sonia having announced that she must go home.

'You seem quite pleased,' observed the Dean, when they were seated. 'Larry has put things to rights in his kingdom; and you, Barbara, have proved that you can be liked for yourself.'

'What's this — about your kingdom, Larry?' asked Barbara. 'You've never spoken of it.'

'He will have plenty of time to tell you,' said the Dean. 'You will be sharing his kingdom. I believe you will both be happy. You must keep it in mind, though, that this ecstasy of yours will have to be paid for if you mean to keep it.'

'We've had no chance to talk about such things,' said Barbara.

'Please go on, sir,' begged Larry.

'It isn't the first cost: it's the upkeep,' pursued Dean Harcourt. 'Just now, your mutual devotion is in the nature of an insurance policy on which you do not have to pay the initial premium until the end of the first year. After that — if you want to keep it in force, you will have to contribute to the security of other people's devotion.'

'I don't believe I understand,' said Barbara.

'Let me put it this way, then. There are three great energies of the human spirit. They are faith, hope, and love. If you want to insure your faith, encourage others to have faith. If you want to be hopeful, inspire others with hope. If you want to keep your love, help other people keep theirs.' The Dean's face brightened. 'That's all,' he added. 'That's everything.... And the lecture is over. Now it is your turn to talk. Larry, did you succeed in painting some good pictures?'

'They were lovely!' answered Barbara. 'He gave two of them to the Wendells, and the five others are being shipped here for you to see.'

'You are to have your choice of them, sir,' said Larry.

'Please don't choose the apple orchard,' said Barbara.

'That one,' observed the Dean, 'is yours, I think.'

'It was on the day we first met,' she explained.

'And where we added a few details to the Pygmalion story,' assisted Larry.

'Want to tell me?' asked the Dean.

They spent some time recovering that first conversation, much to Dean Harcourt's amusement.

'It was great fun,' said Barbara. 'The story brims with possibilities.'

'I wish you had been there, sir,' said Larry. 'You would have thought of many more problems confronting these people.'

'It isn't too late for Dean Harcourt to make some observations,' suggested Barbara.

Dean Harcourt was thoughtful for a moment; then smiled, and remarked dryly, 'Of course, Galatea would be something of a novelty, for a few days. Pygmalion, proud of his handiwork, may have bragged a little when presenting her to his friends. . . . "I want you to meet Demetrios, dear. Demetrios, this is Galatea. I'm sure you must have heard about her."' The Dean paused and directed a meaningful glance toward Larry.

'Naturally,' said Larry, accepting his cue. 'The whole town is talking about it. Congratulations, Pygmalion. Fine job — if I may say so.'

Dean Harcourt nodded approvingly and turned toward Barbara with a slow wink.

'It's getting to be somewhat embarrassing, Mr. Deme-trios,' pouted Barbara. 'I thought I had been invited to live — but I see that I'm just a fine job that Pygmalion has accomplished.'

'Nonsense,' scoffed Larry. 'You're famous! Everybody knows about you. People will be talking about you for thousands of years.'

Barbara shook her head.

'No,' she declared. 'It's Pygmalion who will be famous. Not that I care. He deserves all the credit.'

'Don't you want to be famous, Galatea?' asked the Dean, gently.

'No — I just want to be like other people. I want to live. I don't want to be tagged as the girl who was chopped out of a block of ivory.'

'Bravo!' shouted the Dean. 'Here we've arrived at the really important problem of people who have been given a chance to live. The sculptor's apt to think that he has a permanent lien on his product. When you bring someone to life, he is just as much entitled to live as you are. . . . By the way, Barbara, you'll be seeing Sally, won't you, before you go east?'

Barbara smiled, rather faintly, and nodded.

'I'm dreading it, a little,' she confessed. 'I'm afraid I won't know what to say to her.'

'Well,' drawled the Dean. 'I shouldn't worry about that. You won't have to talk much when you see Sally.'

It was nine o'clock. Larry had returned to the hotel. Barbara, having telephoned to her Aunt Vic, was awaiting the arrival of the ancient limousine which her mother had always referred to as 'Aunt Victoria's hearse.' It would creep over to the Drake where Barbara, with her luggage, would re-embark for the fine old home — and an extended address by her elderly relative.

'I know she is going to scold me,' mumbled Barbara, when word came that the car had arrived. 'And it will take hours.'

Dean Harcourt chuckled a little.

'I think it would be a pleasant arrangement,' he said, idly, 'if people, who have lengthy reproaches to offer, would deliver a mere sentence or two — and then ask leave to print the rest, the way they do in Washington.'

'Shall I suggest that to Aunt Vic?' laughed Barbara.

'If you do, you needn't quote *me*,' said the Dean.

After Barbara had left, Millicent arrived. She had asked for an eight-o'clock appointment, but Dean Harcourt had told Talbot to phone her that he would not be at liberty until nine.

It was easy to see that something had happened to Millicent. The Dean gave her both hands and she took them eagerly.

'You needn't tell me that everything is all right now,' he

said, gently. 'It's written all over your face. **I'm very glad.**'

She sat down in the big chair, took off her hat, shook out her yellow curls, and smiled happily.

'What I came for, Dean Harcourt, is Katharine's address. I want to write her a letter. I want to tell her about my work, and how happy I am. And I mean to tell her, too, how badly I feel about the way I've treated her.'

'No,' said the Dean, thoughtfully, 'not that. You tell her all about your job, and your happiness; but, if I were you, I'd leave that old sore spot alone. It will heal, if you don't pull the scab off. Katharine will be delighted to know that you have found work, and are in gay spirits. Are you employed in the basement?'

'Yes — and it's so interesting that I don't realize I'm tired until the day is over.'

'Very good. You tell Katharine that. It will heal all the hurts you gave her when you belittled her work.'

'I'm anxious to see her,' murmured Millicent. '**I wish she would come home.**'

'Tell her that.'

'It was pay-day today. I had only worked three days, but I was paid, too.' She laughed a little. 'Four ninety-eight. Think I'd better send it to Katharine? She probably isn't making much where she is.'

Dean Harcourt shook his head.

'Better not. You would get some pleasure out of that, but it's too early to begin paying off the debt — in money. Take it easy. She has been your benefactress for a long time. She will not want you to send her this pittance, when she knows that you need it.'

'Would you be willing to write to Katharine, Dean

Harcourt, and tell her that Mother and I are anxious to make amends, and urge her to come home? She'll do anything you say.'

'No,' said the Dean.

'You mean, it's my problem?'

'As far as I can see,' said the Dean, 'there isn't any problem. There was a problem — for all of you — but you've solved it. It was a problem of self-respect. We have all had the idea bred into us that we should participate in the world's work. If we fail to do it — either because we won't or can't find something to do — our personalities suffer. That was what ailed you, Millicent. You were in the grandstand, watching other people play the game of living. You booed when somebody muffed a forward pass. Now that you are in it yourself, you won't have many opportunities to see other people's mistakes, for you will be fully occupied with your own responsibilities.'

'It's too bad,' sighed Millicent. 'Millions of people with nothing to do.'

The Dean nodded regretfully; then, brightening, he asked, 'How are you and Sally making out with your dramatics?'

'We haven't begun yet,' said Millicent. 'Sally wants to postpone it for a while. And I'm just as well pleased. It's quite fatiguing, working in a store. Part of it is an emotional fatigue. Women come with their small children and look at things with a pathetic wistfulness. Sometimes they bite their lips and seem to be counting, probably trying to figure some way to stretch the last dollar. It makes you want to hand them whatever it is — and say, "Here — take it along. It's a present!"'

'And what *do* you say — if anything?' asked the Dean, sincerely interested.

'I say, "Perhaps you can buy it the next time you come in. We always have them in stock, you know." I think that makes them feel a little better.'

'You're probably headed for the Personnel Department, Millicent, or the Bureau of Adjustments.'

Millicent rose, put on her hat, and prepared to leave. She went to the Dean's side and held out her hand.

'I'll always remember what you did for me,' she said, softly. 'You taught me how to live.'

'Come in and talk to me, occasionally, my dear,' said the Dean. 'My task is not always so rewarding. You make me want to keep on trying.'

Millicent went down to the Northwestern Station to meet her, three days later. It was Sunday morning. They hugged each other for a long time, and when their eyes met they were both in tears — and smiles. It was a tender moment.

'So glad! So glad you're back!' murmured Millicent.

They came arm in arm down the long flight of stairs and followed the crowd around to the taxi-court. Millicent tipped the red-cap.

'Let me,' Katharine had said, but Millicent seemed bent on taking charge of things.

'You're tanned,' said Millicent, when they were seated. 'You know you tan beautifully. It's very becoming.'

Mother was sitting in the porch swing. She came out to the taxi. Millicent paid the driver. Katharine slipped an arm around her mother's waist. Then she kissed her, and Mother cried.

When they were in the house, Mother began whimpering herself into a sad scene. She sat down and swayed back and forth in the squeaky old rocker, blubbering, 'And to think

— that we treated you — so mean — you had to run away. Ohh!'

'Now, Mother,' said Millicent, firmly, 'we are not going to do any of that! Katharine is home, and we're glad — and she's glad. Let's try to be happy.' She produced a handkerchief, which Mother — still sobbing — found inadequate. Resorting to her apron, Mother took her nose in both hands and blew and blew until it seemed she would blow her brains out. Just before the final blast, her daughters, standing solicitously before her, exchanged glances. They tried to keep sober faces, but it was no use. Katharine grinned; not much of a grin; just a mere involuntary twitch of the lips. Millicent saw it, and found herself suddenly filling up with giggles. She was hanging on to them so hard that they puffed her cheeks, making her difficult to look at without smiling. When the ultimate detonation came, neither of the sisters was able to bear it without collapsing. They hurriedly tiptoed out to the kitchen, put their arms around each other, and laughed until their eyes were wet.

'I'm ashamed,' gasped Katharine, when she was able to whisper.

'So am I,' agreed Millicent, appropriately. But they both felt that they really had something in common, for the first time in their lives. Mother was their baby. They would join in bearing this burden.

Breakfast was all but ready. Mother, having pulled herself together, dished it up.

They wanted to know all about her life on the farm, and Katharine was glad to tell them. And they listened. She told them about the work she did, and the girls she met, and the droll sayings of Uncle Andy; about the dairy; about the frequent trips to dusty little Axton.

'And what did you do in the evenings?' asked Mother.

Well — in the evenings there was bridge, sometimes; and listening to the radio, and phonograph records.

But she didn't tell them about the picture. For it seemed like a picture. Every night, as she lay half-awake, on her cot in the single-story barracks assigned to the girls, she had done a little more work on the picture, filling in small details.

As for that strange, warm, half-suffocating sensation she used to have when she was trying to be a little brick — it was all gone; and that other feeling, very much like it, was gone, too — the feeling of bitterness toward her family. All gone. The picture had crowded it out.

She wasn't sure why she always thought of it as a picture; for Katharine herself was in it; at the very center of it, indeed.

It was Sunday morning, in the picture, and she was back again in Trinity Cathedral. The people were coming in, quickly, quietly. The organ was playing. It was the Bach Prelude 'Out of the Depths.' She thought that would be an interesting coincidence, because that was what the organist was playing when she had become conscious of Phil's presence beside her. (Later — in the picture — they had both remarked about that. 'How funny!' Katharine would say. 'It was the same piece.' And Phil would smile and say, 'That *was* odd; wasn't it?')

So then she would be shown down to her accustomed seat by the usher who would recognize her, and she would kneel, and the organ would be playing 'Out of the Depths.'

In the picture, Katharine had to reach out, every little while, and pull some sensation back into it that was on the point of escaping; such as the music. It was difficult to keep this Bach Prelude going while you were on your knees waiting for the really big sensation. She could feel the little rustle of clothing and books as the people came into their seats and knelt.

And now the usher was seating someone beside her. Katharine would not turn her head or open her eyes. Presently her neighbor knelt, and she was conscious of a light touch on her arm; a rough coatsleeve; some tweedy sort of stuff. And then the picture would make her heart pound hard; for she could smell a faint, almost imperceptible odor of an antiseptic. (Later — in the picture — she would speak to Phil about that, and he would laugh when she told him she loved that smell.)

And pretty soon — in the picture — the choir would come singing down the aisle, and they would stand, and Phil would smile into her eyes, and reach for her hand — and give it a little squeeze that meant 'Now — we've got each other! Nothing can part us!'

'I expect you're very tired,' Mother was saying.

'Not very,' said Katharine. 'I slept quite well on the train.'

'Any plans for today?' asked Millicent, kindly.

'I want to go to church,' said Katharine. 'It has been a long time since I was there.'

'Why don't you go with her, Milly?' said Mother. 'You girls have been apart for weeks and weeks.'

'Don't make her do that!' said Katharine, firmly. 'She doesn't like church — and I don't want her to be bored.'

Katharine's throat was dry when she left the bus, in front of the Cathedral. She had a feeling that something very important was about to happen.

Everything was exactly the way it had always been in the picture; her joining the crowd ascending the steps. Her usher met her and smiled. When she heard what the organ was playing — Bach's 'In Thee Is Joy' — Katharine's heart almost stopped. True, it wasn't exactly the same one, but it was Bach — and that was close enough.

Now she was in the old seat, second from the end. She knelt, bowed her head, and closed her eyes. She felt a curious sensation of warmth on her upper arm, as if something vital, living, was almost close enough to touch. There seemed a little rustle near at hand. She inhaled very slowly, concentrating, wondering if she could detect that odor. She wasn't sure. The processional was advancing, but she was afraid to open her eyes or stand. The hymn was growing in strength. She couldn't remain on her knees any longer. Murmuring a fervent little prayer, Katharine rose. The hymn was, 'For All the Saints,' and they had come to the third verse. The little boys were screaming, 'Oh, may Thy soldiers, faithful, true, and bold.'

Katharine reached into the pew-rack; and, drawing out the hymnal, found the place. Her eyes were so flooded with tears that she could hardly see, but something kept saying to her, 'Stop it now, Katharine, and sing!'

So she sang. Nobody heard her, for her voice wasn't very strong; but she sang. She glanced up, and saw Mr. Simpson and Mr. Talbot on either side of the Dean, assisting him to his pulpit chair.

She squeezed the tears out of her eyes and joined the people as they sang: 'And hearts are brave again, and arms are strong. Alleluia!'

Although assured by Dean Harcourt that Sally had risen

jauntily from the humiliation she had experienced in Hollywood, Barbara wished the luncheon they had arranged for,
on the telephone, didn't have to occur. It was inevitable
that Sally's misadventures, during her brief stardom, would
be discussed, and Barbara had no taste for it.

Nothing was more painful, in her opinion, than confes-
sions, complete with sighs and tears and pitiless self-
scourgings.

She had said as much to the Dean, that morning,
and he had agreed with her. 'Most of what passes for repentance,' he declared, 'is remorse, and remorse is largely
self-pity. When people have made serious mistakes, and
have demoted themselves in their own esteem, it isn't
very good psychology to encourage the surrender of whatever pride they have left.'

'Shall I say, "Oh, Sally, forget it!" — if she begins
punishing herself about the Hollywood affair?'

'Well — that's a little too casual, I'm afraid. But we
are discussing a mere academic question, Barbara. Sally
has already forgotten it. It is doubtful whether she will
refer to her troubles. If you have been expecting to see
her moping about, with bedraggled plumage, you will be
happily disappointed. She always was incandescent. Since
her Hollywood mishap, she seems brighter than ever.'

They met at the Palmer because it was close to the big
store. Barbara arrived first. Presently she saw Sally sailing
in, radiant and resourceful, crossing the lobby with quick,
confident steps. When fully twenty feet away, Sally opened
her arms wide, as if prepared to gather in a large flock of
Barbaras.

'My lamb!' she murmured. 'So very good to zee you
after this lawng, lawng time.' She slipped an arm through

Barbara's, and they fell into step en route to the main dining-room.

'Why, Sally — I believe you've grown taller!' exclaimed Barbara.

'It's the shoes, my pet; the stilts; hard on the feet, perhaps, but good for what you call ze morale. Listen!' Sally suddenly slowed their steps and lowered her voice to a husky whisper. 'Do you know what?'

'No. What?' replied Barbara, wide-eyed with interest.

'I'm taking French lessons.'

'Oh? I thought maybe you were French — and had just begun taking English lessons,' teased Barbara. They both laughed.

It was Barbara's party, but Sally led the way. Pausing at the doorway, she confronted the impressive head waiter with a detached smile.

'Two?' he inquired, holding up that many fingers.

'*S'il vous plaît*,' murmured Sally, absently.

The head waiter bowed, led them to a centrally located table, turned the 'Reserved' card face down; and, presenting them with menu-cards, scraped himself away.

'You zee?' said Sally, taking up her napkin. 'We get zis fine table.' She laughed delightedly. Bending forward, she continued, with guarded voice, 'And I'm getting good, too. This woman is a native Parisian; has been here only a couple of years. Boy! — she has style! Class! She has all the little — little you-knows.' Sally did a brief agitation of her pretty head and slightly lifted a shoulder as if it hurt. 'Of course,' she went on, 'I'm not speaking very well yet — but I can do almost everything else.'

'What's it for?' inquired Barbara, when Sally paused to inspect the menu.

Moving the vase of primroses to one side, Sally leaned far across the table, and shaped her expressive lips for a secret.

'Psst!' she whispered. 'I'm going French — permanently — in a large way. And when I'm good enough, I'm going to work for *Sonia!*'

'Isn't that marvelous?' cheered Barbara. 'How nice of Sonia to want you!'

'Psst!' warned Sally, patting her lips with a fingertip. 'That's the secret! Sonia doesn't know it yet.'

'Sally,' said Barbara, almost reverently, 'you're wonderful!'

THE END